T0115160

The
School Teacher
and
McGuire

SIMMA LESLIE

iUniverse, Inc.
Bloomington

The School Teacher and McGuire

iUniverse books may be ordered through booksellers or by contacting:

iUniverse
1663 Liberty Drive
Bloomington, IN 47403
www.iuniverse.com
1-800-Authors (1-800-288-4677)

Because of the dynamic nature of the Internet, any Web addresses or links contained in this book may have changed since publication and may no longer be valid. The views expressed in this work are solely those of the author and do not necessarily reflect the views of the publisher, and the publisher hereby disclaims any responsibility for them.

ISBN: 978-1-4502-6545-4 (pbk)
ISBN: 978-1-4502-6546-1 (ebk)

Printed in the United States of America

iUniverse rev. date: 11/16/2010

This book is dedicated to my beautiful daughters Rudya and Idenne.

Prologue

She felt herself flying in the air. The air felt like an entrance to a doorway of the unknown. She landed in a world of mud. It covered her body, but her face was raised above the sucking mud. Her hat flew off in one direction and she lost her pocket book. The pocket book contained all of the money she had, fifty cents.

The mud embraced her like a lover clinging to her tightly as it rose higher around her body. She could feel it creeping into her body, ready to take control of her existing being. Her new clothing was like cement encasing her body. It was stiff and unyielding, like a coffin ready to grasp her last breath that she would breath. There was no way out for her, only the end of her life as little as she knew it.

Why had she never had any happiness? It seemed that her whole life revolved around misery and lose. There was no way she was going to live or have any happiness in her life as she knew it. It was over. She closed her eyes and felt the tears coming down her face. She could not stop crying as the tears mingled with the watery mud.

She had been so proud of the clothing she had worn. It was the first time in her life that she had real clothing to wear and it fit her like a glove. The clothes were made for order for her. The clothing was so pretty that even the nuns had stopped to stare at the change in her looks. She was so use to wearing old burlap bags made into dresses, and here she was in real clothing. That was why it happened to her. She remembered the nuns telling her "Pride goes before a fall." She had been so very proud of her clothing. She had been so puffed up about her looks. In the small mirror by the altar, she looked liked a lady of means. She looked like the rest of the ladies who came to the nunnery to worship. She had a shape in her new clothing that she did not know she had. She had always thought she was straight as a board.

Even her hair had been different than the way she always wore it. It was always in one big braid down her back. She felt the heavy braid as she worked, but never thought of it as something strange, until she was dressed in her new clothing (to her new, but really throw away clothing of some rich women) . Sister Mary had fixed her hair into braids and wound them around her head. She felt like a queen for the first time in her short life. How strange it was to feel her hair wound around her head. A whole new world opened for her inspection.

She stopped thinking, and felt the cold fingers of the mud pulling her into its depths, into the life she would never know. She was jinxed and there was no way to save herself. She was one of those people that the story of Job was all about in the Bible. Testing her belief and strength in the Bible, just like the nuns had told her. She was not good enough for this life, and so she hoped that the next life God, the Lord would take her under his wing and maybe, just maybe love her. She knew in her heart of hearts, she was not lovable.

The nuns had told her often enough, that she was not worthy of any real life. She was miserable and she was not worthy to live. She was left to do the work that no one wanted to touch. She was like the Indian untouchables that no one wanted and no one noticed. In fact, everyone hoped she would leave the world and not touch them.

Was it too much to hope that someone would like her, not love, but like her? It was the end of her world as the mud sucked her deeper into her shame and into its heart. There was no escape, for the world did not want her, and so she was about to put her face into the foul mud and end it all. There was no use going on in a world that hated her.

Her mind whirled into a pool of mud. She was part of the earth. She could feel the pull of the earth in her soul. What had she done to deserve this rude rush to leave her life without ever knowing the pleasures of the earth. She had dreams of coming to a new place with a new life. There was her father, a man she would love with all her heart. She had no one else to love. She dreamed of when they met, her father would hung her tightly. He would say he missed her so much and he loved her with all his heart.

She bunched her fingers into a fist. She wanted to fight the fates, but she knew it was useless. She was destined to die without ever having lived. She wondered why she was born. Maybe, she was born just to die?

She thought back about her life. As long as she could remember she had worked so hard and long. But, in the corner of her mind, she did remember a dress that floated out in ruffles. It was a fairy dress, that blew in the breeze. There was life in the dress, joy and love. She remembered shoes that shone in the sun, all black and shiny. She remembered a ribbon in her hair, The ribbon was so soft and it was like a golden sunset. She thought of arms that held her with love. The dress, the shoes, and ribbon put there by someone who loved her with a full heart.

Her nose became clogged in the mud. She closed her eyes and thought this is the end. Nothing more can happen to me. I am finished. I have ended a life the was no life.

Brad McGuire rode up to the coach stop on his big black horse, Chip. The horse was as black as a cave and larger than any horse in the area. The horse was fast and quick. The horse got his name because McGuire was a gambling man. He carried a deck of cards in his pocket to show he was ready to gamble.

Even though he was a gambling man, he was a rich man. No, not from the old plantation that he grew up on, that was long gone. He owned property. Brad McGuire owned the brothel, hotel and saloon. As a gambling man he knew he was lucky to have all these edifices Thanks to his uncle he was rich in property. In truth, he didn't know the first thing about his properties. He was the son of plantation owners and he was spoiled rotten with their love.

Chapter 1

MᴄGᴜɪʀᴇ ᴀɴᴅ ᴛʜᴇ ʜᴏʀsᴇ ᴀᴘᴘᴇᴀʀᴇᴅ as a shadow in the bright sun of the day. Brad was known to wear black only. Even his scarf was black silk, as he grew up with the finest life had to offer. He was a Southerner, and in his old life, he lived on a plantation, but that was before the war. His father and mother were aristocrats of the South. Their house was the finest in Virginia and they entertained the cream of society.

The house had thirty white columns around its exterior. The house itself was three stories high. The first two stories they lived in and the third story was for the various slaves that worked in the house . The house spread out like wings of a bird. It was crammed with beautiful things from Europe.

The McGuire's were very rich and educated. The father, James, held degrees from the Universities of England and Paris. He spoke French and English without an accent. The family was proud, rich and educated They expected loyalty from their friends as well as their slaves. They never thought of the slaves as humans, but as a staff who were expected to work only for their welfare.

His mother loved both of her children, but loved Brad the best. It was too much to ask the McGuire's to change with the times. Their only son was fighting for the South. They had owned slaves, but that was the way of life at the time they lived. The slaves were treated kindly for that period of time.

Brad lived the life of a plantation owner, happy go-lucky without a thought of tomorrow. It was the life he was born and bred to live. It was the life that was bestowed on the children of the rich. Everyone believed they were the superior race. Even they knew as surely as God was in his heaven, that the people in the North were an inferior class of people. They were just a money grabbing lot that belonged to the lower class of humanity. The people of the North had no idea of gracious living or even the joy of literature and parties.

McGuire knew the war had changed his way of life forever. Slavery was never an issue with him. It was something that he was brought up to believe as his right. He did not fight for the South because of the slaves, he fought because he loved the land he lived in. He fought for states rights.

It was the war between the states that made him a gambler. It was the only trade he knew and what he did growing up as a rich plantation owner's son. He was a man who knew two things that counted; one was that he became a crack shot during the war and the other was to gamble for a living.

The carpet baggers took everything they could lay their filthy hands on. The government seemed to agree with the tough treatment that was given to the South. They, the South, were trouble makers of the worst kind and deserved to be whipped into shape.

He had the most beautiful sister, Helen. Songs were written about her loveliness. He loved his sister and knew it was his place in life to be responsible for her. She was a handful when his parents were alive, but now, she was just a pain in the neck. She flirted with every man be they young or old. His sister was the belle of the ball. She had suitors upon suitors. Every eligible man in the county wanted to marry her. She was destined to be a wife of a plantation owner and be looked after in the extreme.

She was graceful and giving to her peers. To everyone else she was the ice princess.

Brad McGuire gambled with a purpose. He had to find a way that his sister was safe. He wanted her safe, but most of all, he wanted his freedom. He was free to roam as he would without a care in the world.

Brad McGuire became a legend in his own time. He was known to be a killer when and if it suited him. He wore his guns low on his slim hips. The silver guns around the hips of McGuire sparkled in the sunlight. He wore his guns as part of his clothing. His guns were repeaters, new for this age, but something he cherished as part of the Western world.

His golden hair peeked out of his black cowboy hat. His hair hit his shoulders and sparkled in the sun. His lake-blue eyes, made one feel they could drown and be happy at the prospect of drowning.

Brad McGuire was a very handsome man, with a square jaw and smile that resembled the sun. He did not want any trouble with the people of the territory. He liked his life care free and untroubled so he stayed away from women.

Brad McGuire's big shoulders shrugged at the sight before his eyes. His muscles rippled in his body ready to laugh. He sat straight and tall in the saddle as his eyes darted towards the stage coach.

Brad McGuire watched the stage as it slowed down to stop. He noticed the back door to the stage opening. No fool would open the door as the stage was in motion. He watched the old stage coach as it swayed over the mud. He rubbed his eyes not believing what he saw.

The black and brown stage coach swiftly entered Cactus Gulch. The stage coach was never on time, yet today it was on time. The stage coach was pulled by six heavy horses. Every one of the horses were washed out brown.

There was no sense using young, good horses on this run to no where. The driver and the guard sat up on the front of the coach. It was strange to see the guard, an old grizzled man with an old rifle. He didn't see much of anything as his eyes were covered with thick cataracts.

Cactus Gulch was situated on the desert, yet near a river and close to the mountains. After crossing the mountains into Arizona the stagecoach started to slow down. Large green tumbleweeds swirled in the wind. They had broken their roots in the wild scramble to be free. When the town was first settled, it hadn't rained in years. It looked so inviting, close to water, mountains and the land was filled with trees for lumber. They cut down all the trees to build their houses. The big thick trees were gone and so there was left a large sandy place that once held trees. These trees stopped the river from the flooding. The towns became flooded and then muddy. The sun steamed down on the town as the mist rose from the ground. Last night a big rain left the town muddy and in some places filled with water from the river rising and overflowing.

The houses in Cactus Gulch were all log cabins with a sand floor. It would be useless to have a wooden floor for the floods would warp the wood. The logs were corked with mud and no glass windows . There was a board walk from the houses to the higher level of the town. Though they talked about moving, the people remained where they lived as they were too poor and beat to move. The fact was, they were waiting for their death.

The driver of the stagecoach, was Rocky Pete. He hated coming to this town. He was short and very thin. He had a large dusty brown mustache that covered his upper lip, and his eyes were a sad brown. He wore a plaid washed out shirt and corded trousers He had on a pair of boots that were once brown but now looked like dirty sand. There was a sadness as he beheld the town. His thin shoulders became stiff as a tear formed in his eye.

The river rose over its banks. It washed out the town, like an eraser. Lilly, his love, was caught in the flood as it streamed passed her house. Lilly was small and fell during the flood.

The water came, a solid wall of pure menace and she was covered in its cloak of foam. The only reason she was found was she did not show up for work. She had worked at the hotel as one of the maids. They had looked only to find the reason she was not a work.

Pete was told about her drowning when he came to town. His love was gone. They were to be married a week from the day she had died. If the town moved to higher ground, he would have never suffered this loss. But the town's people, the crazy fools, kept their houses right where they had built them. They valued their houses as if the houses were made of gold. The fact of the matter was, they had no money to start over again. Who would pay for their move, and most important of all, why move?

Rocky Pete and Lilly his love were to move out of this crummy town. He had built a house in another town where they would live without shoveling mud out of the house every time it rained. A home that he dreamed about where he would live and love with his wife. That dreamed was dashed with Lilly's death. He turned into a bitter man without so much as a dream to guide him.

These houses that they valued above all else, had the cracks sealed with mud The mud was washed away when the town flooded every year. Mud was the ruler of this town. All of the houses had a dirt floor, which became muddy with the rains. They would shovel the mud out of the door. Their wooden furniture scared and cracked by the floods took the floods and just looked beaten as the people who lived there.

The hotel, saloon and whorehouse were all on higher ground so they never flooded. They also had wooden floors and furniture from the Eastern, Europe and in the whorehouse, furniture from China. Brad McGuire inherited all of the houses from his Uncle Thomas McGuire.

Thomas McGuire was the black sheep of the family. He hated plantation life. He wanted more of things on his own. He fought with his father over everything, and finally he left the home that was to be his when his father died. That was how the younger brother, Brad's father, became the plantation owner.

Thomas went West way before the Civil War and he loved and gambled his way across the country. Thomas had golden hair and blue eyes He had a way with people, especially, with women. Because of that, he gained a reputation of daring and of risk. He ended up building the whorehouse, the casino and the hotel. At first he was awhirl wind of work, but lately, he let things slide, because of a woman. It was a woman he did not care about.

His hotel, gambling casino and saloon lost all their main people once he died. They knew without a doubt, that the new owner did not know anything at all to carry the business that Thomas built. They left, and Brad McGuire did not know the faintest thing about what he should do. He had not learned the ways to run a big organization. He loved to ramble and gamble and have fun.

The hotel and saloon were wooden buildings that were painted a bright white. Thomas knew enough to bring in people who mattered, but did not want to be tainted by the whorehouse. The hotel once had a real cook. But the cook left with the death of Thomas Now, the hotel had a kitchen no one knew how to use.

Brad found a cook who had cooked on cattle drives, fried steak and potatoes and made coffee in an old pot. Most people hated to eat at the hotel. When they came, most brought their own food. The worst thing happened, men with money found other places to go and stopped coming to McGuire's places.

Thomas smiled and showed his white teeth to an advantage. He smiled often to the ladies. Thinking back about Thomas, Brad McGuire wondered how he knew what to do and when. He decided the Madam of his house owed him for letting her be Madam.

Trouble came to him by way of Black Hawk. Thomas thought he had the quickest draw in the territory. Thomas had fought all over the West. When

Black Hawk challenged him to a duel, Thomas laughed and accepted. The duel centered on who the madam of the brothel loved the best.

They met outside of the general store and stood facing each other. Thomas raised his gun, but Black Hawk was faster. Before any one could breathe, Black Hawk fired and Thomas lay on the ground. They buried him in a grave and took the cash from the whore house he had in his pockets as payment.

The madam of the house did not even shed a tear for Thomas. She smiled at Black Hawk and they went into the whorehouse to make love. The madam, Nancy, was fat and had triple chins, but she knew how to love a man and make him happy. Black Hawk did not care for the Madam, but he took everything that came his way. He made love to Nancy without a thought about Thomas being dead and buried.

No one would bother the outlaw, Black Hawk, Thomas left a will and everything went to his nephew Brad McGuire. They found Brad McGuire gambling in a small town in New Mexico. The word spread to all the gambling halls and Brad McGuire heard the news. Brad McGuire went to Arizona. He, the new owner of property, thought he found what he looked for in life.

Nancy was the drawing card of the whore house. Black Hawk was finished with Nancy, before she could even say his name. He found a pretty girl in Mexico. Nancy knew in her heart of hearts, that the only reason Black Hawk wanted her was because he wanted to rile Thomas. She left for a more promising place. She should have stayed with Brad, but it was too late to turn back. Brad was left with a few girls and no madam, and then the girls left also.

The church flooded, but the church was only used once a month. The reason it was used at all or built was that the priest came to the church once a month to render service, confessions and weddings. He was a fat man, with a bald head and he wore his black Cossack all the time, and sandals without stockings no matter how cold the weather. He had four churches he preached in, plus to marry the couples that were living together and waiting for him to come.

There were children from the marriages, and so the town people decided to build a schoolhouse, on higher ground. There was no sense having to scoop out the mud from the school house every time the river flooded A lovely one room school house, with a second floor for the teacher to live in. It had a heavy door for the winter time and they also built narrow steps to the second floor The room had everything built into the bed room., a bed, and a built in wardrobe, and hooks to store a winter coat.

Trouble came as they could not keep a teacher any length of time. All the teachers they hired, found some cowboy or rancher, to marry before school ever started. The school house became a ghostly presence, with spiders and scorpions taking up residence.

The stage coach entered the town. The six brown horses blew out of their nostrils and the mud in the road splattered up their legs. Pete smiled to himself that anyone would be so dumb enough to live here with the flooding, mud and the desert filled with green tumbleweeds.

Pete understood the dangers of the desert. He had lost his true love here because of the river. Water was precious and slimy, the sneaky river drew people here. Once they were at Cactus Gulch they were too tired or poor to move on. He understood that he would have no riders on the way back, because he would have had a telegram by now.

Inside the coach, Samantha Tringle straightened her little brown hat which she titled to the side of her head with the sway of the coach. The hat was etched in velvet and had a bright red feather standing tall and straight anchored by a velvet band. Her hand brushed her ebony black hair that she wore in a tight bun at the back of her head. She tried to braid her hair as the nuns did but it was useless and so the bun. She did this to make sure there were no loose ends sneaking out of the bun. She wanted to make a good impression when she met her father and of course the people of the town who gave her this job. She did not know what her father looked like, but she remembered a blur of a man leaving her at the Nunnery.

She noted the blue river as it ran its course. Around the river, she saw many gray birds with a strip down their wings that lined the shore.

She wondered how the meeting would go when her father saw her. He might hug her, or kiss her, or would he just stare at her and wonder why she was here. The Abbess insisted she go to him no matter what happened.

She knew she should not be so happy about her clothing, as it was sinful to be so proud. But, she never remembered owning anything as fine as the clothing on her back. The nuns found this outfit that a rich lady had donated into the clothes barrel. Luckily, they had seen it first and had thought about her leaving. The clothes fit her perfectly. Samantha clapped her hands as she saw how well the clothing fit her. Samantha twirled around and around in her new clothing. Sister Mary looked disapproving of her antics. Samantha bowed her head to show she was sorry. She was afraid they would take this new clothing away from her.

"You know better than to show off vainly. What are you thinking to dance about?" asked Sister Mary. "You clapped like a clown as you saw the clothing fit you. As if made for you. But it is not a reason for you to show off. Perhaps, we should take the clothing back."

Samantha felt pain in her heart. "I am so sorry Sister Mary. It must have been the evil that you told me lurks inside of me. That is why no one wants me." Tears flooded Samantha's eyes. She looked down at the floor hoping no one saw her tears.

Sister Mary looked at her closely. Samantha hung her head in shame. Sister Mary said, "Well, you know you are very bad. We told you no one wants you. Even your father threw you away. We have worked hard to save your soul, and suddenly you are dancing. I can not believe all of the years we wasted on you."

"No, Sister Mary, I was not dancing. I-I let the bad inside of me out. I must listen to you all the time and not let it happen again. I must be thankful if anyone is nice to me because I am a terrible person and deserve nothing from anyone."

Sister Mary turned on her heel, Sister Mary let her keep the clothing. 'Watch how you act in the future." Sister Mary left the room.

Samantha felt like a million dollars. The jacket and the skirt were made from the finest thin brown wool. The jacket fit her tightly around the waist and had large puffed sleeves. The jacket made a sharp v going down to the waist and was held secure by a silver button. The starched white blouse had ruffles around the high neck. The skirt fit snugly around her hips and then flared out into a graceful circle. Her high-topped shoes shinned like glass.

There was no way she could feel any better, than to touch the clothing she was wearing. Never could she remember feeling so rich in sprit and soul. She was so use to the old clothing she wore that itched and scratched. She was a new woman now, with a job and about to see the father.

She sat swaying and smiling to herself inside the coach. She was the only passenger left from Saint Louis. Something inside of her wondered if Cactus Gulch had been her home before she left. She wanted to sing with happiness, as she would have a real family finally, maybe her father would love her, have a home— The nuns were never wrong, something bad would happen to her because of her pride.

In her trunk she had her winter coat and two sets of underwear, and another blouse. How lucky she was that they had an opening for her in the town her father lived and worked in. Her father had a job as telegraph operator and he just did not have time for her. The nuns had taken her in, but they kept telling her the reasons her father left her, was she was useless and incompetent.

McGuire watched the stagecoach enter the town. He patted his horse Chip, who swished his long black tail. He was surprised the stage came only about once a month and here it was. His long fingers tapped gently on his black saddle that was covered with silver.

McGuire watched as coach started to pull to a stop. The door to the coach swung open. Samantha looked out as the bright sun hit her eyes. She could see nothing as she swung her foot out to the first step. Her heel caught in the step and the next thing she knew she was flying through the air as the coach pulled to a full stop. She saved her eyes when her hands shot out to stop her fall. Her little brown hat with the little red feather sailed away into the mud and her little brown pocketbook sunk into the muddy road.

She the mud wrapped around her body and part of her face. She looked up and all she saw was a sea of mud. She felt the mud dripping down her chin.

Watching the disaster, and wanting to laugh at the display in front of him, McGuire simple looked. Across the muddy street stood a thin stooped man wearing a red plaid shirt and red suspenders holding up black, baggy corded pants. His face turned white as he watched this spectacle. He stood there not moving just shaking his head. McGuire laughed out loud and his white teeth gleamed in the sun He urged Chip down into the mud. Chip splashed to where Samantha lay in the mud. McGuire tried to pull the poor creature out of the mud by her jacket. The jacket seams gave away from the water and mud.

Quickly he leaned down and grabbed her hair that had fallen out of its bun. His strength pulled her out of the mud by her hair. He saw her hands go to her hair to stop the hurt.

"What are you doing?"She cried, as her hands went to her head and the mud streamed down her body.

McGuire looked at her as the mud dripped from her chin and nose and half her hair around her face. He couldn't help himself, he laughed at the mess of mud sliding down her hair and face.

The stooped thin man looked at Samantha "Samantha?" he queried.

"Pa?" said Samantha as the tears fell from her hazel eyes. She felt his hate radiated from his face.

"You – you are all mud," Pa said in disbelieve. "What else could I expect of you?"

His face, filled with distain. His lips were small and straight like a ghostly presence. His eyes were filled with hate, that radiated the hot heat of his passion like live snakes. He turned away from the sight of Samantha like she was dirt.

Samantha watched as he walked away from her as if she was contaminated. She watched as he did not look back or smile. She knew terror in her heart that he did not like her or even care what happened to her.

McGuire swung down from his big black horse. "Better go into the wash house and get rid of the mud on you," he said. He just couldn't believe anyone with an ounce of sense could open a coach door while it was in motion. He knew he felt sorry for her, and her expectations of her father.

"Washhouse is right this way. You need a good wash. I'll make sure no one else comes into the washhouse while you're there."

Samantha looked down on her dull mud colored clothing. She was left with nothing to wear.

"Hey, Billy, will you let this lady use the washhouse and not let anyone in? You watched her fall. Well stop that laughing right now." McGuire said as his eyes crinkled in delight.

Billy was a fat small man with a merry face. Samantha looked at him and could not stop crying. He was laughing so hard he was doubled over. She looked at McGuire who was laughing also.

Samantha heard the nuns say, "Pride go before a fall." She hung her head as her dark hair dangled around her face. Was it so wrong to want something pretty?

Billy stood by the door of the washhouse. He laughed so hard he felt it in his stomach. "Yeah, I saw it all. Funniest thing I ever did see. She can use stall number two. I was getting it ready for Captain Ed, but I'm pretty sure he won't mind. Will you Captain Ed? Stop laughing and answer me. Guess the whole town saw what happened"

Captain Ed, could not believe the girl that stood in front of him, covered with mud, could be thrown from the coach like a rag doll. Captain Ed stopped laughing long enough to look at her. "O.K. by me. She can have my place. You can give her my hot water and towel also. Yes, Miss. I guess you need it more than I do."

Captain Ed started to laugh so hard; he felt he would choke. He took off his glasses and wiped his eyes. "This will go down in history. Funniest thing I ever did see."

Billy stopped laughing, and he motioned for her to come into the washhouse. She felt so embarrassed; she did not know to hide.

Samantha looked at Billy and McGuire. She saw McGuire smirk, but there was nothing else she could do but go into the bathhouse and get rid of the mud. She followed McGuire as he led her into the bathhouse. She hunched her shoulders like a lost dog. He gave her a handkerchief to try and wipe some of the mud from her face.

"I'll bring your trunk so you can change," McGuire told her.

"I have nothing to change into. In my trunk is only some underwear, a coat, and a white blouse," Samantha replied. "I only have this one outfit. What shall I do, or wear? This suit is ruined, my hat is gone, and the fifty cents I had is gone. All my money sunk into the mud." Tears fell faster down Samantha's face. She used McGuire's white handkerchief to wipe the tears from her face. The handkerchief turned into a black ball of coal, which made her face even blacker.

"Well, try and get rid of the mud. I'll come back with some borrowed clothing." McGuire said as he could hardly hold back his laughter His blue eyes ate into her body, a steak ready to be eaten.

Samantha went into the bathhouse. She looked around to make sure there was no one else inside. She saw several tubs of water. She saw the sign that said "Tub 2". She peeled off her clothing like dripping cement. Her underwear stuck to her body as she worked to pull them off. There were some thin towels over a rope stretched across the room. She heard McGuire talk to someone about not coming in for awhile.

She looked down at her skirt and jacket. Her skirt and jacket were ruined. She gagged at the idea they would never be wearable. They were ripped and shrunk.

She stood for awhile without a stick of clothing on her body. She wondered if they would still want her as a teacher. She stepped into the tub of water as it lapped around her legs. She sat down. The tears ran down her face as she washed her body and face. She never felt such luxury having a bath of all clear water to begin with that had not been used by the nuns first.

Samantha lay back in the dirt filled bath water wondering what she would do with no other clothing to wear. She was stunned as she thought she had no where to sleep or eat. The door to the bathhouse opened and McGuire walked in. His blue eyes took on a shrewd look, as he examined her in the wash tub. Her body curved in a smooth line like a Greek goddess. Her black hair outlined her innocent face. McGuire watched her body calling out for seduction. He felt his manhood grow tight. He was ready to jump into the water with her.

"What are you looking at?" she cried as she pulled the first towel she grabbed and stepped out of the tub. She held the towel in front of her.

He walked over to her and plunged her back into the water. He took the towel and threw it on the floor. "You are a ball of mud. Face facts."

His face showed disgust at her actions. Samantha felt her face turn red, but she sat still in the water.

"Got to wash your hair, you sure got loads of hair on your head. Did I hurt you when I pulled you out of the mud by your hair? Here let me soap up your hair for you and then use the bucket here to get the soap out of your hair."

McGuire felt a tightening of his pants as he stepped forward dropping the clothing he held and the trunk with her other clothing in it. He scrubbed her hair but he was looking at her body. He threw the water over her hair and then he hauled her out of the tub. She pulled a towel from the hanging rope in front of her body. He took her slim waist into his hands and held her captive. His hands felt the rough towel covering her front, but his hands felt the warm skin of her uncovered firm rear. His fingers danced lower down, touching her inner core and then his hands caressed her back.

He bent his head over her lips; he kissed her softly. He pulled her closer and kissed her lips with a passion and his tongue pulled her lips apart as it slid into her mouth. For a second, Samantha's body seemed like melted wax, she felt herself desiring that this would never end. They said all men were bad and took advantage of all women. She must stop this at once. Her body shook with the fever of wanting.

Samantha pushed him with all her might. Her hazel eyes were green gems set in her flushed face. His blue eyes stared at her as he released her waist.

"Here's the clothing I brought you. It's just stuff from the girls at the whorehouse. But it will cover you." McGuire said and turned on his heel and left the room. Samantha felt she could not breathe. Never in her life had someone kissed her, let alone felt her body. She felt the world spinning around. She had lost her clothing, no money and a man had caressed her bare body and kissed her for the first time in her life.

She quickly opened up her trunk. She removed her winter coat and found her other pair of burlap underwear. She looked at the clothing McGuire had brought. The skirt was a crimson red, tight around her waist, hips and thighs. The skirt pasted itself against her slim body. The blouse was made of blue lace cut so low her breasts tumbled out. The orange jacket made her breasts stand out. She pulled off the blouse and kept on the crimson skirt. She got her other white blouse out of the trunk and put it on. She finished by putting on the orange jacket. She pulled her hair into a bun and wisps of her hair framed her delicate face.

She could not face the thought of the jeering people. She looked for a way out of the bathhouse, but there was only one way in and one way out. She could not stay in the bathhouse forever.

Her mind spun to the kiss McGuire had placed on her lips. Her body turned to jelly thinking of the kiss.

She slowly walked out of the bathhouse, and her eyes scanned McGuire as he leaned against the wall. Her heart bumped and jumped as if she had raced down a hill.

McGuire watched as she came out of the washhouse. She looked like a woman of the night, and yet, she looked like a Dresden doll. McGuire was use to every woman wanting him. He was built slim and tall, walked like a panther, and his face was rugged.

Every girl that came to the whorehouse wanted him whenever he would be free to let her love him. Loulou, the new madam, was his mistress. LouLou came out of no where and settled down into the whorehouse she wanted no other home. Brad McGuire and LouLou found they liked each other, they became lovers. Brad McGuire had slept with almost every married woman in town but he like a homing pigeon came back to LouLou. He desired this woman he had rescued from the mud, wearing a whore's red tight skirt that accented her figure and white blouse which made her look strange, half whore, and half angel.

"I look like a freak," Samantha said as she watched him looking at her. "I can't teach school in this outfit, what am I to do?"

Her Pa turned around and felt the anger raise in his body. This clumsy girl was his daughter. "I have no place for you to stay. Actually, I don't know why the nuns sent you to me. You can stay over at the school even if it hasn't been used in years. I don't care, and I don't want anything to do with you. I didn't ask for you to come." Clarence, turned his back and walked away.

Those bitchy nuns sent her to me. Guess they were mad because I never sent them any money. I had hoped they would never find me, how they did is a mystery to me. He bunched his hands in his pockets as he thought of how he hated Samantha. He could strangle her. Maybe with her having no clothing and no room, she would go back to those nuns. Only way they could have found him was through the Priest.

McGuire looked at her and handed her a cloak with a hood. "I took this from Loulou. I hope she forgives me. But I'm a gambling man and I think she may never know I took her cloak. Put it on, so no one will see you in that red skirt."

Samantha looked at the cloak and pulled it around her shoulders, and put the hood up around her face. Her face flushed with shame, She just knew that everything she had wished for, laid in waste. The tears gathered in her eyes and she wanted to cry, but she held back. It just not right for her to be happy.

Chapter II

SAMANTHA LOOKED AROUND. SHE SAW the mud surrounding the town. The town looked like it bathed in mud or perhaps floated in the mud. All the houses were wallowing in the mud. Even the Church was covered with mud. Dark, dirty looking mud that seemed like the church had been plucked into a bowl of pudding.

There was no green around the river. They had cut all the trees and used the few weeds that grew around the river to stuff into the logs of their houses. She though of the mud that had entrapped her into its embrace. The mud was laughing at her and telling her it would find her one day.

Her eyes raised above the mud to the rise in the ground. High up on the rise of ground she saw the dry goods store, the saloon and beautiful white mansion. The mansion had white columns and windows. The windows were covered with crimson velvet.

She looked at her feet, still muddy after her bath. Her shoes had been lost in the mud. Heavens only knew where she would find shoes that fit her feet. Lucky for her, the cloak hide the horrible outfit she was wearing. The cloak swept the boards and gathered some mud on its edges. She pulled the cloak closer to her body.

Her eyes darted to the colorful mansion. Fine folks must live there, she thought. Samantha looked at McGuire. She pointed to the mansion. "Who lives in that mansion? I bet they are very rich folks."

McGuire gave a lazy smile. "That my dear love is a whorehouse. Are you interested in earning some extra money?"

Samantha was not sure what a whorehouse was but it didn't sound like it was good. She certainly wasn't going to ask Maybe they were maids and earned their pay. She knew of no other way people earned money. She knew how to clean up things, so maybe if they didn't want her as a school teacher she could be a maid.

Samantha turned around to face McGuire. She dug her bare toes into the boards of the walkway "Am I suppose to stay at the school house? Or maybe they don't want me any more after all the mud and my ruined clothing. I made a fool of myself."

"Don't think the school house is quite ready for guests. Been bare for over two years. I know they still want you as a teacher. They have no one else that answered their ad." McGuire looked at her. Man she sure was pretty. "Mrs. Weatherspoon is a widow. She could use extra help and has five children. She is a seamstress. She could sew you some clothing. I know you have no money, but out here, people help people."

Samantha handed McGuire the lace blouse she had not put on. She nodded her head. "Mrs. Weatherspoon sounds like a life saver, if she will have me. I'm just evil and no one wants me. Maybe the evil is coming out and that is why I fell in the mud." Samantha watched her Pa walk away. Her heart thumped like an empty barrel. "Even my Pa hates me." She whispered.

Her Pa sure did not look like he wanted anything at all to do with her. Samantha's hazel eyes watered. She fisted her hands. She did not try to wipe her eyes, but the tears came tumbling out. To her shame, her hair that she had pulled into a bun was falling away into long stands of wet hair. The nuns would know right away she was a fallen woman.

McGuire trod like a panther up to Samantha and towered over her. He took her slim hands into his big band and she could feel the chills run up and down her spine, "Hey, don't cry. We'll see you housed and get new clothing and all. It's not so bad. Worse things happen to people than falling in mud. Be glad you wasn't killed or maimed. The schoolhouse just isn't ready to put any one up. Mrs. Weatherspoon needs money and can't pay for schooling for her children. Her children can't read. You will be a God sent to her."

"I have no money," Samantha said as she looked at him. How could she tell him, she cried because her Pa just walked away from her without showing he cared. She knew in her heart of hearts, that the nuns never lied. He never wanted to see her again. Was that the reason he looked at her like poison?

McGuire pulled her forward and shook her slowly. "Hey, come back to the world." He took hold of her arm and steered her down the boardwalk that barely lay over the mud. In some places she felt the mud trying to trap her again.

McGuire held Samantha's arm as he walked. He smiled at her with his dazzling smile. Samantha looked down at his gleaming. sun caressed. black leather boots. Samantha noted a small house that was built slightly on the level of the boardwalk with the mud surrounded it like a lover. The boardwalk reached out to all the houses The board walk was warped and in other places lacked boards. She looked up and noticed the pathetic house ahead of them, that could not hold more than two people.

"This is the house I was talking to you about," said McGuire.

He knocked on the door and in a few seconds the door opened. and Mrs. Kate Weatherspoon stood tall and broad. Her face was dominated by her large nose and her tree brown eyes. She smiled with yellow teeth from chewed tobacco.

Mrs. Weatherspoon looked at her with an open mouth. "What in the world?"

McGuire said, "Kate, this here is Samantha, the new school teacher. Guess you heard what happened. It sure was a bang up way to come into town. She needs help as you can see really badly. Seems her Pa, is Clarence the telegraph operator. He sure doesn't want her. She has no clothing, no shoes, and no where to go."

Kate looked at the red skirt that Samantha was wearing. She shook her head.

"Got the skirt at the whorehouse," said McGuire.

"Looks it," said Kate.

"Any way, the school house got to be cleaned up before anyone can live in it. I hoped you would help her out. I know you have one bedroom and the loft is for the kids, but how about letting Samantha sleep in the loft also? Look at her, she is smaller than Mike."

"That's just it. I can't have Mike and her sleep in the loft." Kate said. "It just is not proper. You know how people will talk.

"Well, let Mike sleep in the kitchen. He'll be nice and warm." Said McGuire. 'Listen, she has a great deal to offer. Like the kids learning to read. She needs a new wardrobe and you could-."

Kate stepped away from the door and motioned them in. Samantha noticed the floor was still wet from the rivers rising. They sat down at the kitchen table and she noted a ladder going up to the loft. There was a pot-bellied stove, a pump and this table with six rustic chairs. Samantha felt the chair she sat in give a small shake as it sunk into the ground.

Mrs. Kate Weatherspoon thought about her staying and what it would mean to her and the children. McGuire stood up and his long legs shifted in the mud. McGuire motioned Kate to the door.

"Look, I'll give you money to buy her some material and make her some clothing, and buy her some shoes and I'll pay you to put her up. Plus, she can tutor the kids for free." Said McGuire as he smiled into her eyes. "Just don't tell her I'm paying you. OK?"

Kate would be getting money, and all she had to do was let Mike sleep in the muddy kitchen. Kate knew she could certainly use extra money. It was hard to come by in this town. "You mean that? Pay me to sew her a skirt and dress and buy her shoes, plus you pay room and board?"

"Yep, room and board. You know you need some cash." He put his arm around Kate's neck. "It will be a good thing for you to do for the town. We need a school teacher. The people will be proud of you doing this."

"What do you get out of this?" Kate asked.

"Nothing, just doing a good deed." McGuire was thinking of the lovely white skin of Samantha's.

McGuire dropped his hand from Kate's neck. McGuire turned to Samantha. "Well, what do you know? Kate here wants to help you in the worst way. She'll even sew you an outfit so you can go outside. In the meantime, I have to hurry back with this cloak and put it back where I found it."

McGuire tipped his hat, and smiled. "Just so you don't worry, I'm not the marrying kind. I want you to know -what happened in the bathhouse. Forget it."

Samantha stared at McGuire. "Do you mean that. You really forgot about it??

"Like I said, forget about it, and be pleased the town needs a teacher," McGuire said as he put his hat back on his head and smiled.

McGuire tipped his hat and walked to the door Kate closed the door and walked over to Samantha who sat looking at her bare feet. Kate went to the potbellied stove. She took two cracked cups down from the cabinet shelf and filled them with coffee. She handed one cup to Samantha.

"Call me Kate. We are going to live together for awhile, so we might as well be friends from the start."

"I'm Samantha and I do appreciate your taking me in. It is not easy to take in a stranger." said Samantha. "You don't even know any thing about me. I swear I won't be any trouble to you."

Kate thumped her cup on the table. She felt the stirrings of guilt in her mind. "You will sleep in the loft with the kids except for Mike. Mike will sleep down here in the kitchen. I'll fed you, and sew you a skirt and dress. No paying, the money that I put out. It is a gift. Some times it is best just to receive. I'll try and get you some shoes at the general sore. You don't want to walk around with bare feet out here with spiders and such."

Kate took a sip of coffee. "Is Clarence Trimble really your Pa?"

Samantha shook her head. "I don't know. But that is what the nuns told me."

"Yes, I truly wonder if he is my Pa. The nuns told me so. He's the telegraph operator for this town. Guess he doesn't get paid much. He never sent any money for clothing or room and board at the nunnery. The nuns had me make my clothing from the burlap flour sacks. This rich lady gave the brown skirt, jacket, blouse and hat I was wearing when I came into town. I felt so lucky that all the clothing fit me. I also got a beautiful pair of boots that are just rotting away some where in the mud."

Kate watched Samantha as Samantha stared at her hands. "Oh, Kate, what everwill I do? What if the town doesn't want me now as a teacher. And the reason all this happened is because of my pride. I should not have been so proud of that outfit.

Kate felt her heart twist inside her breast. This poor girl didn't have much of a life. Kate stood up and poured some hot water into the pot that had the coffee grounds in it. She mixed the water with the coffee and then refilled the cups.

"Drink up. You can clean the old school house out and then go live in it. School is suppose to start in September which isn't that far away. I'll make you some clothes for you to wear. Right now you look like a -"

"Yes, I know. I look like a clown." Samantha looked down at her bare feet.

Kate did not want to tell her she really looked like a whore. A young and beautiful whore that men would pay anything to have, especially she thought McGuire.

Samantha twisted her fingers. "I had hoped my Pa would be glad to see me after all the years. Do you remember my living here when I was a little child?" Samantha stopped speaking and looked at Kate. Her brow wrinkled in thought. "Kate, what is a whore? McGuire mentioned it, and I pretended I knew what he was talking about, but I didn't"

Kate looked at her as if she came from outer space. "A whore is a woman who sleeps with a man for money."

Samantha gasped. She knew she made a wild impression on everyone who saw her fall in the mud, but a whore?

Kate shrugged her shoulders. She didn't understand why her father left her either.

"No you didn't live here. I'd remember. You lived some place else, and I sure don't know where. Your Pa came here about five years ago. Didn't you know that?"

Samantha shook her head. "The nuns never told me anything about my family."

"Just where did your Pa leave you?" asked Kate.

"With the nuns in St. Louis. They told me how I was evil and that was why my Pa left me there. He never paid them any money. Then they found out where he was and got me this school teacher job. I don't know how they found out where he was."

Kate leaned on the table with her arms. She stared at Samantha and wondered what had her life been with the nuns.

"Why is a whore bad if she only sleeps with a man? Married people sleep with one man, and he pays the bills," said Samantha as she looked into the brown eyes of Kate. "I never heard tell of a whore, or person who takes money for sleeping with a man."

Smanthat put both hands together. There was so much she did not know. What if it annoyed Kate?

"A whore is a girl who lays down and lets men do whatever they want with her. They get paid to let men do things to them." Kate answered as she looked unbelieving at Samantha. "I better go to the general store now and get you some black cotton for a skirt and some blue gingham for a dress. That should tied you over. Let me measure your foot."

Kate took a piece of paper and drew Samantha's foot on it. "You can get yourself another blouse later if we can't clean the one you were wearing. Let's just get you started so you can go clean out the schoolhouse. You can't be seen in that crimson skirt and - never mind. I'm off for the material now. Just make yourself at home."

Kate picked up her shawl from the bed in the bedroom, then went out. Samantha sat at the table, not knowing how to make herself at home. She picked up the coffee and drank a little.

McGuire watched as Mrs. Kate Weatherspoon left the house. He walked up to the door and knocked. Samantha got up from the table. She opened the door and stood there spellbound when she saw it was McGuire. Her mouth opened and her large hazel eyes danced with wonder.

"Aren't you going to ask me in?" asked McGuire as he grinned. Samantha motioned with her slim hands for him to enter. She felt her mouth go dry. All she could remember was what happened in the Wash Hall. Her face turned red at the thought of him seeing her without clothing.

She pushed at her black hair Her huge hazel eyes begged him to like her.

McGuire's face filled her mind and heart. His nose was like a picture of Roman Gladiators that she had seen in books. His blue eyes drank her into his soul and she felt herself falling into his web. She remembered how she felt when he had touched her bare skin. He was the kind of man that loved a woman and left her behind, no ties binding him, she knew this in her heart.

The crimson skirt flared around her bare feet as she walked to the table in front of him. He felt desire fill his very body. Before she could sit down, his arms shot out and pulled her against him. He could feel her breathe against his face. Her eyes looked like a trapped animal, frightened, yet seemed to ask him to kiss her. He pulled her closer. His mouth captured her mouth, and held her prisoner. He kissed her with passion, deep and hard. His tongue went around her lips until she opened her mouth so that his tongue could capture hers. Her body trembled at his touch. Her breath came in gulps and she closed her eyes. She was in heaven, a heaven she never knew existed.

He pulled away from her lips and stared at her face. Her face was flushed and her lips were full from his kisses. He knew he had to leave or she would be completely lost. He dropped his hands that held her. "Damn," he said as he turned away and walked out the door.

Samantha stood like a stone as he left. She had never felt so hot and cold at the same time She clasped her small hands and looked down. Her petite frame shook.

She remembered her Pa standing in front of the nuns. "She's a no good girl. I don't want her. If you don't want her, then throw her into the street. Look at how she is dressed. Like a princess. Bah, that was her mother. Nothing too good for this kid. Probably stole the dress. Her mother always with other men."

Sister Margaret looked at the thin man standing in front of her. "You her Pa?"

Clarence Trimble shook his head. "Hard to say. I don't want her. I never want to see her face again."

Sister Margaret looked at Samantha. "Who's to pay her board? Her Clothing?"

Clarence Trimble just walked out the door and did not turn around. He didn't want her, and never would. He damned Samantha's soul to the devil.

Clarence wondered why he bothered to take her to the nuns He should have wrung her neck and left her in El Paso. The only constellation he had was that he would never see her again. He walked out of the nunnery knowing he was free from ever having to think of Samantha.

The nuns looked at a chubby five-year old child, dressed in a frilly pink dress. The dress had yards and yards of lace ruffles. She looked like a little doll in her pink dress. She wore little Mary Jane pattern leather shoes. There was little pink stocking with lace outlining the top of the stocking.

Sister Margaret looked at Samantha and said, "You think the dress makes you beautiful. You are an ugly, fat child. Your Pa doesn't even want you. Not that I blame him. Did you steal the dress? Even your Pa doesn't know where you got this dress. Well, answer me, from where did you steal this dress?"

Samantha looked up at the nun and her mouth quivered. "I don't know. I just was wearing the dress when my Pa pulled me into the train and brought me here."

"Well I never. You are a lying child. No wonder no one wants you." stated Sister Mary. "You think your pretty with your shinny shoes? Answer me."

Shifting and hanging her head down, Samantha said, "No Sister. I do not think I am pretty."

"Look at her. She can't even look a person in the eyes. Wonder what she is trying to hide now. Look at those shoes. Patent leather no less. I bet she sneaked into someone's home or store and stole all this clothing."

Sister Margaret's mouth turned down. "We will show her how to dress here. The worst thing of all, is no one is paying for her stay. She is like a wart on the face. No earthily good to any one. Yet, it is our Christian duty to keep her here regardless of the money that should be paid."

Sister Mary and Sister Margaret started to take off all of Samantha's clothing except for her shoes and stockings. When she stood naked in front of them they poked her belly. "Had lots to eat, look at how fat she is. How much rich food did you steal?" Then they pulled off her shoes and stockings.

"We'll show her how to dress in fine clothing." The sisters laughed for the first time.

Samantha didn't know if she should look up or down, but she felt so humble without any clothing on. The ruffles pink dress was hers. She did not steal it. She was dressed like she always was. Her mother made sure she wore pretty clothing. She had no idea where she got the clothing, because her mind became a blank. She was so afraid her mouth felt like cotton,

Sister Mary walked over to Samantha with a burlap sack in her hands. "Here put this on. We don't need to look at you naked. You're a fat pig. Should we call you piggy? But soon, your bones will show and we will know the Lord forgives you, your lying life. You don't need any shoes here or underwear. You can wear this dress and be thankful. Thank the Lord we will feed you."

Sister Teresa entered the room and looked at Samantha and walked over to her. "What is she doing with these pink ribbons in her hair?" She pulled the ribbons from Samantha's hair making sure she hurt her. "Pride goes before a fall. I can tell you have too much pride. Don't count your chicken that we can trust you. We can see how vain you are already. Why else would you wear ribbons in your hair? You are here to work and pay your way. Be thankful we do the Lord's work."

Samantha looked at the nuns. All she could see was their black outfits waving in the little breeze that swept through the room. Her mind spun and she could not find answers to her questions. Suddenly she felt her world turn upside down. She fell to the floor and she knew nothing more.

She could feel the strong arms pick her up and carry her to a bare bed. It was a box of a room but she was alone. Her small body was thrown on the bed. She heard the hiss of breath as she opened her eyes a slit. It was Sister Mary who had picked her up and carried her here. She looked at Sister Mary's face and she saw it was the face of disgust. Sister Mary was not one to like her.

As the days past, Samantha lived in fear of the nuns. She was made to scrub the floors. That was the first chore they gave her. Her little hands turned red from the lye and soap. The nuns acted as if she was always bad and putting on airs. She heard them saying, "Disgusting, the child is disgusting." She remembered the pink dress with lace and the shiny shoes.

The burlap bags given to her as she grew scratched her delicate skin. She could not imagine why her skin was delicate. She saw her pink dress. It was wrapped up with a pink ribbon. The nuns gave her pretty pink dress to some rich lady as a present. The nuns said they had bought it for the rich lady's daughter. The dress was hers.

"The burlap dress scratches my skin," said Samantha to Sister Mary.

"La de da, the queen of lies has spoken. What she needs is the taste of the rod to make her understand we will not take her airs any longer. You know you are not to talk to us in this convent."

Sister Mary went to the cupboard and brought out a switch. She held the switch in front of Samantha's eyes. The switch was a dead tree branch that had many thin branches that would blister the skin.

"Do you see this? We will have no more of your airs here. You will learn respect." With those words ringing in Samantha's ears, she felt the blows of the switch on her legs, her hands, and her body. It cut into the burlap dress. Samantha was numb with pain. "Please, I am sorry. The dress does not scratch. Please. Thank you for giving me the dress."

"We don't like liars here,' said Sister Mary as she continued to beat Samantha until Samantha fell to the floor in a faint.

She was told to collect the eggs in the chicken coop. "Be careful that you do not break any of the eggs. We sell those eggs, so every egg is very important to us. Those eggs give us money to buy what we need."

She went into the little yellow chicken coop and the chickens saw her bare feet and started to peck at her feet. She was so scared. Never before had she seen chickens up close. She wanted to cry, but she knew by now the nuns would beat her for crying. She waved her hands at the chickens. They pecked her legs harder. One rooster kept pecking at her bare big toe. She swung her hands to make them go away.

The chickens continued to peck at her feet and she fled the place in fear. The nuns whipped her. "Can't you even do a simple job? What is the matter with you? Are you stupid to top it all off? Samantha watched in terror as blood flowed out from the whipped places on her arms and legs.

Sister Mary was very cross. "Can't you do anything you are Just told? This is the first job we given you to do by yourself. Some one was always there to tell you how to do it. You are too lazy, and stupid."

The nun slapped Samantha across the face. She looked down at the floor. She did not dare look up at the nun and show her the tears that flooded her eyes. The blood still streamed from her legs and arms.

"Go out and collect those eggs," shouted the sister as she slapped Samantha's face harder this time. Samantha bowed her head and her shoulders slumped. She went back to the chicken house. She was scared of the chickens, but more afraid of the nuns.

The chickens pecked her with sharp beaks, but she collected the eggs in her skirt. She started to go back into the nunnery when the rooster flew into her face. It started her so much; she dropped one of the eggs from her skirt. The rest of the eggs rolled around in her skirt as she clutched the dress closer to her chest.

The egg fell to the ground, and spattered with the shell and egg mixed together. She looked up and saw Sister Susan gasp. Sister Susan ran down the steps to where Samantha stood. She wanted to give Samantha a beating right there and then, but the eggs were much to precious to lose.

The sister took the eggs from Samantha's skirt. She hurried up the stairs. "You stay right there and do not move." yelled Sister Susan.

Samantha stood very still. She knew she was going to be punished severely. There was no help for her. She had dropped an egg after they told her to be careful.

Sister Susan came down the steps after a short time. She held a switch in her hands. She beat Samantha as she stood in her face, her stomach, and her back.

"Now," said Sister Susan, "you will say penance for a week, and it will before the sun rises. Do you understand you clumsy girl?"

She was very careful after that to make sure the eggs never fell again. It was her duty now to collect the eggs every day. Every day her legs were pecked at until they bled. Her legs were bloody almost all day long, but no one cared or noticed. She could hardly walked on her feet because the rooster pecked on her toes.

When she became seven they said she had to milk the cow. The cow was so big it frightened her. They showed her how to milk the cow at dawn. So Samantha milked the cow the first time but did not see the step out of the barn. She fell. The milk spilt. The nuns were so angry with her that they put her in a small, dark closet and fed her bread and water for a week.

It was so dark and she had to pee. She did not see anything to pee in so she did it on the floor. The next morning the nuns beat her with a stick for peeing on the floor because it ran out of the closet onto their floor. They showed her a jar to do her duty in.'

"I did not see it, it was so dark," Samantha whispered.

"Feel it in the dark," said Sister Mary. "Do you expect people to wait on you, oh yes, I forgot you are a queen in disguise. I remember the pink dress you came in that you stole."

She learned to read and write because there was no talking to her in this Nunnery. They wrote lists of her chores. Sister Mary taught her to read and write so she could read the lists She never saw any men in the Nunnery and she assumed that the world consisted of all women wearing black when they got older.

Many a night she cried in her narrow, hard bed. It had one thin blanket and during the winter she froze. She wore the one burlap dress until she out grew it and then she made another larger one out of burlap. Finally, she grew too big for burlap bags, so they made her a dress from some gray material that was baggy and had no shape.

They wanted to cut her hair, but she would not let them no matter how hard they beat her. She screamed and shouted, and would not let them cut her hair. They gave in and said she could keep her hair if she braided it around her head and wore a cap so it would not show. This was her only luxury; Over and over they told her that vanity of vanities was a sin.

No one spoke to her unless it was to tell her the job she did was not good enough The years rolled by. One day, the head Abbess called her to appear before her in her office. Shaking with fear that she did something wrong again, she stood at the door of the Abbess's office.

"Come in and sit down," the Abbess said. She pointed to a red, wooden chair that was situated in front of her desk.

Shaking with fear, Samantha came into the room and sat down in the chair, the Abbess had indicated. Samantha looked around the room. The wood shone and there were large sofas and tables that held books and flowers scattered around the room. Dark black crosses covered the walls. The desk that the Abbess sat behind gleamed in the light coming from the window. The Abbess was dressed in black and she looked long and hard at Samantha.

"It is time for you to go to your father. You can read and write. You will go as a teacher. You will be leaving tomorrow. That is all."

Samantha started to cry. "Please let me stay here. I don't want to leave. No one will like me. I can try to do harder work."

The Abbess was a large woman with cold gray eyes. She looked at the cringing girl. "You will do as I have said. I want you to go to your father. I got you a job as teacher in the town he lives in. What else do you want me to do? Carry you there?"

Samantha looked at the Abbess and lowered her eyes. "I will do as you say, you Holiness."

Yes, the Abbess thought, it was time to send the girl to her father. He never paid. He'd be surprised when he saw the girl. Did he think they did not know where he was? They kept tract of him all these years. It was the Priests that made sure it was him, so they could send Samantha to his town.

That night, the nuns went to the clothes barrel to see what they could find for her to wear. They found a jacket, skirt and two blouses, plus a pair of black boots. The skirt was so soft and flowing. Samantha's hands could not get enough of the soft feel of the material. She tried on the clothing and boots and everything fit her as if it was made for her. She felt like a fairy princess. They even found a petticoat for her to wear under the skirt. She still wore the burlap underwear.

The next morning they took her to the stagecoach that was bound for Cactus Gulch. They put her on the stagecoach with some hard bread for her to eat along the way. She was shocked when she saw other people dressed in colors that were not black.

The men hanging around the stagecoach winked at her. Her face turned red with embarrassment. As she watched the women, she saw every color or the rainbow in soft materials. Suddenly, she thought of her pink dress. It was the man in the black suit that had made sure she had that dress.

She would see her Pa again. He left her because he had no money. He loved her. The nuns did not understand why he left her. She had someone who loved her. She could not think what Pa looked like. It flashed in her mind, and she remembered the screaming and the tears that took place before she was brought to the nuns. Someone told her Mom was dead. It was when Pa brought her to the nuns. She sure didn't recall the funeral. It seems strange that she never thought of her Ma being sick. She did remember beautiful dresses of many colors floating about. She wondered why she thought of those dresses and her Mom.

Tears came to her eyes as she thought about her Pa. All she remembered of him was a shadow. He acted like he hated her when he brought her to the nuns. She could remember something like his telling the nuns to keep her. He wanted nothing to do with the child.

She smoothed the bun on the back of her head. She made sure the little hat with the red feather sat at an angle. Her large hazel eyes took in every cactus or wild flower. Samantha smoothed down her skirt and jacket.

She looked out of the window as yellow flowers grew in several places. She saw the many different types of cactus that grew. Some cactus was big and fat, but others were tall and skinny. Much of the desert extended into the mountains. The mountains were covered with pine trees. There was such contrast, that Samantha never even dreamed existed in the world. Shyly she watched the other passengers in the coach. They all seemed so confident.

When the coach stopped the people got off to eat and to wash and dry their hands. All she had was the dry bread the nuns had given to her. She hoped they would not mind if she got a drink of water from the barrel. Shyly she asked if she might take a drink of water without paying for it. She was told to take all she wanted. She only had fifty cents in her purse, and she did not want to spend on something foolish like a drink of water. She left the coach and went to the barrel and dipper to get a drink of water. She drank deeply from the dipper.

One of the men noticed her drinking the water. "Haven't you got money to eat on?"

Shyly she looked down at the dipper. "I have bread, thank you." she said.

"Here," said the man, "I didn't finish my meal and there is a piece of steak there. Have it."

Samantha shook her head. She wanted the steak. She was so hungry. The hard bread did not appease her appetite. Then she thought about it, and she looked at the man. "Thank you, I am hungry."

She ate the meat and felt so much better. It was the first time she ate meat. It was so strange to the taste. After that she noticed when the coach stopped the people left the coach to have a meal. The man who gave her the steak bought her a full meal, before he left the coach. "I wish you luck," he said as he tipped his hat and a haze of sorry filled his mind. "You will need it.".

For the first time, since she boarded the coach, she became afraid of the world she was facing alone. She had never been anywhere before and she had never spoken to any one but the nuns. She shivered. She thought of the man and the meals he gave to her as an angel that watched over her.

<h1 style="text-align:center">*Chapter III*</h1>

"WHAT IS WRONG WITH ME?" Samantha stretched her hands and raised her head from the table she had been laying across. She looked at the doorway. She saw five pairs of eyes staring at her. They were all different heights, but they looked alike. Was she still in her dreams?

No one spoke as they looked at each other. Mary, who was 16 years old said, "Are you in a play or something?"

Feeling like a bug under a microscope, Samantha shook her head. "Who are you?"

Mary, her brown hair streaked with gold glared at Samantha. "We are the Weatherspoons who live here. That says more than you can say. Who are you?"

Mary just humped. Her silver eyes glared. "You look like some of those ladies that live in the whore house. Are you a whore? Why would you be in our house? Does my mother know you are here? You look ridiculous in your outfit."

Shaking her head to clear it, Samantha just stared at Mary. "I'm a new school teacher for the school, I think. That is before I fell into the mud."

The three girls were all dressed in pink calico. She could tell that Mary was the oldest, not much older than she was. The two boys smiled a very large smile.

"Oh," said Mary. "Cat got your tongue?"

"I am not a whore, I am dressed this way because I have no other clothing to wear. Your Mother told me to wait here for her to return, and to make myself at home. What make myself at home means, well I declare, I do not know."

John had a silly smile on his face. "You are the one that fell into the mud."

"True, and ruined what clothing I owned. I had this blouse and some underwear and a winter coat, but that is all in my trunk. Mr. McGuire got me out of the mud. Everything I owned was lost in the mud. I am a total mess. But your mother said she would make me an outfit so I can go out."

The five children just laughed and laughed. "Saw the whole thing as it happened," said Mike a strong man of seventeen. "Any way I'm Mike, seventeen years old, that is Mary who is sixteen. The rest of the hoard is John, fourteen' Sally who is eleven and Kate, who is named for my mom, is seven."

"Pleased to meet you all," Samantha said as she stood up to shake their hands.

"You should have seen her," said Make, "She looked like a mud pie. All drippy and the mud even ran from her nose. It was so funny. I think everyone in town saw the show."

"We didn't see it," cried Sally, who had hair as white as snow. "I was doing chores for Mrs. Grass."

"I didn't see it either," said Mary as her silver eyes flashed. "I missed the best shows in town. Nothing ever happens in this town."

"How did you fall in the mud?" asked Kate.

"Foolishness," said Samantha, "Pride goes before a fall." Samantha thought of the nuns and how they would be pleased to know she was so clumsy.

"Lucky that McGuire was there to save you. Most of the people here would just be pleased to watch you flounder in the mud," said Mike. "Of course, I was thinking of saving you but McGuire got there first. I would have waded into the mud and pulled you out. I really would have."

"Thank you," said Samantha as she looked at Mike with interest. She noted he still wore that silly smile. She knew she was a sight. "Anyway, I am I hope, your new teacher, and I mean to do the job. I always finish what I start, in spite of what the nuns say."

"Your Catholic?" asked Mary.

"I really don't know," replied Samantha. "I must be. The nuns brought me up. Why would I be with nuns if I wasn't?"

31

"Are you staying with us?" asked Helen.

"Yes," said Samantha. "Your mom said I could sleep in the loft with you all, and Mike would sleep in the kitchen, if it is alright with Mike."

Mike puffed out his chest. "I am the man of the family, and I like to stay in the Kitchen. That way I can be sure who comes in and out."

Mike walked over to the trunk and picked it up. "Sure is light. I'll take it up to the loft for you. Glad you are staying with us. Makes us special."

"I don't think people will think it special after my falling in the mud. I can just imagine what they are thinking. My pa just walked away."

"YOU have a Pa here?" asked Mike.

"Yes, he is Clarence Trimble," said Samantha. "He left me with the nuns when I was five years old."

"Why would he do that?" asked Mary "He's the telegraph man. I never thought much of him. He stays by himself a great deal of time. In fact, I say, all the time."

Samantha just looked at the children. "I was about five years old as I said, but I must have been one messy person. That's why he left me. The nuns said I was so terrible, no one wanted me. I must be terrible to fall in the mud as I did. I don't think anyone else would have fallen like I did. It is because I am not liked by anyone in the world."

Mary looked at Samantha. "Well, we may be Catholic. We like what we are, whatever we are. The Priest comes only once a month here. Anyone could fall in the mud here. It is all around us when it rains. It comes into the houses. It comes inside the church. Do You think you could attend our church?""

"I think a Priest is someone I had seen once in awhile." said Samantha as she sat down again. "I just want to teach, and I want my Pa to love me. I surely will attend church, especially with a Priest there."

Mary sat down and looked at the floor which was swept clean of mud. "Yes any body could fall in the mud. I wish I had seen you fall. It must have been a rare experience."

Samantha felt her face flush. A rare experience to be sure for the whole town. And look at her now, dressed like a …what? She watched the children look at her. maybe her life was just a terrible mud bath to begin with.

Chapter IV

KATE WEATHERSPOON CARRIED PACKAGES OF material, and a pair of shoes. She walked in the door and saw her children standing and staring at the new teacher. The new teacher looked so stupid in her outfit but manners held her for a moment, and then she just laughed.

"You all met I see, so there is no reason to put off having dinner. You are a sight there Samantha." Kate said. "Never did see any one look like you do."

The children all looked at Kate and smiled, and then they roared with laughter . It was all right; because Kate, the mother was laughing also.

Samantha put her hands over her face. Then she started to laugh. It was funny when she thought about it. No one could explain the sight she made in her costume.

"My goodness, I am like a caterpillar and a butterfly all at once." laughed Samantha.

"Guess you heard Mike, you, Mike will be sleeping in the kitchen. Rest of you in the loft. See you took Samantha's trunk upstairs already. Mike is it OK with you?"

Mike nodded his head. He knew he really wanted Samantha to stay with them. He thought that as long as Samantha stayed in this house it would be heaven. He felt his heart pound. Mike thought of all the joy that Samantha would be part of his family.

"We might as well eat now," said Kate. "Mary set the table. Stew has been on the stove all day so it should be mighty tasty."

"Please, let me set the table," said Samantha. "I want to feel I am doing something right this once. I seem to get into trouble without thinking. Maybe I just should stop and not move. I am so undesirable."

"Nothing wrong with you child. Just nerves. Be my guest and set the table. There are no great shakes of dishes. They sort of don't match," said Kate. "They cone from here and there."

Samantha smiled and started to open the doors to be little closet and took out the dishes. She started to set the table. Kate took some dough she had laid out and started to roll the dough into small rolls. She stuck them in the oven.

Samantha looked out of the window and ran outside. She saw some lovely golden dandelions. "Oh, they are so pretty and gold," she cooed. "I never saw such beauty before."

She came back inside and found a chipped mug on the window still. She put the flowers in it. She poured water into the mug, and placed the flowers in the middle of the table. "I remember flowers in the middle of the table some place in my life. But it was not with the nuns. The nuns did not believe in things that did not work. "

Kate dished out the stew from the pot on the stove, and took the rolls out of the stove's belly. There being only six chairs, Helen and little Kate shared a chair. They all started to gobble their food.

"Aren't you going to say prayers first?" asked Samantha.

Everyone looked at her. Kate looked at the question and then she smiled. "Oh, yes of course. Children put your hands together and we shall say a prayer with our new teacher."

"Don't you say prayers all the time? I wonder do you all know how to read and write?" asked Samantha.

They all shook their heads. "No, we never say prayers. And none of us can read or write," said Mike.

Samantha smiled and looked around the table. "We must thank the Lord for the food on our plates. We will learn our alphabet first and numbers and I shall read you stories from my Bible that the nuns gave to me. I am not worthy of loveliness. The nuns were so stern. This house is so warm and loving. We shall start tonight on our lessons. It will be fun to talk to someone who cares. And you do know the stories in the Bible?

Kate shook her head as she held her spoon filled with stew halfway up from the plate. "No, the priest comes a short time here and he just don't have time for stories. Even if we do have a church! He just comes like once a month then to marry people, you know people who were-you know. Any way, he stays and says some stuff, we never listen to."

"You will love the stories from the Bible. They are what kept me alive. It will be such fun for all of us. It will be like the family as I always thought it should be. I heard the stories in church. The nuns were big that everyone must go to church and pray. Especially me, as I'm so unlovable."

After the prayer, Samantha picked up her spoon; and dug into the stew. The stew was delicious. It was something she never tasted before. So she filled her mouth, and savored the feel of real food. She took a big bite of roll. The fresh texture of the roll filled her with joy. She had never eaten anything so good. She was so use to eating hard bread and maybe a little hard cheese if there was some left over on someone's plate.

Mike rolled his eyes. He hated to be cooped up inside and just sit. He didn't like going to school and doing some thing with a pencil, but to be near Samantha it was worth it. Maybe she'll give him private lessons. Mike though as he pulled his hand through his thick brown hair. He could smell her sweet breath and feel her arm as she moved. They sat very close together at the table.

Little Kate, who sat with Helen, reached out her hand and touched the orange jacket that Samantha wore. "So pretty. Can I have it when Ma sews you up a new outfit?"

Sally was plump and pushed little Kate's hand away. "You know better than that. We are not suppose to say anything about how someone dresses."

Little Kate looked at Samantha. "I love flowers. It is so special to have flowers on the table. I still want the orange jacket. It is so different."

A pink blush covered Samantha's face. She had dreamed of a house with flowers. It was so wonderful to have the children around her and Kate, so kind and good. "I'll do the dishes," said Samantha She really did not know what to say about the orange jacket. It was not hers.

"Oh, no you don't. It is Sally's turn tonight," said Kate as she smiled because it suddenly seemed to her that the world had changed in just that second. She had been promised house money, and she would have someone to talk to in her own house.

Sally hurried doing the dishes. The whole family sat down at the table and Samantha smiled. This was the first time she was the center of attention, not counting the time she fell into the mud.

"Tell us a story now, not tomorrow.,"said Kate.\

Samantha picked up her Bible.

"I shall read you about Noah and the flood," said Samantha. She started too read. The family sat silently still listening to the story. When the story was finished the children clapped their hands.

"Why did you read the story of the flood?" asked Kate.

"Because this town floods all the time I am told. Look at me, I look like a rainbow. All colors," said Samantha.

*   *   *

Clarence Trimble walked slowly back to his telegraph office. He just never expected to see Samantha again. He just wanted her gone and out of his life. They weren't supposed to tell her anything about him. He should have married and had some children. But no, he was so timid that people would find out about him and what had actually happened.

There was no doubt in his mind that Samantha had to go. He had to do something so that she would disappear. Something slick like he did before. Some how, he was not to get the blame. This must look like he is innocent again. He could do it, but he had to think, and do it soon. Before people got to know her too well.

Chapter V

McGuire looked like a long shadow, dressed all in black. Samantha wore her new black skirt and the crimson skirt and orange jacket were returned to the whore house. Her white blouse had been washed and looked fresh and clean after its mud bath. Her skirt fit her small waist and then flared out in a circle, and her tucked in white blouse had buttons down the front with a high collar that touched her chin. They rode in a black buggy that McGuire owned. They rode slowly to the schoolhouse.

The land lay stark but it was not barren. Here grew different types of cacti. The Salt brush trees had grayish leaves that were surrounded by clusters of papery, 4-winged fruit. A Yucca's white fragrant blossoms filled the air with perfume. They swayed gently in the breeze like a ballerina ready for a dance. Samantha held her breath as she never had seen any thing as beautiful as the swaying Yucca She felt the breeze telling her to live and love and be among the living.

It came to her that the desert was filled with beauty. She gazed at the blue mountains in the distance. The world was beautiful and she was glad the nuns made her come here. It seemed to be waiting for a special event.

The brown horse came to a halt before the discolored schoolhouse. The color of the school house seemed to blend into the dirt and dust of the land. The horse blew out a deep snort. The schoolhouse seemed out of place in the middle of nowhere. The schoolhouse was situated on a sea of sand, cactus and probably snakes. It was bordered with wild grass like a bride waiting at an altar for a groom that never came. Large round tumbleweeds danced in the wind.

The chimney was crooked as an old man leaning on a cane. The splintered door did not even fit the door frame. The building crouched ashamed that it was standing. She suddenly sensed the schoolhouse dragging at her and waiting for her to enter. She detected a feeling like it was going to devour her. Something bad was going to happen here. She could feel it in her bones. This was to be her home or maybe her grave.

The schoolhouse leered at Samantha. She felt the shivers go up her spine. "Am I suppose to live in this? It is so spooky and well, it looks like it hates me right now."

McGuire looked at the building. "Yes," was all he said as he helped her down from the fine black buggy. The horse gave a small jerk to the reins. McGuire pulled the reins tight on tied it to the hitching post.

They walked over to the building. Samantha picked up the black skirt she was wearing with her starched white blouse. She certainly didn't want it to get all dirty and dusty. Her boots were shinned but she noted the dust gathering around the edges of her boots. She wondered if she should have worn older clothing, but then, where would she get older clothing? Beggars can't be choosy she thought. She wished she had the fine brown suit that she had come to town in.

The door squeaked open as McGuire touched the handle. It was ready to fall down. Samantha took a deep breath and walked into the building. She timidly looked around the room. She gasped as she saw spiders, mice, scorpions, dirt and then a smell like someone was dead in this room. She backed out quickly still staring at the mess. She backed right into the arms of McGuire. His hands felt strong and protective around her waist. He held her tightly as her body smashed into his. His hands went up around her breasts. She turned her head to protest his touching her. Still holding her breasts in his big hands he bent down and slowly kissed her. His thumbs rubbed her breasts as his kiss deepened. Samantha felt like she was melting away as her mind twirled into a mist of desire. She had never felt this way before. Her breath quickened and she shut her eyes. He pulled her body closer to his body as he turned her body into his. His heat surrounded her.

She felt the rubbing of his fingers on her breasts. Her breasts felt heavy but sprang into erect positions. He leaned down and kissed her mouth again.

His tongue darted around her lips until her lips opened. His tongue went into her mouth. She let out a little cat like sound. Then she sucked at his tongue. It was like nectar of the gods that she had read about.

He pulled her body closer and she could feel the muscles of his body. The hardness of his manhood pressed against her stomach. "Open your eyes, little one," he growled.

Samantha opened her eyes. She looked deeply into his lake-blue eyes. They dragged her intensely into his caresses. His hand went to her hair and took the pins out of her bun. Her hair tumbled down around her face. Her hair framed her face like waves of delicate lace. Her face was white like a cloud, floating in desire. He could feel her body against his body.

"I want you," he said as he smiled into her eyes. Her eyes grew huge. Something was not right. McGuire continued to talk. "You are so pretty. I have never held a woman as pretty as you in my arms."

All at once her mind shuttered and she pushed McGuire away with her small hands. She knew she was not pretty. The nuns told often enough how ugly she was. She could not imagine why she felt so wonderful in McGuire's arms.

McGuire looked at her and smiled. His sky-blue eyes twinkled as he still held her by her breasts. "You seemed to like it. Shall I continue?"

""No, No, stop," Samantha's voice turned to steel as she pulled away. She looked at him and remembered the mess in the room "Please, release me."

His hands dropped from her breasts and he smiled as his white teeth glittered in the sun. "Tell you what. I'll have some of my people come and clean the whole place up. Even get you a new mattress. Can't say what has been living in those old mattresses. Would you like that?" He gently caressed her breast again with his thumb. He could feel her tremble as he touched her. He dropped his hands. He took her arm and headed back to the buggy. "Of course, I think you should think of something nice to give me for my troubles."

Stepping into the buggy, Samantha looked at him. She picked up her skirt as she slid across the seat of the buggy. She saw his eyes go down to her slim ankles. "I have nothing worth giving to anyone."

"I beg to differ with you. You have loads of things I want from you.," said McGuire as he jumped into the buggy. He turned in his seat and took her face into his hands. Samantha caught her breath. McGuire kissed her lightly on her lips. "Until later," he said, "I'm pretty sure you will give me what I want without any question."

He watched her face and could see the desire in her hazel eyes. Maybe it was not desire, but a wish to be wanted and loved.

Samantha looked down on her lap. Tears welled up and rolled down her cheeks. McGuire looked at her and gave he his handkerchief. "Hey, it's not that bad. Seems you like getting me to give you my handkerchief," he laughed. McGuire suddenly felt like a fool. What was he trying to do to her? In his mind, he knew what he was trying to do, and he knew she was so vulnerable. She wanted someone to love her so badly and all he wanted was to get into her body. Still he wanted Samantha like a burning brand in his chest. For the first time in his life he felt like he could settle down with the right woman.

*   *   *

Back in the weeds, where no one could see him, Mike crouched and watched as McGuire kissed Samantha and held her breasts with his two hands. He cursed. He wished he were older. Hell, he was 17 and he knew Samantha was only 17. That sure wasn't any difference in their age. Maybe he could tell her that he was 18, and she would look at him the way she was looking at McGuire and let him kiss her. It made his whole body heat up. God, but Samantha was so beautiful. Why did she have to hide her hair in that tight bun? He rubbed his eyes from the fine sand that blew and stung his eyes as he watched. He watched as Samantha put her hair back into a bun. He looked around carefully that there was no rattle snakes around. "McGuire can take her hair down," thought Mike aloud. "Yeah, but he will do more than that to her. I have to save her from McGuire. He'll take her virginity away."

*   *   *

Mike was not alone, though he thought he was. Not far from were Mike hid, Black Hawk watched the new schoolteacher. His dark eyes were hooded like a snake. He usually liked big women, but this schoolteacher, she was something he could really like to get his hands around. Now this lady, she was too pretty to be left alone in that school building. But it was dirty still, and then when she moved in, why he would move. She would just love what he had in mind for what he would do to her. For the first time, he felt he could just eat the woman alive like candy.

The Golden Eagle some called McGuire. He would kill any man who trod in his path. That man had a bad temper; and sure could shoot straight and hit what ever he aimed at. McGuire just never did like anyone fooling with his possessions. Black Hawk would make sure that McGuire was far away when he took this angel. It meant loads of money to Black Hawk to get the new schoolteacher.

*   *   *

Clarence Trimble sat in Mrs. Kate Weatherspoons's kitchen drinking some coffee and eating a cookie she had baked. Kate wore a shapeless cotton dress that made her round body look fat. Clearance's eyes roamed around the kitchen.

"You think she will be all right here? You think she'll stay. Maybe after she sees the schoolhouse she will leave," Clearance said.

"Can't see any reason for her to move. She seems happy to be here, near you," Kate replied as she sat down and looked at Clarence for the first time since she knew him. He was stooped from the job she guessed. She heard their pay was very good. He sure could afford to look after Samantha, instead of McGuire doing it. She watched him fiddle with his cup. She knew he wanted to say something, but he did not know how to bring it up.

"I mean, well, that McGuire. You know his reputation. And he seems to be always looking at her," Clarence said as he sipped coffee. "You think he wants her for his whorehouse? She's sort of innocent, she would be better off in another town, or back with the nuns."

Kate looked at him. He was spooky as hell. She looked up into Clearance's cow brown eyes. Kate looked at him closely and it seemed she saw something hiding there in his eyes.

"Guess it will depend on your daughter what will happen. We sure can't stand by her all the time," Kate said as she stared into Clearance's eyes. "But it seems to me, you should be taking care of her. I don't see why you don't."

Clarence cracked his knuckles. "Hey, Clarence," Kate said "how about us all going to the spring dance. You know there is a dance in the Saloon and park tonight. Doesn't happen very often. We all can get away and go. Samantha could meet some other men. Maybe you're right about McGuire, she should meet other men."

"No, No! Meet other men. Let her go some place else. Why meet men here? No, I'm not going to any dance so Samantha can meet some men." He started to say, but Kate cut him off.

"It's all settled. You take Samantha and me to the dance tonight. Then you introduce her to some other men. We will have a great time." Kate smiled as she looked at him.

"No, Samantha should leave this town. You saw how she entered. They'll all laugh at her tonight. No man will want her," Clarence started to say as he slumped further into the chair.

Kate cut him off. "Don't you want to go to the dance?"

Cadence fiddles with his hands. "No. I have to be at the telegraph office and-"

"Forget it for this night. Anyway, we are going to the dance tonight with you or without you," Kate said. "Oh my Lord, here comes Samantha and McGuire in McGuire's black buggy. I wonder what he was doing to look like he won the horse race? You don't suppose, no, Samantha looks decent and she doesn't have a button out of place."

McGuire jumped off the buggy then put his hands around Samantha's waist. He swung her off the buggy. Her skirt flared out showing her shapely legs. He looked down into her face as his hands still held her waist.

"So what did you think?" asked McGuire.

Samantha pulled away from his hands and ran into the house. She was surprised to see her father sitting at the table with Kate. Not only that, but she knew they had watched her being swung off the buggy. Her face became red as a rooster's comb.

Kate and Clarence looked at her, but did not say one word. Finally Kate got up from the table. "How about some coffee?" she asked.

Samantha nodded her head. She sat down next to her Pa. Clarence stared out the window. Clarence got up from his chair and walked to the door. Kate gave Samantha a cup of coffee. "There's a dance tonight in town. Every one will be there. I think we should go." Kate said.

"I have nothing to wear," said Samantha.

"Ha, I finished your blue gingham dress. It will look just right at the town dance," Kate said as she lifted the cup to her lips. "Besides, you will meet some other folks from town, and especially those who have children for school."

"What ever you think. Will you be at the dance with Pa?" asked Samantha.

Just then Mike walked into the house. He looked at Samantha with a hurt look. Clarence stood by the screen door not moving.

"Just where have you been young man? Kate shouted. "There is work to be done here, and you were nowhere to be seen."

Mike shrugged his shoulders and bounded up the ladder to the loft. Kate looked at Clarence at the door. "Wonder what got into him,"said Kate "Maybe he has some girl he wants to take to the dance. He's old enough."`

Clarence stood by the door as Kate turned to him. Clarence looked at Samantha and raised his voice. "Thanks for the coffee, Kate. I got to get back to the telegraph office. Been gone too long. No, I'm not going to some stupid dance and neither should you, Samantha. Everyone will be laughing at you the way you came into town."

Clarence looked at her without saying a word. Kate looked at Clarence in shock.

"I think you take your job too seriously. Think you should take time off. You don't have to there 24 hours a day. I don't think you should be at the dance tonight. It would be too much for you to have some decent fun." Kate picked up her coffee cup and put it in the sink. "What are hiding from?"

"Good riddance is all I can say," yelled Kate. "I hope you are not at the dance tonight. You would mess everything up. Reminding everyone about Samantha falling in the mud."

Clarence walked away from the door. His face was gray. He would have to leave town before-but they found out about him; but then if Samantha left-He hated them. There was no way that they would change his world. He rubbed his face with his hands and his eyes closed. He plucked at his red suspenders and pulled up is baggy pants   In the kitchen still, Kate smiled at Samantha. "Come along child, let's see how the dress I made you looks. Might want to add some lace and bows to the dress."

Pushing back from the table, Samantha put her cup into the sink and followed Kate. Kate took out a light blue gingham dress with lace on the bottom hem around the long sleeves. The sleeves of the dress were puffed from the shoulder to the elbow, and became very tight around the arms. There was a velvet bow at the waist that emphasized Samantha's small waist. The skirt of the dress had yards and yards of material flowing out. "I have never seen a dress so beautiful." She picked up the dress and her hands slowly stroked the material. "It is so soft," she whispered, "and three petticoats. I had a petticoat once with the brown suit."

Without being told, Samantha slipped out of her black skirt and very starched white blouse. She put the dress and petticoats on. She stood waiting for Kate to say something. Kate looked at Samantha. She was beautiful. Kate was stunned at how lovely she looked. The soft blue color was just right for bringing out Samantha's dewy white skin.

"Think it will do," Kate said. "I like the petticoats. They really make your waist seem life it is ten inches round. I made three petticoats if you noticed."

"You think I look all right? The nuns always said I have eyes and a mouth that look too big. I always knew I was ugly. But they were sort of kind to me. They fed me and let me sleep on a wooden bench. Kate, I was so lonely there. Why couldn't my Pa let me stay with him? The only people who are nice to me are you, your children and Mr. McGuire. He thinks I should leave town because I embarrassed him and he thinks every one will laugh at me."

"No one will make fun of you. Trust me," said Kate. She sat Samantha down on the bed. She sat down next to her and hugged her. McGuire isn't the marrying kind, so why is he so kind to her. What does he want of her? McGuire doesn't do any thing he doesn't get the best from. I sure don't trust that man. She is so lonely, and she will do anything so someone will like her, let alone love her. I have to be sure she meets some nice men tonight.

"Come along girl," Kate said in her loud voice. "Let's get out of that dress and save it for tonight. You will be a fine teacher, don't worry. Everyone will love you."

Samantha smiled. "Oh, Kate. Thank you for making me this wonderful dress. I never had anything so pretty. And Kate, thanks for holding me, You are the first person I can trust. You are so honest and willing to help any one in need."

Kate looked at Samantha as she took the dress off, and tenderly smoothed the material. Kate felt like such a liar. McGuire was the one who paid for the material and her time to make the dress. McGuire was the one who gave her extra money for her room and board.

"Kate, you should see that school. It is like a cesspool from China. It was terrible. I saw it and stepped back right into Mr. McGuire's arms. It was so embarrassing. I don't know what he thought. But he said he would get his people to clean the place and he even said he would get a new mattress and paint the built in bed for the room above the schoolroom.

"Have you seen the room above the school room?" asked Kate. "It is only a bed and a built in chest with three drawers. There is no place for a lot of clothing."

"Very funny," Samantha said. "I only have this black skirt, two white blouses and the dress you made for me. The slips are real white cotton with lace. They are so soft and beautiful. All I had was a burlap dress, until I grew to big for that and then they gave me a cotton dress that was way to big all over. Burlap is so hard and scratchy. Oh, Kate, you are so wonderful making me those things. I hope I can repay you one of these days to show ho much this means to me."

Kate looked down at her hands. Should she tell Samantha that McGuire paid for the cost of the cloth and the sewing? "Listen, at the dance tonight, let your hair down, and wear this big blue bow that will pull your hair into a long, black cascade of midnight. It is time you stopped putting your hair into a bun like an old maid."

"Kate, the nuns said that wearing my hair lose was wanton."

Kate looked at Samantha. "You know, those nuns don't sound like they liked you very much. Did your Pa pay them to keep you?"

"No. They said I was a charity case, and they didn't make a penny on me. I had to do work. Always work no matter how young or old I was. Pay for your room and board they would yell. They believed idol hands were the devil's workshop. Some times I wanted to just sit and watch the sun sink into the land, but they always had me doing something. Weeding the garden, helping the cook, making beds, cleaning out the horses, feeding the chickens, scrubbing the floor. They taught me to read and write well enough so I can be a teacher. The reason they taught me to read and write was because no one was suppose to talk to me. To get back to the something funny, they sad, it was about Pa. Kate, they told me where my Pa was. I was so surprised, but they said he deserved having me find him." I found out later that they knew where he was from the Priests they were living in the West. They really wanted to know where he was. But why they wanted to know, they never told me. Why would they want to know where my Pa was, when he wasn't paying them a cent?"

Kate took Samantha's hand into her large hands. "Well, don't worry about the past now. You are here and you are going to be a great teacher. In fact, most teachers don't last long here. They all seem to marry. We are short of women. Right now the one all the men are flocking to is Ginger. She's the daughter of the dry goods storeowner. She is sort of pretty, but kind of tall. Yes, I can see what you're thinking. Mary? But my Mary is still young. But with those silver eyes, I just don't think she will be unmarried for long. Now don't ask why I'm not married. It is a long story and one-day I will tell you about it. But it just isn't something to shout about. In fact, I would say it is boring."

Samantha looked at Kate and smiled. "There was no way I was going to ask any questions tonight. Maybe tomorrow will do. Honestly, Kate, I am so happy right now to have such a wonderful dress. Even my Pa not paying attention to me, don't seem too terrible. I have a song in my heart because of you. For the first time in my life I feel almost pretty. Would you believe even McGuire said I was pretty? Can you imagine a man like him saying I'm pretty?"

Kate looked at Samantha and thought how pretty she was. The nuns sure did a number on her to make her think she was ugly. She was a pretty as the sun rising in the morning, the smell of honey suckle in the evening, and the moon at night.

Still she worried about McGuire, and then she worried about her taking the money he gave to her.

Chapter VI

THE MOON WAS A BIG, yellow ball, shedding light on the park. The lanterns around the saloon were colored red and green. The swinging doors to the bar were man sized. Inside, there was a large mirror, the length of the wall, which reflected the polished tables and bar. On one wall was a painting of a naked lady leaning back among the colored pillows with one leg raised in front of her, and her breasts jutted out.

TABLES CIRCLED THE DANCE FLOOR, but the town women did not enter the saloon. The whores were dressed in simple dresses that reached the floor, and it was almost impossible to tell them from the town ladies, except they had kola around their eyes.

LOULOU LOOKED AT THE TOWN people and smiled. She watched McGuire as he strutted about the park. He was showing the town ladies all he was worth, like his golden hair, his tan skin, and his slim waist. She watched as the ladies all looked at McGuire with lust. He was a very pretty picture of what the women wanted in their lives, new blood, and a real man. They loved their husbands, and were glad they were married, but the look of McGuire left them panting. LouLou was glad that McGuire was her man. He might roam, but he always came back to her, like a homing pigeon.

The town ladies ignored the whores. They put their food and blankets on the tables around the park. The bar was open, and the men thought nothing about going into the bar for a drink. The doors of the bar swung merrily to and fro as the men entered and exited. They expected the women to forgive them tonight as it was a special night for the town. This was a dance to enjoy.

Multi colored dresses of cotton swirled to the dance music under the stars. The three fiddles played music loud enough to be heard all through the town. This was just a night to have fun and laughter. It was a night that came too seldom for it to be ignored.

The whole town was there, including babies less than a year old to oldsters in their nineties. Just for a few hours they let themselves be young and gay.

Kate, the five children and Samantha came into the park. The girls were wearing cotton dresses in red and green that had tight bodices and swinging skirts. These were new dresses for the girls, as they had out grown all their other clothing. They wore a big red bow in their hair.

The boys were spruced up in clean denim pants and red plaid shirts. Hair was slicked back and shone in the silvery light. As the music played, so did their feet tap out a tune. Every one could feel the beat of the music as the crowd danced and talked and fiddlers played.

Kate and her small troop brought their food to a large table that was filled with food that every one present had brought. The table groaned with roasts, chickens, potato salads, beans, breads, cakes, and cookies. There was no silverware or plates around because every one brought their own utensils.

Kate proudly placed her chicken with the other chickens, her bread with the other breads, and then proudly she put out her ham at the head of the table. She knew she was noted for her great ham. Kate proudly looked at the ham and knew it would not last long. Everyone wanted at least one slice of it.

The Weatherspoon girls screamed as they saw their friends. They had not seen some of their friends in over a year. They ran to each other and hugged each other with a passion. They smiled and tears came to their eyes. It was so great to find their friends again.

"When school starts this September, we will see each other more often. It will be great to learn to read and write. I miss you so." cried Mary as she twirled around and round and her skirt made wide circles as she twirled.

"Mary, do you think we will have a school finally?" asked Doris her friend.

"We have the school teacher living in our house. It is so great. She reads us stories every night, and she is teaches us to read and write. I can hardly breath with the wonder of it."

Doris looked at Mary with so much worship. "It is something I wanted to learn. Do you think if I came over sometimes she would help me?"

"Oh, she is wonderful and kind. Of course she would help you," cried Mary.

Mike stopped listening to the girls and looked at Samantha. Mike stood next to Samantha and thought it was time to ask her to dance. He just had to get up the nerve. He stood preparing a speech to ask her to dance. His palms sweated as he rubbed them down his denim pants. He gazed around the park and saw McGuire.

McGuire stood out dressed in only black. No way was Mike going to let McGuire dance with Samantha. He watched McGuire smile as the women simpered and the men smiled broadly. Each couple had to tell him about the food they brought and how they loved the dance and the music.

The air teased with the smells of food, perfume and sweat from the dances. Kate looked around and saw Ted Malone. Ted was tall, over six feet, with hair the color or rust, and eyes so very black they looked like obsidian. He was talking to the daughter of the man who owned the general store. She was a pretty, a tall girl with brown hair and a smile a yard wide. Ginger was wearing a dress of white cotton. It had a low cut top that just skimmed her breasts. The bodice was tight around the upper part of her body, and the skirt came into a wide circle as it reached the floor. It made her seem to float in the silver light.

"Ginger," said Ted, "you look mighty fine tonight. You are surprised that I came tonight, but hey, it was time to relax. Right-only once a year."

Ginger looked at him with worship. "I had hoped you would come. I miss you when you are not here."

"I believe you, Like you need some man," laughed Ted "You have every man in town in love with you. When are you going to chose who to marry."

"In case you don't know it, I have chosen. It is just the man don't know it yet," said Ginger with a sigh.

Kate wore a green cotton dress that was not fitted, but still it floated around her wide body. Kate pulled Samantha's arm. "Come on, I want you to meet some people of the town." Kate said as her large nose sniffed the odors of the food every where.

Mike opened his mouth to ask Samantha to dance with him, but as he looked, she was being pulled in another direction. Mike knew when he was out maneuvered. His mother had won again as she always did. Mike could kick himself for waiting so long to ask Samantha for a dance. Always a dollar short when it came to girls.

Kate tugged Samantha to where Ted and Ginger were standing and talking. Ginger sulked as she watched Kate march over with the pretty new schoolteacher. Sparks flew from Ginger's eyes as they advanced towards them.

Ginger gave a fake smile. "Howdy."

Ted looked at Samantha long and hard. He felt his heart turn over. This was the prettiest lady he had ever seen. He gulped and smiled broadly. "Sure glad to met you."

Samantha looked down to the floor. She felt like she had interrupted what ever they were saying.

Kate smiled, "Want you to meet the new schoolteacher, Samantha. This is Ginger and Ted."

Ted looked at Kate. He didn't know what to do. Kate said, "Haven't seen you in over six months. What have you been doing?"

Ted looked at Kate, then Ginger and then he concentrated on Samantha. "I have been working on the ranch; branding, and getting ready for a cattle drive. I'm tired of cows and thought I'd come to the dance and let some steam off. I am really glad I came to town. So glad to know you Samantha."

Ginger looked up into his dark eyes. She put her hand on his arm. "I think we should dance."

Kate took hold of Ginger's hand, "Bet you heard of the grand entrance Samantha made when she came into town?"

Samantha's face turned brick red. Would anyone ever forget how she fell into the mud?

Ted looked at Kate. "Quite a triumph. Everyone is saying how brave Samantha was. I sure am glad to meet you."

Samantha looked up into Ted's dark eyes and smiled. "I was so afraid that people would hate me,. You know for what happened."

Ted shook his head. "No way, No one could hate you," Ted said as he took Kate's hand in his. "I'm just tired of being by myself. I came into town when I heard there was to be a big dance. Thought I should start to see other people in person besides cows. I'm meeting people. People I want to get closer to."

Kate laughed long and loud. She pulled Samantha in front of her.

"Thought you all wanted to meet her. This is the first dance she has ever been to Bet she don't know how to dance, but it don't matter Samantha needs to know people here about. Ginger, you about her age, perhaps you could help her fit in?"

Samantha smiled. She felt she was being welcomed which is something she never felt before. Kate continued speaking.

"She was in a convent since she was five. She sure needs to meet the people and see the town. Maybe you and Ted can help introduce her around?"

Ginger looked up at Ted. She sure didn't need or want any competition, but Ginger was a sweet girl, so she smiled and figured what ever was to be would be. She felt sorry for Samantha being in with nuns and having no fun.

"Sure, glad to met you. Maybe we can do something's together. I sure can help you with some things at school. This is Ted's favorite song. We must dance. Be right back."

Ted pulled his hands off Ginger. "Where are your manners girl? We have to make Samantha welcome here, and we sure can't leave Kate here with her face hanging out."

Ginger twisted her fingers. She turned to Samantha. "Sorry, I was a bitch. Really glad you're here. Maybe you should dance with Ted and I'll keep Kate Company. He can introduce you to some of the other men here. That are single that is."

Ted looked a Samantha and his heart was humming. "Yes, it is my favorite song. So will you dance with me? Ginger forgot she promised this dance to Ray. That Ray is always after Ginger, she's so pretty. I'll walk Kate and Samantha back to their table."

Ginger laughed. "I did forgot about Ray. Sorry, but I do have to keep a promise." Ted put his big hands on Samantha's small back. "Come on, stop looking like you lost your way. No one is laughing at you."

A firm shake of her head and Kate looked at Samantha. She had to admit Samantha looked like a lost soul. Samantha stared at the floor, thinking about how she entered town. She knew everyone would laugh at her. Maybe she should leave the town. She didn't know how to dance.

Ted looked down at her as he held her hands. His body felt paralyzed just looking at her. He knew right then he had found the woman that he wanted to spend the rest of his life with. How was he going to tell Samantha, especially as they just met? "Come on smile. It was funny the way you came into town. No one cares. All they want is a teacher to teach their children. So forget the past and let's enjoy the dance."

Samantha looked into his dark eyes. Something queer happened to her. She felt her body tremble and her heart begin to sing. She had never felt this way before. Was she having a fit? Was she sick? Was she just wishing that Ted would look at her and love her as she heard about in story books?

Chapter VII

Ted turned to Samantha and pulled her into his arms. He felt the heat spread thorough his body. This was love, he never believed could happen to him. "I love that song," he said, and wanted to add, I love you more. Strange, he had hoped that he would met the girl of his dreams some day, and now he did.

Samantha stood stiffly in his arms. She looked into Ted's black eyes. She felt a chill course through her body. "I can't dance, I never was allowed to dance. It was sinful to dance or listen to music. I would be a burden to you to dance."

With her shoulders hunched, Samantha peered up at Ted. Ted smiled and pulled her closer. "I shall be the first to dance with you. I am honored. Just follow my legs. I'll go slow and you can feel my legs as we dance. Press your legs next to mine."

The music was playing "Old Suzanne" and Ted swung Samantha out into the dance floor. He held her tightly around her small waist as if she would disappear at any second. They whirled in time with the music. She stumbled. Her body pushed into his broad chest.

His lungs seemed to stop and he could only smell her sweet odor of lavender. The soft breasts rested against his hard chest. He wanted to pull her closer to his body, but was afraid she would resist. She was lost, and did not know what to do.

She looked up at him. "I told you I never danced before."

"Forget it. You are the best thing to happen to me. I wish you could stay here forever." said Ted. "In my arms, I want to protect you from any thing in this world that would hurt you."

Samantha's heart pounded in her chest and she had difficulty catching her breath. She felt like a Princess and Ted was the Prince.

He stared down on her. "Do you have a boyfriend?" Ted held his breath. He knew McGuire had taken her under his wing. He only hoped that Samantha thought of him as a friend, not a boyfriend.

"A boyfriend. I am glad to have a friend that I can trust. Yes, I guess McGuire is my friend. My father is the telegraph operator, but he does not want to know me. The nuns said it was because I am so ugly."

"You are beautiful. The most beautiful person I have ever set my eyes on. I could look at you forever and ever. You are precious to me, and I have only just met you." said Ted. "I want to know you, really know you."

Samantha looked deeply into his eyes. She felt like she was falling down into a well of kindness that she never knew. She shook her head and continued to lean into his body as the music stopped.

Ted dropped his hands from around her body. He wished he could hold her forever and ever. He leaned his face close to Samantha. "I want to be your friend. In fact, I like to be more than a friend to you. But please, let me be your friend."

"I want you to be my friend. I have such a funny feeling about you. I don't know what to say. I have never felt like I do now," said Samantha.

Ted shook his head in wonder. "Maybe you feel that way because you have never had a friend. Someone to count on, to love, to be free to feel wanted."

As she turned to leave, her new dress flared out around her ankles. She looked away from Ted. Then his hand fell lightly on her shoulders.

"May I have another dance with you?" asked Ted.

"Oh, Yes. I would love that," said Samantha as she once again turned and looked into the dark eyes of Ted. "I do not know how to dance. But it felt so good. So wonderful It was like I was walking on air."

Mike stood at the Weatherspoon table and watched Ted and Samantha dance and then he watched them talk. He felt cheated. He promised himself he would have the next dance. Mike looked around and saw McGuire throwing his charm around by laughing and talking to everyone. Still, he was closely following Ted and the way he held Samantha. Mike thought that at least

McGuire isn't dancing with Samantha. What ever was he to do to make her notice him, Mike.

Ginger stood with her arms out ready to dance with Ray. Jim Ray was from the Bar X ranch and came over and took her into his arms. "You dance like a goddess," Jim said. He looked at her with his shiny brown eyes and white hair bleached by the sun. "You forgot you were to dance with me? I think of you all the time, you know. I love you. Come on Ginger, smile. You are so beautiful when you smile."

Ginger looked at Jim for the first time. Not as a friend, but as a suitor. She smiled shyly. She did like Jim and his sense of humor and his take charge quiet attitude. She liked Ted and she liked Jim and maybe some other men. It was fun to have them all want her.

Ginger was a girl that men liked. She was honest, and sweet, and she tried to help anyone in need. She looked at Jim Ray and for the first time she heard the pounding of her heart. Was she in love with Jim Ray?:

Kate looked at Mike standing by the table. She walked over to him and put her arms out to dance. Mike took her out on the floor and they danced.

Kate stared at Mike. "You look lonely. Why not find some girl to dance with. Cat got your tongue?"

Mike growled. When would she mind her own business and let him alone? Mike bunched his muscles. He was a man now, and he did not have to take her nagging all the time. It was time to put a stop to it, but not at the dance. He would not spoil it with a fight with his mother.

Samantha smiled as the rhythm beat into her head. Ginger knew his favorite song so they must be married. She turned to Ted and looked deeply into his eyes.

"Are your children coming to the school when it opens?" Samantha said as she looked closely at Ted. "You and Ginger look so beautiful together. How many young ones do you have?"

Ted answered in a voice showing his displeasure. "We are not married, not even engaged. What made you think that Ginger and I – well, we are good friends. Have been since we were little."

Samantha felt her face turn crimson. "I am sorry. I just thought- It was the way she knew your favorite song, and the way she looked at you."

Ted cut her off. "Glad we are talking about dancing. I get to hold you close. When I hold you, I hold a piece of heaven in my hands. Do You understand what I am trying to say? To change the subject, I heard tell the new teacher was little, and you just come up to my shoulder. Do you think it will be hard to control some of those kids. Why some of them are over six feet tall. Maybe, you need a man to protect you. I want to apply for that job."

Samantha looked down at his boots. "You think I can't handle the students? Remember, I was brought up with the nuns. I can handle anything."

He put his big hands around Samantha, as the music started to play. They started to dance to the tune of the fiddle. As they danced, he wished Samantha would stumble and fall into his chest once again. His manhood came alive as it seldom did for any woman. He was madly in love with Samantha, who he only knew for less than a moment in time.

He felt something, he had dreamed of feeling, but didn't suppose it would happen to him. He wanted to take Samantha into his arms and kiss her, and keep her safe, and protect her forever. "Sure. You can teach. I said control. They all will be in love with you. You need a man to take care of you. Honestly, you don't need to teach. You could marry me."

Samantha smiled up at him. His black eyes sparkled back. "Marry you? I hardly know you."

Ted laughed. "I think you are adorable. Look, I'm not poor. I own a ranch. It's a big spread and a woman who-"

Her big hazel eyes suddenly sparkled with glee, "Look, I'm dancing, really dancing." Her laughter tingled like bells. She wanted to throw her hands out and shout. "I feel like I am floating on the clouds. I can't believe, I am dancing. I never dreamed that I would dance."

She twirled around by herself as she felt Ted's arms loosen around her. She was so proud of the fact that she was dancing and it was easy. She heard the music in her soul. She went back into Ted's arms. She was laughing with wonder.

Holding her tighter around the waist, Ted took Samantha's hand into his free one and kissed it. He pulled her gently closer to his body as he bent down next to her face. Samantha wanted to tell him, the music and his holding her made a storm flowing through her body. He slowly put his hands into her hair and drew her closer. He bent down and kissed her pink lips. His insides turned to water, as he wanted more and more of her. Samantha did not pull away, but she let the heat fill her body.

They glided with the music and Ted held Samantha closer still. He could hear her heart beat, or was that his? He wanted to keep her to himself and away from any other man. He hated McGuire because he knew that, McGuire had saved her from the mud and helped her in the school. He wanted to kiss her again.

Samantha looked up at him. He was so strong. She could feel his hand as they lay around her waist. His eyes were so black; they looked like endless pools of oil. Ted smiled down to her and without thinking she smiled back to him. Butterflies filled her whole body, and she wanted to shout to the world, something wonderful had happened to her.

She looked at his stern lips. They were so straight with anger, and then he smiled at her. Her heart beat time to the music and the feel of his hands. She wondered what he was thinking that he looked so stern. He smiled at her and her world burst full of flowers.

His smile brought sunshine to her heart. She had never felt wanted before, but now she felt like the world had opened to her.

"Can I come and call on you? One doesn't court here but a short time. It's not like in the East where it takes years."

She heard his words and could not believe anyone would want to call on her. Court her? The pressure of his body made her senses swim. "Samantha" he whispered. She looked up at him and he moved his face closer to hers. He was set to kiss her again. At that very second a hand came to rest on his shoulder.

Ted looked over his shoulder and there stood McGuire. "Cut in now. You had her long enough,"

McGuire took hold of Samantha's waist and pulled her over to him. "Stay away from that man, he just likes to find his joys with any woman. Never means what he says. You know he's with those cows all the time. Any woman looks good to him after looking at cows so long."

Samantha felt her heart skip a beat. "I look like a cow?" she said. She had believed Ted and that he would call on her. But McGuire was always there to help her. She should be grateful that he cut in. But, she did not trust him for some reason. He smiled too broadly. She hated him with his quick smile and his broad shoulders. She hated McGuire for busting her dreams. It was in that moment of time that Samantha realized she did not even like McGuire.

Then she remembered every thing that McGuire did for her. How did she think bad meanness against him. She should be proud that he even noticed her. She was unholy to think anything about McGuire, but bless the day he saved her.

Ginger watched the whole scene. She was going to make the most of it now. She stopped dancing with Jim "I need to talk to Ted, I hope you don't mind."

Jim looked at her as she moved away from him. Jim was a fool to be in love with Ginger. He wondered if Ginger would ever notice him as anything but a friend? He was going to have to show Ginger that he cared for her, really cared enough for her that he wanted her as his wife. Why was she always chasing after Ted?

Jim wasn't poor. He saved every cent he earned so he could buy a ranch and raise children. He wanted his children's mother to be Ginger. He knew she was ready to marry, he wanted it to be with him. Ted and he had been friends since they were children and even before they started what little school they had. This was not a place that education came easy, as all the teachers seem to marry as soon as they came. Most of the children had to go somewhere else to school. That's how Ted and he learned to read and do arithmetic.

Ted bought the ranch from his Pa who died. He was lucky to have a Pa that had a ranch. But Jim had no such luck and that was why he saved every penny he earned. He would have a ranch, and he would have Ginger, his dream. He knew exactly what ranch he would buy, and he had started the process of buying it for right now. All he need was Ginger the mother of his children, and his dream wife.

Ginger swayed up to Ted and smiled at him. "I meant that this was our dance, and it turns out it is different music, but still our own dance. We can still dance it even if the song has different words I think they just play whatever they feel like. " Ginger put her arms around Ted's shoulders and smiled a him. "Come on, the music will soon be over and I know you are hot for that little schoolteacher."

He watched as Samantha danced with McGuire. Ted took Ginger into his arms and started to dance with her. Samantha felt blood run through her chest. He was so very nice and now he was with Ginger. He did say he would call on her. What did 'call on' mean anyway? He and Ginger seemed so right for each other. She noticed he did not hold Ginger as tightly as he had held her when they dance. Why did he hold her so tight, was it to be sure she followed his steps? Because he really liked her, or even better still, he loved her. What would it be like to be loved by someone?

The night rumbled on with laughter, dancing and eating. McGuire was talking to her, but she really didn't hear a word he said. Her mind was a thousand miles away, thinking, and wishing that Ted really liked her.

She danced with McGuire and then Ted came over and took her into his arms. She felt his strong hands on her waist. Ted looked down into her eyes.

"You're the type of woman I have always looked for," Ted said and pulled her closer to his body. "I just never thought I would find the woman of my dreams. Do you know I dreamed of you before you ever came to town? Do you believe in love at first sight?"

"Oh," Samantha uttered as she looked into his dark eyes. It was possible to fall in love at first glance. She knew she had. She just knew McGuire made up stories to suit himself. He was a story teller, not a liar, but he liked to believe what he said, true or make believe.

She did not know what to think. She had no experience with men. Were they making fun of her? Ginger watched the two closely. She knew her dreams of Ted and her had ended. She could tell he was falling in love with Samantha and all he though of Ginger ever was as a friend. Ginger thought of Jim. There was a man's man.

Ginger wondered why she never noticed how much attention Jim had paid her. How much he had tried to please her.

Samantha's heart was pounding so fast, she thought she would faint. Her face felt flushed.

"Are you all right?" asked Ted.

She shrugged her shoulders. "Please, I need to sit down."

"Would you like me to get you something to drink?" asked Ted as his hands caressed her hands.

"Please," said Samantha. As soon as Ted left, McGuire was at her side. "What is Ted doing? Are you all right? You seem flushed. Did he say something that he shouldn't?"

Samantha looked at him. He looked so worried. He was carrying what she thought was a glass of water. Samantha reached up and took a large swallow from his glass. The liquid burnt a path down her throat. She coughed and could not breathe. Her heart pounded in her breast and she could not catch her breath.

"Better drink some more. You need it. Help you think about what you're doing," said McGuire. "Especially about Ted. You know that you can count on me for anything. I am here to help you."

She shook her head, but McGuire took the glass of gin and put it up to her mouth. "Swallow," he said. "I want you to forget about Ted."

At that moment Ted came back with a glass of lemonade. He watched McGuire holding the glass of gin to her lips. "Hey, what are you doing McGuire?" yelled Ted.

"None of your business, Ted. I found her first, remember that," McGuire said as he turned to face Ted. "I mean to keep her from you."

McGuire put his hands up to fight. Ted followed suit. Kate came over and grabbed Samantha. "You fellows are trying to ruin the first dance Samantha has ever been to? Come on, Samantha, I'm taking you home. You don't need these bully men around you."

Samantha rose as the park spun around her and she held tightly to Kate's hand. Kate started to walk away from the party but Samantha stumbled and almost fell. Ted and McGuire looked at each other.

"I'll be darned," said McGuire. "I sure didn't want to ruin her first party."

Ted started to follow Kate and Samantha. Kate turned around and yelled at Ted, "Don't you give me any guff. Stay away from her tonight, both of you."

Samantha's world spun out of control and she could hardly walk. She leaned heavily on Kate's shoulder. Mike watched for a second and ran over to his mother.

"It's that McGuire. He gave her gin. I saw him give her that glass of gin. I can't believe he would do that to her. Here let me carry her. I'm pretty strong and big." Mike picked up Samantha and he cuddled her into his arms. He felt her body so warm and tender. She was so light and small. He carried her down the path to their house. Mike never took time to help anyone and least of all the girl who took his place in the loft.

Kate felt like there was something she should know and know. Was Mike in love with Samantha? Was that why he was acting crazy?

Mike touched heaven as he carried Samantha close to his chest. Her hair fell into his face and he smelled her sweet smell of lavender. He secretly caressed her small body as he cradled her in his arms. He pulled her body closer to his chest. Samantha sighed and smuggled against him. He knew he was all man as his manhood struggled in the tight confines of his pants.

Chapter VIII

Ted watched Samantha, Kate and the children leave. He had an ache in his heart. His Grandparents started the range many years ago, when winds howled and wild animals ruled. Ted made the ranch expand, until it was huge. He built the house which was two stories with many bedrooms and painted white. It had a big living room with a fireplace. The kitchen was inviting for someone to cook and sit and just visit in its confines. It was ready for a home full of children. He wanted Samantha, as badly as rain needed for the crops.

He surprised himself that he could love so quickly. He felt that Samantha was his, and some how he had to prove himself qualified to have her.

Ginger and he were friends from when they were toddlers. Both their folks had been fast friends. Ginger, when she was older, would come out to the ranch and they would ride together. Ginger was a great rider and a real friend. Could it be that Ginger had expected him to marry her?

He never tried to kiss Ginger. He never even held her close, except when they were dancing. Ginger lately had been coming out to the ranch. He didn't even notice how many times she came to visit.

His housekeeper had been the one his folks hired. They had built a special little house for her and her family. She cooked up the most wonderful meals when he was home. She always brought out lemonade and home made cakes whenever Ginger visited.

Could it that his housekeeper wanted another woman in the house? Ted just stood and watched Samantha and Kate and her family until they had disappeared. His heart lurched as he watched Mike cradle Samantha. He didn't care about anything just as long as she was his. Rage covered his mind as he watched Mike cuddle Samantha near his chest.

Ted was tall and built like a bull, but he was shy with the ladies. He had dreams of a woman that was his and his alone: someone petite and beautiful. His rust colored hair was always wild looking. His eyes were so black they looked like holes in the ground. His mouth was stern, but he had nothing to laugh about since he was young. Would a woman want to live a life on this ranch with hardly any friends around.

He was out so much of the time on the range, because he hated coming home to an empty house. He would be home with bells on if he had a wife, and that wife was Samantha. On the range, he had people to talk to that understood him. Even they had a home to go to after a drive, or a lady to love.

The moment he saw Samantha, he knew this was the woman he had dreamed about all his life. The woman he had waited for to enter his home. Not with McGuire standing there ready and willing to help her. McGuire and the ladies just clicked the second they saw him.

He acted differently with Samantha. Was he going to ask her to marry him? Was he finally going to love only her? He didn't have a chance if McGuire was going to really love Samantha.

Ted thought about LouLou. McGuire had LouLou to love and he always came back to her no matter what he had done Maybe, McGuire would just be a friend to Samantha. Not by a long shot, Ted thought. McGuire was smitten with her. He could see it in his eyes and the way he held her. He noticed Ginger coming his way. He better let it be known that Jim was wild about her. That Jim wanted to marry her. Jim was such a shy man when it came to women, if he told Ginger that Jim loved her, she would stop trying to trap him. Ted was shy, but found the strength to tell Ginger abut Jim.

Ted saw McGuire from the corner of his eye. McGuire stood right next to him before Ginger could make it to his side. They looked at each other, sizing each other up. They were the same size, but McGuire drew people to him like a magnet.

"How could you give Samantha gin?" asked Ted.

"Hey," McGuire smiled and said, "she grabbed the glass from my hand. I never though of giving it to her."

"Yeah, sure. I believe you, I saw you put the glass to her lips." Ted said as he balled his hands into fists. He wanted to smash McGuire in his pretty face.

"Come on, what's the big deal?" asked McGuire. "Kate will take care of her. Plus I told you, hands off. She's mine. Where were you when she needed help?"

"I just met her, and I'm going to marry her. How about that?"

"I don't think so," smirked McGuire. "Maybe I met the woman of my dreams and I will marry her. You're a casualty of nature, all bull and wild hair and dark eyes."

Ted's face turned red. What McGuire said about him was true. He was no prize catch, but he was a hard worker. He loved but once, and he loved forever. He wanted Samantha, but he doubted that she would want him. A misfit. A mistake of nature.

Ginger stood still watching them. No one got close to McGuire. He drew people to him true, but no one knew much about him. Why was McGuire so close mouth about his life? Had he a mother, a father, sisters or brothers? It seemed he knew about money and how to acquire it and use it. He must have to come from wealth. He dressed too well and he knew what suited him.

Ginger walked over to the two men, and put her hands on both their shoulders. "Loosen up will you. Samantha will pick who she wants. She is a big girl. This is a dance, so let's have fun,"

Both men looked at her. She was a power in this town, with her Pa the owner of the dry goods store. Ted coughed. He put his hands on Ginger's arm. "I need to talk to you."

McGuire walked away. Ted looked at Ginger in her eyes. "I have to tell you Ginger, Jim is crazy about you. Why don't you give him a chance? I-well, I- I've fallen for Samantha."

"I will give Jim a chance," said Ginger as she smiled. "I've been thinking that myself that Jim is sort of special. Do you think he will ever get up the nerve to speak to me?"

"I think that you have to sort of push him."

Ginger nodded and started to walk over to Jim. To her surprise, Jim was walking over to her. He held out his hand and took her hand. "Let's dance," he said.

Ginger smiled at Jim. She never noticed how good-looking he was. Time to settle down, she thought, and Jim was a good honest man.

Jim pulled her into his arms and bent his head. "I can wait no longer for you Ginger." Jim kissed her right on the dance floor. He felt the passion build in his body. He could not stop kissing her. Ginger opened her mouth. Suddenly, she felt like she was in heaven.

Ginger raised her head and looked at Jim. "Oh, Ginger, I love you. I have always loved you. Please say you love me."

"I love you, Jim, I really do," said Ginger.

Ginger looked at Jim. "I have always felt love for you, but I didn't let it ripen. It was held tight to my chest. It took you long enough to say something to me."

Jim swelled. It was worth the effort it took him to tell Ginger he loved her. He loved her for so long, and he never told her.

"First thing we got to do, Ginger, is get married. I have waited for you long enough. Let's set the date and do it?" said Jim as he looked into her eyes, and was surprised to see they were full of love for him.

"About time you said something that makes sense," muttered Ginger. "We have to talk to my folks about the wedding. I want a big and wonderful wedding, with everyone invited in town."

Ginger snuggled into his arms and her body trembled and felt his strong hands encase her. His hard frame held her body nestled close to his.

"I have enough money saved to buy a ranch. In fact, I am buying a ranch right now. I had hoped you would marry me. I love you so. I wanted to give you something special. I bought the O'Leary ranch"

"Oh Tom, it is perfect. I always liked the O'Leary ranch. It was a place I played in and loved. It has a wonderful old house that needs fixing, and I love to fix things as you know."

They looked at each other as if they had just found a gold mine. It was so strange that they fell in love at this time and place.

Chapter IX

THE DAY AFTER THE PARTY, Ted called on Samantha. His boots reflected light like a mirror. His blue denims were pressed and clean and his red checked flannel shirt was open at the neck. His rusty hair standing every which way shone redder in the sun and his black eyes shot out warm fires.

"I have to leave tonight. Cattle got to be pushed up to the tracks. That's what happens when you own a ranch. I have a big house with a rambling porch all around the outside. There are shade trees and a place to plant a little garden. Maybe it could be flowers or vegetables growing in the rich soil. I have a great housekeeper, Gabe, who would love to see me married. She's about sixty-years old, but she can cook. Her daughter cleans the place. It needs furniture, that would be up to the woman of the house. Samantha, please wait till I come back before you do anything. Especially with McGuire! Try to think of me."

Samantha looked at Ted who looked so manly and honest. She noticed how tall he was and how broad his shoulders were. She wanted to take her hands and straighten out his rust colored hair. McGuire had helped her so many times. What in the world was she thinking? "Ted, I wish you won't talk about McGuire like that. He has helped me so many times. He was the first one to save me from the mud, and find a place for me to live. He is even now as we speak, cleaning up the schoolhouse for me."

Ted shuffled his feet, and moved closer to Samantha. His hands reached out and held her shoulders. "I don't mean anything bad. I'm so jealous of him, because he is close to you. I just, oh, Samantha, I just want you to think of me. Maybe marry me. Can you do that? I mean I do love you, and want to marry you. I can not think of anything but you."

Ted pulled Samantha close to him. He felt her small body against his. He bent his head and kissed her softly on the mouth. She didn't know what to do because the world did not stand still but went round and round in her head. Ted put his arms around her body and kissed her hard and long. She knew she loved Ted. She closed her eyes as warmth flooded her body. For the first time in her life, she knew what she wanted – love. Samantha started to kiss him back, but then she pushed him away. She was foolish to feel love for this man. Maybe McGuire was the man she should be thinking about. McGuire saved her from the first time she came to town.

They stared at each other. Samantha looked deeply into Ted's black eyes that sparkled like mountain fire. His mouth did not look so stern. It looked inviting.

"Le's take some horses and ride out into the desert." Ted said as he took her hand. "It's a great day for going into the desert and see the cacti in bloom."

"I can't ride. Never have. It seems that I really can't do anything you do. It shows that we are not made for each other. I bet you go kissing every girl you meet."

"You're right. I never would kiss Ginger the way I kiss you, because I do not love her. I love you. I never kissed Ginger in my life." Ted took another step closer to Samantha.

"I said, I don't ride a horse. I am afraid of them. They are so big and scary." Samantha turned her face up to Ted's face.

"I'll teach you to love horses," Ted said, then raised her face to look at him. "I mean I'll teach you to ride. It will be a joy. I don't go around kissing every girl I meet. In fact, I never felt the way I feel about you."

"Please, I don't want to ride." She turned away from Ted. Her dress flared around her legs. She spoke over her shoulder. "I think I better go in." She could not control the trembling of her hands, so she clasped them together. Then she turned and faced Ted. "All you do is try to kiss me. I don't know if it is right or wrong."

"Wait," Ted yelled, as he grabbed her waist and pulled her towards him. "I'll get us a buggy and we'll just ride out to the desert and back. We'll see the wild flowers in bloom. Samantha, there is nothing wrong in kissing someone you love."

"Ted, I don't think I can go riding with you, so, I-"

Ted smiled again. "Hey, I promise I'll be good. Just let me get to know you."

Ted just knew that if he could get her alone she would open up to his love. He never knew love, but it burnt in his heart now and his body was on fire. He had to leave, but he wanted to leave her thinking of him, and maybe, thinking of him alone.

Her heart pounded so hard, Samantha knew she could not just stand here. She never had a man ask her to ride in a buggy so humbly. She rode with McGuire, but he didn't really count. He never asked humbly. He just ordered. But Ted, was something she had dreamed about. Some how he fit every dream she ever had. She knew McGuire only as a friend who helped her, not as a man who would marry her and dream of family and love. She could not imagine McGuire with a family and a home.

"All right, I'll ride in a buggy for a short ways. Ted, I don't want you kissing me again. It's just not right." Samantha's face turned bright red. The reason she blushed was because she did want him to kiss her and hold her.

"I'll be right back with the buggy. Samantha don't you dare run and hide. I promise it will be fun."

Ted jogged back to the hotel where buggies were for rent. He ran into the hotel and got a picnic basket filled with food and wine. He came back to the house. Samantha was standing right where he left her. She was wearing her black skirt and starched white blouse. Ted jumped down from the buggy and walked over to Samantha. He picked her up as her hair fell into his face. He felt her waist, so tiny, and he pictured her lying next to him in bed without any clothes on. She would be velvet smooth. Her body would be stark white against her black hair. His dream burst as he looked at her sitting in the buggy and staring out at the desert. God, just give him a chance with Samantha.

The sun shone and they looked into the sky at the sunshine, and then they looked at each other. Ted slowly had the horse pull the buggy out into the desert. The ride was slow and smooth and Samantha began to feel more secure in the thought of riding into the unknown. The flowers were small but all yellow and purple flowers filled the desert sand. For the first time in her short life, she felt the hand of God on her arm. A smile filled her face with the wonder of the world.

Ted noticed the smile and he smiled to himself. This was going to be one of the best days in his life. He was with the women he loved and she was happy.

McGuire watched from the doorway of the saloon as they rode out of town. His mouth scowled. He had planned to keep Samantha all to himself. Certainly not married, maybe as his mistress. He just was not the sharing type of man.

Ted let the horse go into a trot. The buggy danced over the rough road as they went out of town towards the desert and the mountains. After about a half-hour, Ted pulled the horse to a stop under a giant tree.

"Surprise, Samantha. I brought us a picnic lunch. I have, chicken, potato salad, pickles, bread, cake and wine. By the way, this tree is what we call our forest. It just takes one tree to make a forest. This is a foxtail or better known as Bristlecone."

"The tree is beautiful. I love it. I have never been on a picnic before. What do you do on a picnic? Do we just eat? I never drank wine; it was for the priests only. Is it like that water stuff I drank at the dance?"

"First of all, we start a picnic off by kissing. Yes, sorry, but that is the start. Wine is no where near that horrible stuff you drank at the dance. You'll love the wine with the chicken and bread. I have a real home, Samantha, we'll have wine every night. You'll love everything I brought. I promise you," Ted stopped speaking and jumped down from the buggy. He then picked up Samantha and pulled her out of the buggy.

They stood very still. Then Ted put his arms around Samantha and kissed her long and hard. His tongue went around her lips. She opened her mouth. Ted let her go and grabbed the picnic basket from the buggy.

Samantha reeled from the kiss and stood very still to get her balance. It was heaven to just feel his lips next to hers. What would happen if I put my tongue into his mouth?

He'd pulled a blanket out of the buggy and put it on the ground in the shade of the one tree. He helped Samantha sit down on the blanket and put the basket down next to her. He took out two glasses of real crystal and opened the wine. He handed one of the glasses to her. "To the most wonderful picnic ever eaten with the most beautiful woman who ever lived. Drink up, Samantha."

The wine tasted sweet. It slid down her throat. She drank a little more. It tickled her nose. She laughed. She took another sip. Ted watched her and put the chicken, bread and pickles on a plate and filled her glass up again.

They both ate every single piece of chicken and bread. The wine bottle became empty as Ted moved the basket out of the way and sat next to Samantha. He put his arms around her and kissed her. They leaned against the tree.

"Open your mouth," he commanded. Samantha did as she was told and she could feel his tongue invading her mouth She followed suit and her tongue went into his mouth. He pulled her closer, and her mind seemed to dance and whirl from the wine and the love she was receiving. She put her arms around Ted. They melted into each other. His hands started to open the buttons on her blouse and his big hand went into the blouse and caressed her bare breasts. He heard her moan. She pressed closer to his strong body. He was about to pull her breasts out of her blouse but he heard something.

The sound of a horse galloping closer and closer, Ted stopped. He looked up and saw McGuire galloping up to where they were leaning. Fire filled McGuire's heart as he watched what was happening. He wanted to tear Ted apart. He could not believe that Samantha had let Ted touch her breasts.

"Hello, there," McGuire called as he stopped inches from where they sat. Ted and Samantha pulled apart. His hair gleamed in the sun as he pushed his black hat back. Samantha jumped up. She gazed at McGuire and stared down at her open blouse. One breast was almost out of the blouse. She could not imagine what McGuire thought. She was a wanton creature. Why did it surprise her, the nuns said she was wonton.

He smelled the wine on Samantha's breath as he came closer to her. "I think you better be going home." He picked her up and put her into the buggy. "Button your blouse, Ted you take her home, or are you going to walk? She's leaving right now."

Ted wanted to kill McGuire right then. His hand went to his gun. He remembered he had left his guns back at the hotel. Ted shook his head to rid himself of his rage. Ted got up and got into the buggy. He knew McGuire was going to ride with them to her house. The outing was over and maybe his chance to have Samantha as his own, his wife, his mate, and his love. Samantha was the woman-child who was so innocent.

Ted felt a slight boil as McGuire rode next to the buggy watching every move Ted made. Samantha seemed to crawl into a hole of her own making, not looking at anyone. Tears slipped down her face and she hoped that neither man saw them as she buttoned her blouse.

"You didn't let Ted do anything to you? Did you?" asked McGuire.

"No, I-I I should not have let him unbutton my blouse. I am so bad."

"No, you are not." said McGuire in a husky tone, "You just don't know what is right now. Just forget it all happened."

When they arrived at Kate's house, McGuire jumped from his horse and swung Samantha down. "Go on inside," he said as he gently pushed her toward the door. Samantha fell against the door and then straightened up as McGuire opened the door for her. Samantha wobbled forward but McGuire put his hand on her elbow and led her into Kate's bedroom.

"Hey Kate," called McGuire, "better come to the house and help Samantha. Seems she is drunk as a skunk. What say you Ted? You wouldn't give her something to make her tipsy would you. Get the idea from the Gin last night"

"What are you doing to this girl? First its gin, and now I smell wine on her breath," yelled Kate. "Have you no feeling for this poor little girl?"

"I didn't do anything. It was Ted who gave her the wine. Go scream at him," McGuire shouted back. "Go figure what he was going to do with her. It was hot, and she drank what he told her to drink. She believed him a good man. But we know better, don't we Kate?"

Ted came to the door and looked at Kate holding Samantha up.

"I'm sorry, I don't know what I am doing. I want to marry her. I never felt this way about anyone before. Forgive me. I wanted her to love me." Ted said as he glanced down at his shinny boots. "I didn't give her wine to have my way with her. I only wanted her to fall in love with me."

Kate and McGuire looked at him as Samantha slipped down to the floor. Kate looked at Samantha laying on the floor, and then she looked at Ted.

"You are honest. You want to marry her? I think that is great.: cried Kate. "She needs someone to look after her. The poor little thing has no one to love her truly."

"Wait a moment," cried McGuire, "What about me? I love her. She has me."

Kate looked at McGuire and shook her head. "You love your self only. You're not capable of loving any one but you."

"Give me a break, haven't I tried my best for Samantha? Haven't I always helped her. Haven't I paid for her room and board and clothing?" screamed McGuire.

Ted looked at them both and picked up Samantha from the floor. "I'll put her on your bed Kate, till she wakes up. I'm sure she just needs some sleep for now."

*　　　*　　　*

The next week, Samantha did not see either man. She felt so bad that she had acted so loose. She missed Ted even if she only knew him such a short time. She had let him open her blouse and go inside to touch her breasts. What in the world was wrong with her? This was the reason her Pa hated her. He could see she was a whore.

As she leaned against the stone wall outside Kate's house, she could not stop chastising herself about her actions. She did not hear the buggy come to a sharp stop almost on top of her. McGuire jumped out of the buggy.

"Hey. Wool gathering?" shouted McGuire as he walked up to Samantha. She gave a quick jerk to her body and looked into McGuire's blue eyes.

Samantha gave him a big smile. She was so glad to see him. "Hello," she whispered. Maybe he forgot she had an open blouse when he saw her on the picnic. Maybe pigs have wings and can fly.

"Come along, your school is all cleaned up. You can move in right now. I do want you to see how lovely it looks. All the work I had the men do for you, I hope you appreciate it. It is worth it, if you like it." McGuire took her hand and then lifted her into the buggy. "You're light as a feather, but you just have to learn to ride a horse. This buggy business is not for around here. Tomorrow, I shall bring a very meek horse for you to learn to ride."

Samantha smoothed her black skirt and made sure her hair was in a tight neat bun. "You look much better when your hair is left loose, or at least tied back of your head in a horse's tail."

Samantha looked at him with half closed eyes. She wanted to tell him that with her hair lose she was a wanton woman. That was the reason she let Ted touch her breast. As long as she kept her hair secure, her body was secure.

Back at Kate's house, Mike watched them go. He was jealous that she was with McGuire. If he hurried, he could be at the schoolhouse before them. He would take the short cut across the desert. He wished McGuire would leave town and leave Samantha alone. Mike hated McGuire because it seemed McGuire had the inner track with Samantha.

Mike knew he was second best in everything that Samantha thought about him. He could try to kiss her, but then, she might hate him for that. Red rage filled his body.

When Samantha and McGuire got to the schoolhouse, McGuire made a big deal out of taking out a key. "Got a new lock on the door for you, besides which, I also got a new stout door. So when you go to sleep, you know you are safe. Don't look so sad. You knew you were going to live in the schoolhouse. I even got you a new mattress and repainted the bed that was built into the wall. Yes, but you have to wait till I show it all to you. Come on. Act surprised at all the wonders I have had accomplished in this old schoolhouse."

McGuire jumped out of the buggy and then lifted Samantha into his arms. He held her and looked into her eyes. He pushed his hat back as his golden hair made a halo around his head. He lowered his head and his lips pressed hers gently at fist and then without thought, he kissed her long and hard. Samantha's head went around in circles. She had never felt so fragile. He set her shaking feet onto the ground, but her arms held on to his shoulders. He kissed her again as his tongue darted unto her mouth.

"Don't," she cried.

Her small hands pushed against his chest. There was no way she could move his body. It was like rock. She wanted to move it, and then, she wanted him to love her. She wanted someone to love her.

"Remember," McGuire said as his hand gently caressed her face, "you said you wanted to pay me for all this work and things I have done for you?. Time for payment is now."

"I know I owe you," she whispered and felt her body tighten at the spine. She wanted him to - to take her, but then she wanted to say it was against her will. She wanted someone to want her.

She twisted and tried to push away, but he held her tightly in his hands. "You owe me. I saw you let Ted touch you all over. So relax and enjoy my loving you. You know you melt every time I touch you. Come on, I saw you love it when someone touches your breasts. I saw you let Ted do it to you. You're the type of girl that likes sex. Tell me you don't melt every time I touch you?"

She looked at his face, and his white teeth glittered in the sun, like wolf's teeth. His large hands covered her breasts. His fingers kneaded her breasts. He slowly started to open the buttons on her white blouse. His hands went into her blouse as his mouth caressed and teased her mouth. He could feel the soft velvet flesh of her breasts in one hand and the other drew her closer to his body. He kissed her harder with passion.

He felt the softness of her breasts like no other breast he had ever touched. He let his fingers roam around the pink tip of her breast. He watched her face as it changed to that of desire and need.

McGuire looked at her eyes, which were twin peaks of daze. She seemed to not know what was happening to her. Her world was a world of feelings and desire. She was not the lost soul of the convent. She was living and breathing a new life. She wanted someone to say "I love you" so very much.

He knew he felt like heaven had descended into his world. He pulled Samantha closer to his body, and he felt his body react to her nearness. He made love to LouLou, but it never felt like this. He could not tell right from wrong at this moment of time. All he knew was that Samantha belonged to him. She was his possession. She was his to take and hold and love.

Samantha pushed at him with all her might. He stood rock solid with his arms now around her waist. "Look into my eyes and tell me you don't like me touching you. And stop thinking of that loser Ted."

"I don't know. I know I am not good. The nuns always said I would do the worst thing in the world." answered Samantha "I like being touched. I like being loved. In fact, I love to have someone touch me."

"No, You were meant to be loved. No matter what they told you. You are at heart a lover. You belong to me. You know that as a fact," replied McGuire.

She gazed into his lake-blue eyes. She could see the passion in his eyes. She could feel the throb of drums in her own blood. She did not know her own mind. At least, she thought she did not love him. She had an attraction to Ted but then she was not sure. He held this attraction that she allowed him to do whatever he wanted with her. He was magic, she could not resist his magic. She wanted someone to want her desperately. She knew that she would not stop him,. No matter what he did to her. All her life, she wanted someone to say they loved her.

McGuire tasted victory. He knew she would not fight him. His heart leapt in his chest. McGuire never took a woman unless he was sure it was what she wanted. He was sure Samantha wanted him, he could see it in her hazel eyes as they turned a bright green.

"I must show you your new bed and mattress now," he said as he picked her up and carried her up the stairs to the little bedroom. "I think that is the fist place we should go. I think you will love it. I bought it for us. It is ours forever."

"Forever," she said in a low voice. "We will use it forever." Her eyes grew large as she looked at him. Was she to be his mistress as LouLou was?

His eyes charmed her like a snake. She just knew she must do as he asked. All reason left her mind as she watched him look at her. It was a miracle that he should even like her.

"Yes, I even bought us a new mattress. Had to make sure there were no bugs in it. Especially as we both will be using it."

"Put me down," cried Samantha. "I don't want this." He laughed as he carried her up the steep steps. She kicked and struggled in his arms.

"Come on Samantha, you know you can hardly wait for me to love you. This is our first time, but we have loads of times to look forward to after this."

As they went up the narrow stairs, Samantha put her arms around his neck. She pulled her body close to his. She smiled and her face lit up like a hundred candles. This was what she craved. A body that loved her, and her alone.

He gently put her down on the bed. He looked at her as part of her hair escaped from her tight bun. Gently he pulled the pins from her hair as he held both her hands in his one big hand. Her black hair cascaded down her shoulders and back making a cameo of her face. Her soft pink mouth was incapable of any sound as he kissed her with passion. He wanted to possess all of her in one big bite, like a jelly apple that tantalized him with its ruby red skin.

His hands reached out to the unbuttoned blouse, and he took the blouse off as he held her in his arms and kissed her neck and her shoulders. He pulled her breasts from the camisole she wore. He bent and kissed each breast. The rosy tip of her breast invited him to linger and sample. Never in his life had he tasted breasts that tasted like candy.

He knew she liked his tasting her breasts. He kneaded her breasts as his mouth traveled down her body. She could feel the tension build in her body. Her body loved what he was doing to her. This was a place she had never knew existed. Her body churned like the waves of the ocean. She wanted to push him away but each second she felt a new sensation. Life could not be so wonderful to her, if she had such feelings. It made her feel like cotton candy. She wanted him to kiss her body.

Samantha felt great waves wash over her mind. She floated in an ecstasy of delight. This was so unexpected, so wonderful, and so beautiful. Her eyes closed at the sensations that rocked her body.

She knew she was being lured by the devil. Like the nuns told her; her hair was evil. It made her feel things that she should never feel. She knew she was wanton, but never this wild. With her hair loose, she lost control. She was a wild animal.

He took off his shirt and pulled off his boots and pants. He stood buck naked in front of her. She had never seen a man without clothing; she had really never seen any real man in her experiences in the Nunnery.

Her face heated up as she inspected him. She noticed his large shaft which stood out big and ugly. Her eyes flicked up and down his body as he stood there. He knew she was looking at him in wonder. Was she doomed to eternal damnation? She was the devil's own flesh and blood.

He came towards her. His fingers pulled her skirt and her pantaloons down. She lay now on the bed soft and inviting with out a stitch of clothing on. He lay on the bed next to her and took her into his arms.

His arms soothed her as he brushed them across her back. She could hardly breath. She wanted to cry and scream at the same time. Her head fell against his chest. His chest was broad and strong.

"Oh, God, you are so beautiful. I wanted you when you looked so funny all covered with mud. I wanted you when I saw you in the bathtub. I have wanted you it seems like forever. You know in your heart that you are mine. I should put you in a box and close it up and open it for myself only. I was so jealous that you let Ted touch you."

McGuire's hands roamed over her body softly and gently. She never felt like this before. It was like syrup gently floating around her body. She closed her eyes and just let the whole sensation flood her entire body. She felt like a leaf, floating in the wind, as he stroked her body. He had never felt a woman who made him think of marriage and children and flowers. He kissed her gently on her lips, her breasts, and then down to her thighs.

He could feel the heat in his own body, but best of all, he felt the heat rise from Samantha. She turned her face towards his and she put her arms around his neck. She ran her fingers up and down his back. He rammed his manhood into her body. He felt the shield of her virginity give way. He stopped for a second. He knew she was a virgin, so why was he surprised. It was because he didn't believe anyone could be a virgin.

But the way she had acted with Ted, he believed she had sex before. He was jealous of Ted. He was just a rough man, without any skill such as he, McGuire possessed. McGuire was her master.

He continued slowly and steadily pounding her as he felt her whirl away in feelings she had never sensed before. He went inside her and out. He felt her push to be next to him. He continued to pull his manhood in and out of her body. He felt her pull herself closer to him. She came and moaned and he came with her as she let out a small sound of pleasure.

He looked into her eyes as she tried to breathe. Her hazel eyes were filled with so much emotion, she never dreamed she possessed. He kissed her before she could say anything. She was so young and innocent. He just had to make it right. The old plantation idea of virginity took hold of his brain. He had no right to take a virgin. He was a man of honor. He had crossed the line.

"Are you going to stay here tonight?" McGuire asked as he got out of bed. He picked up his pants and shirt. His mind seemed to stop thinking as he looked at her. She was like a world he never entered. She was what he needed the most and wanted so very much.

He dressed slowly as he knew Samantha was watching him. He knew her eyes raked his body in wonder. He could picture what she was thinking. She was thinking he should ask her to marry him. But what of LouLou? And what about his freedom? He had to leave now or he would say something he would regret. Marry? When had he started to think of that?

Shame darted into the heart of Samantha. She did not know what to say or do. She had expected McGuire to ask her to marry him, but he was dressing. He was leaving.

He looked at her lying naked in the bed. He gazed at her like nothing of importance had happened. She was an insult to womanhood. She could feel his shame for her run through her body. She was like all the whores in his mansion. She had spread her legs without thinking. Samantha quickly got out of bed and dressed.

She had wanted love so badly that she would do anything for it. She had sold her soul. She was a wanton woman now. What right had she to think of Ted and his face. Ted would never understand what she felt, or thought. She was evil to the core. She had a wonderful feeling about all the love of McGuire. She had wanted it to never end.

"I'll see you out." she said. As her hands twisted into her skirt, she didn't believe what she had done, Not only that, she had enjoyed it. Samantha raised her head up to stop the shame she felt from showing. She didn't love him, yet she let him take her virginity. He never asked her to marry him and she wanted to die.

They walked single file down the narrow steps. She felt like a prisoner going to her execution. McGuire turned toward her. He wanted to say something. Anything to make her understand that this was the most wonderful thing that ever happened to him. He heard the pounding of his heart. He would wait till he was in more control. Samantha was too shy to find out things for herself. She just let life lead her around as it would.

He watched as she hung her head in shame. She raised her eyes and stared at him. What he had done to her was his fault and he had to make it right, no matter what. He watched as she lowered her lids to hide her tears.

Her mind was twirling around the fact that she was a willing partner to McGuire. She didn't even try to stop him. She liked the feeling of his holding her and loving her.

Samantha turned her head away from McGuire. She could not bear to look at him. Some thing in her wanted him to love her, and her alone. She did not follow him to the door of the school house. She stood frozen on the stairs like a Greek statue, void of emotion. Tears streamed down her face that she did not even feel. Lost, in a world that hated her.

McGuire reached the door to the schoolhouse. McGuire put his hat on and turned to take her hand. There was no hand to take. Samantha had not followed him to the door. She stood by the staircase. Her eyes were lowered.

He could almost see the tears in her eyes. He felt his heart lurch in his chest. What had he done to that poor little girl?

"Better lock the door when I go," said McGuire. "It is safer to have a locked door if you plan to stay. Would you like for me to take you back to Kate's?"

Samantha stood very still. She would stay here for awhile. She would stay until her world stopped falling apart. Then she would take her time to walk on back to Kate's house. She had to tell someone what she did. She had to clear her mind that it was a spur of the moment idea that took over her body.

"I'll stay here for a time," she said in a shaky voice. The stairs spun around in her mind like a ladder to hell.

Samantha nodded to herself, and watched McGuire leave. She let the tears come down her face. Her heart cried bitterly; she had just ruined her life. Then again, she had never had the sensations she had witnessed about her body.

Somehow or other, she felt the pounding of her heart as she thought about what she had done. She pushed her hair in back of her ears. The long locks were unruly and she kept her hands in her hair. It was her hair. She should cut it, and maybe she would not be so wild. She was able to do as she pleased and no one could vouch sake her and she wanted someone to love her. It did not matter that it was only for a moment in time, it had given her a release from fear and loneliness.

Outside, Mike watched McGuire leave. He knew that McGuire had his way with Samantha just as he did with all the women. It won't surprise him any, if his own Ma had sex with McGuire. He cursed him, and he wished he was like McGuire. He was no little kid, but a grown man. When would people recognize the fact, that he was gown? His own Mother thought of him as nothing but some overgrown kid.

Mike flexed his muscles. He felt his manhood rise up and he knew it was for Samantha. He loved her with all his being. How could he make her see that she was his love? How could he make his mother notice that he was a man?

The prick of the cactus made him stop thinking of himself. He had to think of Samantha and how he could make her love him. He looked at the spick of the cactus in his thumb. He pulled out the hurtful little thing that hurt like blazes. He watched as the blood flowed from his thumb.

He watched as McGuire rode away from the schoolhouse. He almost stood up as he thought about going into the schoolhouse. His eyes darted to the side of the school house. and he saw them. He saw Black Hawk and Jose the Coyote, riding up to the door of the schoolhouse. Their horses looked like they were well rested. As if they too, had waited for McGuire to finish his loving with Samantha. It was a play of people in the wings waiting for their part to begin. They knew she had given herself to McGuire. They both got off their horses. They swaggered into the schoolhouse.

He watched as the door to the school house stood open. He wanted to scream to Samantha to hurry up and close the door. Lock it. His eyes scanned up to the two men. He sensed the chill of terror run through his veins.

Mike was scared and hoped they would not see him. He stayed hidden behind the cactus. Once again he was struck by the cactus. He had better take care not to fall face into it.

Those two men were not to be fooled with as they could shoot an eye out of a flying bird. Mike could not think why they wanted Samantha. A cold thread of fear ran down Mike's back. They were going to do mean things to her. As much as he hated it, he had to get McGuire to come back and save Samantha. It was too much for him to handle. He felt the cold creep into his veins. Maybe he was just a yellow belly hunk of a boy still. He realized that McGuire could handle these men. He was afraid. If he had a gun, well, he would shot those yellow rat men. Yes, he would.

Mike slowly slide around the cactus and the mesquite tree he had been spying from. He worried about Samantha. He slithered down the bank of the desert sand that he lay on hoping there were no rattlers around. The sand stuck to his clothing. He tried to brush it off, but the thorns of the cactus dug deeper into his hand. Mike crawled on his knees until he was out of sight of the schoolhouse and then he stood up and started to run.

Mike's heart was pounding with a mad idea that if he saved Samantha, she would like him better than anyone else. He wanted to be her knight in shining armor. It was his first chance to prove that he was brave and stout of heart.

Mike felt the hot sands of the desert hit his face. He knew he was lifting the sand as he ran. He had to take care that he ran more smoothly. He ran like a man that was afraid of his own shadow. Take one step at a time, and think of how fast he could run. He was a good runner. He pictured his running smoothly and faster now, and he did run faster. He must as he had to save Samantha his one true love.

Mike ran his hand through his hair and felt a wave of courage enter into his heart. He was going to show the world that he, and he alone would save his love. If he had a gun, he would have done it all himself. But, without a necessary tool he was useless. He would get McGuire to save Samantha, and McGuire would tell her how he. Mike, saved her life.

He dreamed of her coming to him and telling him how proud she was that he saved her life. He was so wonderful and -he ran on and on.

Chapter X

BLACK-HAWK SWAGGERED INTO THE SCHOOLHOUSE. He was enormous. He was six feet four inches tall, and wide as an ox. He cast a gigantic shadow on the floor. His eyes were dead fish brown and his mouth was a thin straight line. He had a big hawk nose. It was his nose that gave him his name. His temper was fierce and he was not afraid of anyone, not anyone but he sure didn't want to fool with McGuire. He took any woman he felt like, except he steered clear of McGuire's women. This time it was an exception. He would be gone before McGuire knew anything. Following him into the room was Jose the Coyote. He was small, only five feet four inches tall and he was as thin as a starving coyote. His hair was wire black. His brown eyes looked as a blank piece of wrapping paper. He wore all black. He tried to look like McGuire, but his style of dress only showed how little he looked like the real thing.

The Coyote was known to cut up anyone who stood in his way with his sharp bowie knife. It made him whole. Cut and slash the people that got in his way, or better still, in Black Hawk's way. It was also known that Jose would do anything that Black-Hawk told him to do as he had no real mind of his own. Black Hawk was not a man to fool with.

Black Hawk stared at Samantha as she stood by the steps. She was the most beautiful woman he had ever seen. He dreamed of someone like her. Someone he could possess and have at his beck and call forever. A person like a story book princess, that was his. He could not believe that anyone would want to have her killed. He could not believe the money given to him to kill her.

He held his breath and just stared at her. He took in her hair, like midnight in the moonlight glow. He stared at her face half hidden by her hands that held her hair. He could feel the tears that were shed. He would show her the true meaning of love. No one would dare take her from him. This was the first time he felt whole and alive. She would be his and his alone. He would kill any man who tried to take her from him. He knew the Coyote expected to share this girl. He would never share his dream with some one as gross as the coyote.

Samantha didn't notice them as they entered the room. She bent over the rail leading upstairs to her little bedroom. Tears filled her eyes and she sniffed so loudly that she did not hear their footsteps coming towards her. What was it she was looking for?

Black-Hawk grabbed her arm and turned her around to face him. She inhaled sharply as she saw him. It was like looking under a bed and finding there were monsters in the world. She breathed deeply. Things could get worse, she thought. I am in the middle of a nightmare, and I shall never wake up.

"What do you want?" stormed Samantha, as she tried to pull away and wipe the tears from her face at the same time. She could not image any one wanting anything from her. She was so exhausted by all of her life.

The Coyote laughed. He loved to watch Black-Hawk with the ladies. He was so big and powerful, but he always made sure he, Jose, got a turn on the ladies Black-Hawk tamed. She was terrified as she looked at Black Hawk. Her eyes were round questions in her face. The both of them were her worst night mare.

Black-Hawk dragged Samantha closer to his bulk. "Have fun with McGuire? He sure loves the ladies. I bet he loved you up good. He's known to love them and leave them. I'll tell you this right now, I'll never leave you."

Samantha's face turned crimson. It was so true; McGuire had just put his hat on and left. He didn't even say a word, not of love, but he closed the door firmly. She had let him have his way with her but she had helped him. The bile stuck in her throat as she thought about all she let McGuire do to her. Not only had she helped him, it felt so good. She had expected more from him. He always looked out for her.

Black Hawk slowly dropped her hand. He could not believe his luck. He was going to have his dream come true. His big hand circled around

Samantha's small waist and he pulled her closer. She shuttered as he drew her nearer to his face.

He bent down and drew her face closer to his by his large hand. He pulled his fingers through Samantha's tasseled hair. His thin lips puckered up and he held her tight as he kissed her. The more she struggled, the fiercer his kiss became. His unshaved face left a rash on her face. She smelled his awful odor of whiskey and sweat. Bile came into her throat. She was going to throw up.

"Yeah, me and Jose are going to take you home with us. We haven't had a woman in a long time in our house. Decided it would be you. Saw you at the dance and wow, we knew you were the one to be our little girl. We'll just train you to do what we want you to do, to please us." Black-Hawk kissed her harder and his hands traveled over her breasts. She gasped as she felt him grope her breasts. It was like he owned them, without the lover's touch.

She looked around at the school room and the white walls looked like a prison. Would she ever teach any children?

Black Hawk did not want to share with the Coyote. He wanted this girl all to himself. But right now, he would not say what he thought. First came the money, and then, his picture of the girl who shared his dreams. He would have to get rid of the Coyote. The coyote had become an annoying fixture to his way of living. It was time he let the man die. The rewards were greater this time, he had the woman he had always dreamed about, the woman that would be his and his alone.

Samantha gulped in air. This could not be happening to her. First she had given her body to McGuire, and now this monster was going to take her some place to be his. Maybe she deserved this terrible life, because some how she sinned badly. Had she sinned when she was a child, before she came to the nuns?

"But don't worry about, McGuire. He won't know anything about it till maybe noon tomorrow when he comes over to take another quickie with you. But, hell, we'll be far away in Mexico." Black-Hawk laughed. He pushed her back, but still held her tightly around the waist. He could see the fear in her eyes. "You'll love Mexico. You'll love waiting on us personally. I would kill you without thinking. One more death does not give me nightmares. But I can't kill some one so beautiful. Still, I will get the money, and we shall live very comfortable in Mexico."

Black Hawk knew he had to keep the Coyote on his side, till they got across the border. He had to act normal to the man.

"Hey, Jose, have a feel. She sure is a little bird." Black-Hawk said as he pressed his big hands over her breasts.

Jose came over and kissed Samantha as Black-Hawk held her tightly. Rage swept over Black Hawk's heart as he watched the Coyote kiss Samantha. He wanted to kill him now.

"Hey, feel those little breasts. She sure needs some meat on her bones. I like it the way it is. Never had a little bird before." Black- Hawk sneered as Samantha tried to twist free.

Jose regarded Samantha. "She sure is a pretty little thing. I think we'll just keep her forever."

Black Hawk wanted to wring the Coyote's neck for saying "we". The Coyote knew Mexico and where to go to live. He wanted to be a ruler of his castle with Samantha at his side. He did not need any extra baggage like the Coyote.

Black Hawk smiled his special smile for the ladies. He never had a lady to think about, most of them had been whores. Now, he would have a lady. A lady that would be his alone and do as he wanted. He pushed Samantha from his grasp in an angry motion.

Black-Hawk picked Samantha up and threw her over his shoulders much as he would throw a bag of wheat. Samantha kicked and screamed and punched as Black-Hawk walked to the door. He whistled for his horse. His big brown horse came over and Black-Hawk gracefully jumped on the horse with Samantha still on his back. He winked at Jose. He saw Jose was smiling. Black-Hawk understood that Jose thought Samantha was getting under his skin.

Black-Hawk gave one lusty whack to Samantha's rear. She felt like a dozen big boulders had landed on her back. "Think she needs one more to quiet her down a bit. Got to show right from the beginning who is boss. Everyone knows I'm the boss, right?" His large hand whacked her once more and made her scream and then she just went limp. Her body sagged on Black Hawk's shoulder.

Jose got on his horse and laughed so hard the tears came to his eyes. Something was wrong, Jose knew it and stopped laughing; it did not sit right how Black Hawk was acting. Jose faced Black Hawk and stared into his eyes.

Jose started to think how nice it would be if he had the girl to himself. He could kill Black Hawk when he was sleeping. He would have the girl and the money. Black Hawk would never think he had the gumption to kill him in his sleep.

"You sure know how to handle a lady," Jose said looking seriously at the limp form on Black-Hawk's shoulder. "Did you kill her? Wait till you really do something to her," laughed Jose. "Then she won't be screaming and crying; she'll end up begging you to stop."

"Aw, just being nice to her now," laughed Black-Hawk. "Want her to get all this out of her system. She'll know that she belongs to me, and no one else." He liked the ladies, and he sure liked her. To think McGuire had her first. He'd have his turn when they got to Mexico and he had the money in his hands already. No sense in coming back to this hick town. Money meant a great deal to him, and this particular lady was what he wanted more than money. He had to think of the way he could get rid of the Coyote, without any harm to him or her.

He knew something was wrong with the Coyote. He sensed the change in his character. So, he thought, the Coyote finally had gotten up the nerve to try to kill him, the Black Hawk? But he knew they were safe until the border Then it was every man for himself, and Black Hawk, knew he was the best man.

His hands roamed over her back. He was sure that she was his and his alone forever.

They rode at a fast pace away from the schoolhouse. "Just think, besides this little bird for our nest, we get a fortune to leave this place. I always wanted to live in Mexico. Bet you can show me some real fun and games there." Said Black-Hawk as he tenderly ran his hands over Samantha's rear.

They were headed towards the mountains. This was Black Hawk's hidden place. He knew the mountains were smiling at him, because he had everything he ever dreamed about All he had to do, was get rid of the Coyote.

"Still can't believe that someone would pay us to take her and kill her. Imagine us killing a bird like her until we used her up.'" The Coyote said as he watched Black Hawk and how he was sliding his hands over Samantha's rear. He burned for this woman. Except, Black Hawk would be dead by his hands before they reached the border.

"We'll leave here tomorrow morning. It will give us plenty of time. McGuire won't be back till noon, and then, he might think she went to visit that Weatherspoon woman. Should give us plenty of time to get to the old mine, get our stuff we hid, and be on our way", laughed Black-Hawk.

Samantha could not make out any words, She was so mixed up she did not know up from down. The pain in her rear made her feel so venerable. Her black hair covered her face as she realized that she was in hell and there was no place left for her to go. The nuns always said that is where she belonged." With her eyes closed, she knew she had gone straight to hell, and she left without going to purgatory The blood rushed to her head. She had a hard time breathing. She wanted to reach her face, but her hands were held together by Black Hawk. She felt his hand slid over her body.

*   *   *

Mike ran as fast as he could to find McGuire. His heart was pounding and he wondered if he would get help for Samantha in time to save her. He could see McGuire's horse up ahead. He knew his throat was clogged up with fear, fear for Samantha. He ran harder and tried to scream McGuire's name, but his breath stopped any noise coming from his mouth. He stopped running and breathed heavily. Then he screamed, "Stop McGuire, Stop.

McGuire pulled his horse to a stop when he heard Mike's voce. He turned and looked at Mike. Mike ran up to him as McGuire turned his horse back and came up to Mike. He stared up at McGuire like a hungry lion.

"What's with you boy?" asked McGuire. He looked at the sand that was plaster on Mike's clothing, and also looked at the deep frown on Mike's face.

"They took her, they're going to do bad things to her," screamed Mike. "I was outside the schoolhouse when they came. I saw them go in and then watched them come out. You got to save her. Hurry." Mike screamed at McGuire. He gestured with his hands like butterflies in the wind.

"What are you talking about? Who are you talking about? You're not making any sense," McGuire said. He looked at Mike as one would look at a crazed person.

"It's Samantha, Black-Hawk and Jose the Coyote went into the school house and I don't know if they are still there. I know they got her." Mike let his voice get louder and louder. His body shook with the knowledge that he was not getting through to McGuire.

McGuire's face turned a ghastly white. He finally understood what Mike was talking about. Black Hawk usually stayed away from any one he took a fancy to. Only when he left the lady fair did Black Hawk move in. His lake-blue eyes tuned to ice and narrowed.

"Get a posse in town to come after me. Every one will come because it is the school teacher we all wanted here. I'm going to get those black hearted men and when I do, they won't be able to say if they are alive enough to tell any one any thing. Tell the posse I'm starting at the school to look for tracks of the men who took her. And I will start tracking them now, before it gets too late in the day."

Mike made a move as if he should track with McGuire. McGuire shook his head. "No get going and get the men to come after me, before there is no light. You best stay with the posse."

McGuire tugged his horse, Chip's reigns, and rider and horse took off in a cloud of dust. Mike stood there for a second, then he started to run into town screaming, "Help, Help! They took Samantha. Some one listen to me. They took Samantha, our teacher. Help, Help."

"Black-Hawk and Jose the Coyote have taken Samantha, the new teacher. She was going to live in the school house now that it is clean. McGuire cleaned it for her. But the scum took her, and she was kidnapped. McGuire said to get a posse and follow his tracks." Mike said in a loud voice. He surprised himself that people were listening to him for once.

Ted had just ridden into town as he decided he could not wait any longer to see Samantha and get her to be his wife. When he heard what Mike was saying, his whole body turned to ice and then to red-hot lava. Before anyone could say a word, he turned his horse in the direction of the school and took off as though the devil was chasing him.

Ted had his insides turn into water. He could not believe that the love of his life was taken by Black Haw, the worse criminal in the whole territory. He could not count only on McGuire alone to save her. Even if she loved McGuire, he had to save her, because he loved her so much.

The sheriff and the rest of the town men gathered their horses and started off. Mike begged the holster to lend him a horse. "Please, I got to save Samantha. I love her," cried Mike. "It's my fault. I should have screamed when I saw them come to her door. I was too scared. I'm a coward. Please, let me have a horse."

The holster looked at Mike and shook his head. "Haven't any hoses left now that the posse is riding. But wait, I have old Nancy. She's a plodder. She would get you there some how."

Mike shook with sorrow. "I'll take her, please."

The holster walked into the empty pad lock. The stalls were covered with hay, but the Horses were all gone. This horse looked sway back and tired before she even left the stall. The horse was Nancy was as old as the trees. The holster saddled the old horse and gave Mike the reigns.

Mike jumped on the horse. He horse stood still like a wooden statue. Mike jerked the reins. "Coward, coward!" He and the horse lopped off toward the school as Mike slapped his legs against the horses hide.

*   *   *

McGuire got to the schoolhouse and slid off his horse and started to slowly look around. He checked inside to be sure that Samantha was not there, lying maybe dead. He found the tracks he was checking for and was about to jump onto his saddle when Ted came galloping up.

"What are you doing here?" asked McGuire as he looked up at Ted on his horse. Something told McGuire he did not want Ted near Samantha.

Ted controlled his anger. "I come to find Samantha, what else? If we are to work together, so be it. It is Samantha that counts, not you or I. I only care about Samantha. If she loves you, then it has to be all that counts."

"Just forget it. I'm saving her. She's mine you know. All mine. You have no reason to be in this. She's mine from head to foot if you know what I mean."

"Did she say she would marry you?" cried Ted, as his black eyes became stones. His chest heaved with regret that he had waited too long.

"Marry her," suddenly McGuire knew he would ask Samantha to marry him. "Yeah, marry me. What is wrong with that? We are so very close. Believe me, we couldn't get any closer."

"Well close or not, I'm here to help find Samantha. Just remember, when we do find her, I'm going to ask her to marry me." Ted said in a low vice. "At least I hope so. Did you take her? No, not now, or ever. I love her. Right now, let's work together to find Samantha. If you are so close, then my asking her to marry me won't matter will it? I love her too much to worry about that." Ted felt the bitter bile in his mouth.

McGuire glanced at Ted. Hell, he did need help if they found Black-Hawk and Jose the Coyote who was he kidding. "Right, let's work together for now."

"What did you find?" Ted asked as he got off his horse. He held the reins of his horse in his hands so the horse would not roam.

Both men looked at the tracks in the sand. They both knew that they were responsible for the abduction of Samantha.

"Their tracks," McGuire answered as he bent low to the ground. "We have to follow the tracks to find Samantha."

The two men moved swiftly following the tracks. "Don't seem like they are trying to hide the fact they took Samantha," said McGuire. "They must feel very safe."

They moved forward following the faint tracks in the sand. "Yeah, but they didn't know Mike was watching the school. They thought they had at least a day or more head start. I wonder why Mike was watching the school?" said McGuire. Mike spied the school from the cactus and the one tree. Thought McGuire.

"If you ask me," said McGuire, "I think he's in love with her also. I guess all of us unmarried men are." McGuire shook his head in wonder, that he waited till now to think of marriage to Samantha.

Ted shook his head. "I just love her, because, I never loved anyone before." Ted's heart lurched as he thought of what Black Hawk might do to Samantha.

Ted looked at the yellow flowers and thought of how Samantha loved flowers, The yellow flowers stood out in the desert just as a beautiful woman stood out in a crowd. The mountains were straight ahead of them and they stretched up to the sky. The sun started to sink into the heart of the mountains. The sun reflected into their eyes. It was hard to read the trail. They stopped,

"I think we lost the trail back there," said Ted as he pointed to a tree.

"It's the darn sun. We have to back track," said McGuire as he turned in horse around.

Both men got off their horses at the same time and started to walk back. They kept their glued to the ground, hoping they would pick up the tracks again.

"We also have to hurry, God knows what they will do to Samantha," Ted said as he examined the earth walking next to his horse. "It's all rock here. That's why we lost the trail. There's no telling where they went."

McGuire shook his head as he bent closer to the rocks. "I know where their cabin is. It's up that mountain, but the shortcut is dangerous. It has narrow ledges and empty spaces that have to be jumped. It will be dark and then it will be more dangerous than in the light. Let's hope that is where they took her."

That was the only hope that was left for them. McGuire knew the way to the cabin.

Both men jumped on their horses and sped up towards the mountain. The climbed the mountain until they reached the first narrow ledge. They narrow ledge of the mountain became very steep.

"Can we make it?" asked Ted as he looked at the dark shadows that filled the ledge.

"We have to," replied McGuire as he whipped his horse towards the narrow pathway up the mountain.

Both men grumbled at the slow pace of their horses, but one slip and it was down hundreds of feet to the bottom.

"How come you think we'll get there?" asked Ted.

"It's a short cut I know, sort of dangerous because we will be riding on this ledge. And this is the first of the ledges. We have three more to go."

Finally, they had to get off their horses and led them up the mountain. It was slow going up on the ledge, as they had to feel their way up and not slip on the curving road.

The next three ledges were done by feel in the dark. The both men felt exhausted from this work. They also had to jump a few places where the trail broke off.

At last their way opened to a wide expanse of trees. They mounted their tired horses. They urged their horses on, but it was useless as the horses were worn out. There in the distance they could see the dark log cabin's outline. It was outlined by the soft glow of the flickering light that came from the one window of the cabin.

They slid from their saddles. They held the reigns of their horses lightly in their hands. They didn't want any noise to alert the men who took Samantha.

The two hunters stopped out from the light caste by the cabin window. They could see the villains horses in the corral.

They tied their horses to a branch of a tree away from the cabin. Quietly the two men approached the cabin. Both men hoped Samantha was in the cabin. They might have hidden her in the mountains. They may have killed her. They were unable to read the trail that Black-Hawk and Jose left.

"They're there," said McGuire as he looked at the bright lights coming from the window of the cabin. For the first time in his life, McGuire felt a pricking in his skin.

The cabin blended into the mountain. Some of the light escaped through the cracks in the trees where the mud had fallen out. There was a single window and a single door into the cabin. There could not be more than one room by the size of the outside of the cabin. The chimney poured out white smoke into the black night. A candle flickered in the cabin.

"We'll sneak up and look into the window." Ted said. "They would never had lit a fire if they expected us. I only hope Samantha is not harmed and is here. They might have killed her."

Two men crawled up to the cabin. Sweat poured from their arms as they tried to be as quiet as they could be. Ted hit a rock with his gun belt as he crawled forward. McGuire turned sharply and motioned for Ted to stay still and close to the ground for a second. Sound carried very far in the mountains. Both men were frozen where they had crawled to on the ground. Black-Hawk or Coyote heard them, they might kill Samantha if she was in the cabin. Minutes passed and no one looked out the door or the window.

The two men started to crawl forward again. Ted held his gun belt to be sure it did not hit another rock. They reached the cabin. Both men held their breath as McGuire slowly poked his head on the side of the window and raised his head slowly. The light blinded his eyes for a second.

McGuire slowly squatted down again by the window. He motioned to Ted to be still. He pantomimed the men were drinking. Both men slowly raised their heads on both sides of the window. They saw the candle on the table. There was a table and two chairs, which Black-Hawk and Coyote sat on, and the bed with the lifeless form of Samantha. The window had no glass in it, and so it presented no problem in looking into the room. A whiskey bottle was on the small table between the two men.

They saw Black-Hawk sitting at the table drinking a whiskey. Jose the

Coyote was getting a glass from the counter. They saw a black and blue mark across Samantha's check. Her hair was a dismal mess around her face.

Black Hawk tapped his fingers on the table. He felt his whole world was at stake, and he had to get rid of the Coyote.

"When you think she'll come to?" asked Jose Jose knew he was in trouble, and was afraid to look at Black Hawk. Jose felt Black Hawk's eyes looking at him differently than they had before.

Black-Hawk shrugged. "Hell, the telegraph operator gave us $1,000 to make sure she never comes to. Like dead! Little did he know we're going to keep her not kill her like he wants." Black Hawk knew that he would have Samantha all to himself. He didn't need Jose anymore. Once he was in Mexico, he was safe.

"Wonder why he wants her dead." thoughtful for once, Jose pondered. Not that Jose cared, but it was what he was expected to say.

"Who cares," Black-Hawk said as he filled his glass and downed his whiskey. He turned in his seat and observed Samantha.

"Hell, we got lots of time. I guess she passed out when I smacked her in the face. I told her to be still when we got here, but would she listen, no. I have to be a little less hard when I hit her," said Black-Hawk. "We could take her like she is, but hell, that's no fun." Black-Hawk laughed. "Besides, I want some sport. Not just a body lying like dead, but some fun of her fighting. I just had to hit her across her ass. Show her I am the master and she better listen to me when I talk. She'll learn to mind her manners with me. She'll find it hard to sit and she'll find she better do as I want because I can do much worse to her body."

Jose went over to look at Samantha. "She is the prettiest girl I ever did see. You will give me a turn, won't you?" Jose touched Samantha's face. His fingers trailed along the black and blue bruise.

"You get away from her," shouted Black-Hawk. "I'm first with her. You don't touch her. Wait, just till I have her. We have to leave after tonight. We might have two days tops before they miss her, but with McGuire and that Ted so fired up with her, I think we only have tonight before we have to move."

Jose sat down and poured some whiskey into his glass. His mouth curved into a sly smile. He sure as shooting had to kill Black Hawk before he disfigured that little lady. He knew this was the first time in his life that he was certain the lady was just for him.

Black-Hawk now had to kill Jose before they left the states and went to Mexico. He hated the thought that Jose would not be with him as he did need him sometimes. Jose knew Mexico, and so he needed that knowledge.

Outside the cabin, Ted and McGuire looked at each other. Ted and McGuire took out their guns. Black-Hawk jumped up from the table. "I heard something," Black-Hawk shouted. Jose dropped his glass of whiskey. He pulled out his gun. Black-Hawk took out his gun from his belt. He snuffed out the candle. He looked to the window. Then quick as a snake he moved over to Samantha. The light from the stove filtered some light giving odd shapes to the few pieces of furniture in the cabin.

Ted and McGuire were afraid to just shoot as they might hit Samantha. They waited in silence and heard Black-Hawk creep to the door. Very slowly they saw the door open. Black-Hawk looked around but the night was dark as a closed coffin.

Jose silently came to the window. He jerked back as he made out the blacker forms of Ted and McGuire. McGuire shot at Jose at the window. Black-Hawk shut the door and moved to were Samantha lay.

"Who ever it is out there, I'm going to kill this girl if you don't give up your guns and move away from here. Toss the guns in the window and let me hear you ride away from the cabin. I'll be listening. Jose, better not be dead or there will be retribution."

Ted and McGuire shook their heads. They tossed in one of their guns and started back down to their horses. They weren't so stupid to give up all their guns, and they were sure Black-Hawk knew that. They both knew Black-Hawk would kill her if they tried to save her now. Black-Hawk never made idol threats.

Had they failed Samantha? Their eyes darted around the woods. All they saw was the dark outline of the trees. They had to have some plan, but their brains stopped thinking of anything but the sight of Samantha laying on the bed, unmoving.

They mounted their horses and rode a short distance away. McGuire said, "I know where the old mine is. We can bushwhack them there."

McGuire started to think of the old mine and its location from where they were now. It would be a wild ride, but it would be worth it, if they could save

Samantha. Besides it being a wild ride, it was dangerous and narrow following a lesser known trail up the mountain.

Ted pushed his hat back, "What if they, well, you know, what if they don't go there?"

McGuire looked at his horses back and he knew defeat. He turned and looked at Ted. He half smiled and knew that all he had was the knowledge of where the old mine was.

"It is our only hope right now. They will head out to the old mine. They don't know we heard them talking." Their horses snorted from tiredness from the long, hard ride.

The two men silently stopped talking as they watched Jose open the door of the cabin. He had a bandage around his head. He whistled and three horses came up the door. Jose started to saddle the horses.

Once they rode away, the two men knew that the window was the escape hatch they had used to open the coral. Black Hawk was big, but he was smart and he must have wiggled out that window when they were riding away. He was one slippery cuss.

Black-Hawk sprang out of the door carrying Samantha as a shield. She lay as if she was dead. "You watching. You better not follow us. I don't need much prodding to kill the girl. That you McGuire? Maybe Ted? Or both? McGuire always seem to be on top of the draw. Who else would it be, come to get another taste of the lady?"

Ted and McGuire watched as Jose and Black-Hawk mounted their horses holding Samantha over Black-Hawk's shoulder. Her body was like a rag doll, just laying without any form. Black Hawk held her body close to his side. He seemed to be guarding the body from anyone that might take her away. She hung there over his shoulder without any life. The two men and the girl galloped away into the dark night. The third horse was to be used for their supplies to Mexico.

McGuire and Ted stared after their leaving. Their hearts heavy in their chests. Some how or other they had fouled up their rescue attempt.

"We'd better get moving to that old mine," McGuire said. "It's a short cut. It is dangerous, so if you don't want to come with me, I understand."

"Of course I'll come. I love Samantha. I would give my life for her. How did he know it was you McGuire?" asked Ted.

McGuire just nodded his head. "We go back a long ways. Someday, we're going to have to kill or be killed by each other."

They trotted higher up going to the East, while Black-Hawk and Jose went towards the West. Bearing East for awhile, the two men silently climbed up the mountain. The trail was narrow and their sleeves touched the rough stones of the mountain. Then the trail turned to the West. Both men felt like failures not being able to rescue Samantha.

The trail was curved in several places, and the narrow trail turned into a nonexistent line. They could not go fast as this trail was so narrow and so indistinct in the black night. The trail turned into a broad meadow with trees.

McGuire and Ted stopped their horses to listen for the sounds of the night.

It was impossible to see anything but slowly dawn started to break through the trees as the sun began to rise.

"Better trail than going to the cabin," McGuire noted as he tried to smile. "now that we're off that Indian trail we are fine. I hope that I am right and they will come here with Samantha."

They rode for a time in silence. Ted was thinking about Samantha and how he might tell her how much he did love her. McGuire was thinking that his life was changing and it was time he settled down.

McGuire pointed to the dark opening in front of them. "There is the mine. It is very old, and seldom anyone goes there. I learned about this mine from my Indian friend."

The black hole was small, and there were traces of neglect about the place. It looked like no one had been near it in ages. It must have been an Indian Turquoise. mine in the days of its first use.

"They'll be here shortly. Find a place and shoot to kill. Watch out you don't hit Samantha! Maybe it would be kinder for her to be dead then to be their woman." Snarled McGuire.

Ted wanted Samantha as his wife. He wanted her to give him children. He knew he was madly in love with her. He also knew that McGuire had helped her with every problem she had. She had let him feel her breasts. She was filled with wine, and hardly knew what she was doing. He was sure McGuire had her virginity. Why had she let him have her, unless she loved him.

Both men found large gray and black boulders to hide behind. Rocks were strewn around the area like a giant had tossed him aside in his hurry to reach the mine. They could hear the rattle of the horse's hoofs in the distance, as the three horses headed towards the old mine.

Black-Hawk held Samantha close to his chest. A cherished possession. Her head was so very close to his body. But the left side of his body was open. There was no way the men would shot. They might hit Samantha. They watched as Black Hawk slowly caressed her back. He kissed her forehead. They had never seen Black Hawk act as he was acting now. He had eyes only for Samantha.

He looked at Samantha's face and wondered why he had hit her so hard that the black and blue blazed across her white face. He shook his head and went back to his dream.

McGuire said a little prayer wishing she was out of the way, Ted raised his pistol. He could wait no longer to save Samantha. He sighted Jose and fired into Jose's shoulder. Jose screamed that Black Hawk. "Tell whoever is shooting at us, that you will kill her."

Black Hawk looked around in a daze. He had to save Samantha no matter what happened to him. He took one foot from his stirrups and laid Samantha down on his saddle with care. He did not pay any attention to Jose. It was only Samantha that mattered to him.

McGuire could not shot at Black Hawk. He was so confused by the way Black Hawk acted and how he shielded Samantha's body. He acted as if he did not care what happened to himself, only that Samantha should live.

"Let Samantha go," cried Tom.

"I will not let her be hurt, who are you?" cried Black Hawk.

"We'll shot if you move." cried McGuire.

"McGuire, I hear your voice. What do you want?" cried Black Hawk "I don't want anything to happened to Samantha. I don't know if she is going to live. I give up. Just let the lady live."

It was at that instant, that McGuire squeezed the trigger of his gun. He did not mean to, but he was so rattled that Black Hawk cared about Samantha. It was too late to stop the bullet that McGuire fired that went into Black Hawk's chest.

Tom held his gun out and fired at Jose His eyes were red with blood and lust for the death of those who had held Samantha and now she might be dying.

Jose let out a shriek as his body fell forward over the horse, Blood spurted out of his neck. His body slipped to the ground and the horse took off in a rush.

Black Hawk felt the bullet in his chest, and he raised Samantha to his face. He kissed her with tenderness. He laid her down slowly as the blood left his body. "Live, oh dream, live."Slowly he slid from the saddle only one foot in his stirrups. At the last moment, he placed Samantha over the horses body.

"Goodbye my dream. Oh my love, I have tried to protect you. May God in his heaven protect you from the scum that is shooting at us." cried Black Hawk as the life blood flowed from his body.

The tension of the moment was not lost on Ted. Ted and McGuire had talked about how they would kill their hated opponents. They had talked about this on the way up.

Ted and McGuire ran towards their horses. They jumped on their horses and raced to where the black horse of Black-Hawks started to kick and turn in circles. Black-Hawk's foot dangling from the saddle was the cause of the horse bucking. Samantha started to slip forward.

McGuire had his horse dash up to Black-Hawk's horse. Ted followed his lead and as McGuire grabbed the horse's reins, Ted pulled Samantha from the horse's back.

Ted jumped from his horse holding Samantha close to his chest. He leaned down and kissed her brow. "Please be all right, My love, be alive and hear me. I love you so." Samantha did not move, just lay in Ted's arms.

Samantha lie still and hardly breathed. Her face was white with the black mark of Black Hawks hand playing havoc on her. Her dark hair hung down like a plays end and the curtain to drawn.

McGuire went to the old mine and found a bucket. Just as he thought, Black-Hawk had left supplies here at his hide out for emergencies. There were rifles, and several sticks of dynamite, plus canteens filled with water. He poured some water into a cup he found with the supplies.

Slowly Ted lowered Samantha to the ground. He watched as she lay so silent and still. He beseeched the almighty to let her live. He noticed her white skin against the back marks that had been made on her face by Black Hawk's hand.

Ted went up to where McGuire was drinking from one cup and carrying another for Samantha. Ted got some water from the bucket and dropped his kerchief into it and then went over to Samantha. McGuire tried to give some water to Samantha, but it only dribbled down her chin. Samantha opened her eyes and stared into the dark, black eyes of Ted.

"I must be in heaven," Samantha whispered. She reached out her hand and touched Ted's face. He smiled as she looked into his eyes. She sighed and closed her eyes. Her mind was whirling around.

McGuire watched. "Did she wake up?"

Ted seemed to see McGuire as an intruder. "I think we better get her out of here. No sense her seeing those dead dogs."

Ted picked her up. She weighed so little. She was just what he wanted for his wife. But what about McGuire?

Ted carried her over to his horse and laid her down gently on the ground. "Are you and she an item? Like are you two going to be married?"

McGuire's blue eyes danced. "I sure hope so. I never saw anyone as beautiful as she is. I want her. There is no doubt about that. If she will have me, I'll marry her. You know, I had her already."

"You haven't asked her yet? What makes you think she wants you. What about your house of prostitution? Will she go for that and gambling? You think she loves you?"

McGuire scrutinized Samantha and remembered all the glory he felt taking her virginity. He never had a woman so innocent. "She'll marry me. I'm sure of that. I could sell the whorehouse if she wants, but that is all. I would do nothing else. I really want her."

"Well, let me tell you something. I want her also. I will do anything to have her love me. I'll not be stopped. I have a beautiful house and make an honest living. I think Samantha would like that better where she could hold her head up."

"Is she dead?" asked the Sheriff.

"No. She's alive. I'm not sure how she really is," answered McGuire. "We shot those bastards. Right in their little hearts. How dare they steal our schoolmistress?"

"Good riddance," said the Sheriff. "We might need some sort of thing like the Indians use to carry stuff to lay her on,"

"No need," said Ted. "I'll just have her lean on me on the trip back to town. I just can't believe the way he acted with her in his hands."

"Wait one moment," yelled McGuire. "I was the one found the cabin and the mine. I get to take her back to town."

"No need to fight over that," said the sheriff. "Her father's here. She can lean on him."

"No," cried Clarence. "They can take her anyway they want. I just came to see if she was dead. The nuns should never had told her where I was."

Ted and McGuire humped. They clearly had heard Black-Hawk say that he was the one who paid Black-Hawk to kidnap Samantha and kill her.

"When we get back to town, I'm going to kill that bastard. But first I want to know why he wants her dead." Ted snarled.

McGuire sneered. "Take your turn. I'm getting to him first."

McGuire and Ted shook with anger. Ted picked up Samantha and handed her to McGuire.

"You're the one who always helped her, so let me hand her to you as the so called first. God, she is so light."

McGuire nodded and pressed Samantha close to his chest. Her skin was so white and her hair was so black. Everyone he ever had in the whorehouse or outside of it were a big women. Why his mistress, Lou Lou was big. She was blonde like he was with eyes of lavender. He just wasn't use to a woman so soft, sweet and pure.

He was a gambler and knew that his fate rested in her hands and heart. She let him take her virginity but would she let him take her? She trusted him, and he had let the trust work for him. He just could not figure out her wishes, but he knew in his heart and soul he was in love with Samantha. He was for the first time in his life truly and madly in love with her.

He pulled her close to his mouth. He wanted to make sure she was breathing. His heart stopped beating for just a second, and then he felt her breath on his face.

She was his, and he would make sure she knew it. He would make her feel her obligation to him, and to him alone. He had done everything for her. She had to pay him back.

Chapter XI

CARDS AND GAMBLING WERE THE only professions McGuire knew. He was not a plantation owner, or heir, he was a blasted nobody. He had a sister safely in England, At least he had enough money to get her to England. He thought he was free of all baggage, until his uncle died. Now he was stuck with his inheritance, of a whorehouse, a gambling casino, and a hotel. He knew nothing about running a hotel; and next to nothing about whorehouses.

Women loved him with his inviting smile and he was received by the men as he could laugh at himself. His Uncle Thomas had to go and die. He died in a gun fight with Black Hawk, over a silly woman.

Uncle Thomas left him all this stuff that he had no idea what to do with. The old Madam who ran the house, took half the whores and moved on to California. He was in real trouble, as he didn't have the faintest idea of where to turn.

The whore house looked like an old fashioned house of the rich and the powerful. Home like entrance and exotic inside. A place that made the senses riot in the colors that vibrated in each room. It was a place of dreams, but without a madam, it was empty and deserted.

Slowly he came up to his whore house and got down from his horse. He tied the reins of the horse to the hitching post and went inside to his office. He sat down and stared out a window. He was lost.

He sat and watched his whorehouse turn into a nothing. No one came to his whore house. Why should they? He didn't have anyone there to cater to their wishes. No one came to his hotel because his cook could not cook.

And gambling, why come to his small town when there was nothing to do afterwards? Here he sat, lost and not knowing what to do, as it seemed his luck had run out.

He heard a knock on the door, and opened it, imagine who would call on him. There stood this big, tall woman wearing a red satin dress two sizes too small on her body. Her red gold hair gleamed in the light. She gave a sickly smile. She hitched up her dress. It showed her long legs to McGuire. She sure had long legs he thought.

"Heard you lost your whores. I'm real good at running a whorehouse," said the lady in red. She squirmed in her shoes that seemed too small for her feet.

McGuire just looked at her. She was big and nervous. She was no great looker. But then thinking of her legs, McGuire felt his body feel hot and heavy and ready to make love to her.

"Think any one would want you?" asked McGuire. He missed the old life, the plantation was one that he missed terribly. All he knew how to do was gamble, and he learned that as a gentleman of the South.

The lady in red smiled. Her face lit up. "My name is LouLou. I know that someone wants me. You look at this dress and think I'm nothing. I can see it in your eyes, your smile. Borrowed this dress to hide. But all this dress does for me is make me look big."

McGuire looked at her and he laughed. She might be beautiful if she lost some weight. She was beautiful when she smiled. Her lavender eyes held hope.

"Sit down," McGuire said as he seated himself behind the huge desk that was his uncles. McGuire leaned back. "How'd you hear about all the whores and the Madam left me?"

"Hey, the West is small town. News travels fast around here. Besides, I met your Madam and girls on the way here. I found them going to Denver."

"Denver!" shouted McGuire as he sat up straight in his chair. "I was told they were going to California."

"Guess they told you a fib," laughed LouLou.

"Hell's bells," McGuire said as he settled back in his chair. "Care less where they go. They left me with nothing much to work with."

"I can help you, if you let me. I know about whorehouses. I'm a smart whore." LouLou said as she opened up her little paper sack and took out a cheroot. She was certain she'd get the job she always wanted. A whorehouse mistress! That was her dream of being on top of the world.

She lighted the cheroot, puffed out smoke and smiled. "I can be a Madam. I can get you my friends to come out here. Like I'm in charge of the place. I can get you some of the best ladies of the night you ever did see."

"Have you looked at yourself lately?" asked McGuire as he looked at her seated in the chair opposite him. She looked bloated with rolls of fat in her red dress.

"Oh, you mean I am fat? I am fat with these pillows inside the dress. This poor dress is straining at the seams. I have been running and hiding for over a month. It was no picnic. I was dodging that outlaw Sam Morales. He thinks I'm his and his alone. I sell myself to no one. If you decide to let me run the whorehouse those are my terms. I do not give myself away."

McGuire laughed and laughed at what she was saying. "Take the pillows out and fit into that dress. What my Uncle Thomas did with the money is a mystery to me. But as far as I know, there is no cash around this place. Maybe he took it out in trade. If Morales wants you. He will find you. He is one smart man, I have heard. You didn't throw him off coming here. I can hide you for awhile, and then you just go on your way. I'm really not looking for trouble. I lead a peaceful life."

LouLou didn't breath. "Perhaps you didn't hear what I said. The outlaw Sam Morales is out to make me come back to him. I may not be safe here with you. Or should I say you might not be safe with hiding me."

"I'm sure he knows right now where you are." said McGuire.

"Would you hide me, then, even though he knows I'm here. Tell him I left. I just won't go to him." cried LouLou.

"I'll hide you if that is what you want. I'm not afraid of any man," muttered McGuire He thought of the war, and the many men who he killed. He felt so empty inside, but now, here was a reason to live. He would rid the world of unwanted men.

LouLou sat like a statue. All at once she heard the clatter of horse's hoofs. She could hear the silver bells attached to his saddle. They sang as he rode. She glanced out the window.

Twisting her fingers, LouLou looked at McGuire. "I think I better hide now. Coming into town right now is Sam Morales. I am so sorry.'

LouLou stood up from her chair and made for the door. "Maybe I'll just give myself up. I guess it is my lot in life to always give."

McGuire stood up. He made a face and took his guns down from the hook they were hanging from. He started putting on the gun belt around his waist.

McGuire took hold of her hand. He pulled her away from the door. "I'll take care of Morales."

LouLou started to open her mouth, and then shut it. She saw his eyes blaze with an unholy blue. She suddenly felt afraid of him. He wore his gun belt low, like a killer.

LouLou turned to face him. McGuire was strapping on his guns. She saw the silver guns shine in the light of the sun.

The outlaw Morales was known to have shot many men without a blink of his eyes. She didn't want to see McGuire killed because of her. "Look, I'm sorry I bothered you. I can't have your blood on my mind. Somehow or other I shall survive. No need to play hero."

McGuire put his hand on her shoulder. He looked down at her, and he opened the door and looked out. He saw Morales on his horse a dappled colored skin. He heard the silver bells ringing. He called over to Morales. "What you want here in this town, Morales?"

Morales did not want to start something with McGuire. He heard all about McGuire and his swift, silver guns. But pride came to his mind, and he could not or would not back down.

"I want my woman. I don't want any trouble with you. Hear tell you have no heart. You would rather fight than let the coin drop. I don't want to cause you any trouble." called Morales. "Just let my woman out here and I'll leave."

"If you didn't want trouble with me, why are you in my town?" McGuire asked in a cool voice.

"Listen man, I know they call you the Silver Eagle because you never miss when you shoot your guns. Just let me have LouLou. my woman."

Morales let his hands wonder over his guns which were slung low on his hips. He once again wondered if it was worth his while to want LouLou.

"You all living together, or something?" asked McGuire in a silky voice.

"No, I want her real bad. Nothing is going to stop me from having her."

Cried Morales. Morales pulled his hat lower down on his face so McGuire would not see how terrified he was.

McGuire smiled. "She says she don't want you. So you better leave before I lose my temper."

Morales in a show of bravo, reached for his gun. Swiftly, McGuire put his hands on his guns, ready to draw his gun. They faced each other and Morales snarled. "You think you're so great? Well, let me tell you, I have shot twenty men and never missed."

"Never missed," said McGuire. "Now is your chance to see if that still is true."

Morales' face turned red. He was scared silly about McGuire and he knew no graceful way to call it quits. He wanted his manhood to stay in tact.

McGuire stood very still. "It's your play, Morales. Put up or shut up. Leave or draw!"

Morales patted his horse. He hoped for some sort of reprieve. He bit his lips to keep from trembling. He knew he was facing a man that could kill him in seconds and never think about it again.

Morales, short with a very dark complexion, still stood very still with his hands hovering over his guns. He shot so many men, what was a silver eagle to him? "So they call you the Silver Eagle. Think that scares me?"

McGuire smiled with his mouth.

Morales hands quickly drew his guns, but McGuire was swift like an eagle, drew his guns and in one motion, fired at Morales and shot him straight through his heart. Morales' shot went wild.

McGuire walked over to the dying Morales and looked down on him. "I gave you a chance to leave. Was this woman worth your life?"

Morales tried to shake his head. He knew he was beat before he even stopped his horse. No woman was worth his life.

Morales rattled in death's agony, then he lay very still. McGuire shook his head. He hated when he killed a human being. The war had changed him. He hoped that LouLou would leave now that she was safe. It made him remember his killing of men. Men of the blue army. who were just boys.

McGuire knew that his Uncle had died because of a woman. He played the field and had a wonderful time.

LouLou just came running out of the door. She stopped as she saw

Morales lying in the sand. She opened her mouth, and tears ran down her checks.

"You don't have to run any more. I would like you to go you know. Yet-. You can stay here, or go wherever you want to go. You don't owe me anything," McGuire said as he smiled into her teary eyes. People needed people in their lives. She needed something badly, he could see that. She wanted to belong to something and do something with her life. He guessed it was to be a whorehouse madam.

"I'm staying. I'm going to be your Madam. I am going to show you the best girls you ever did see. I'll get all my friends and not so close friends to come on down here. We are going to be the best whorehouse in the world, in fact, I think I'll just buy a new dress as Madam of this elite establishment."

"Hell, LouLou," laughed McGuire, "just stay the way you are in that red dress. Don't think I will ever think of you except in that red dress."

LouLou looked into McGuire's lake-blue eyes and smiled. "You and I are going to be really fast friends. There is nothing I won't do for you and its not because you saved me from Morales. It is the way you didn't demand payment for what you did for me. No one has ever given me anything, but you gave me a choice. Dignity!"

McGuire laughed and pulled her into his arms. He looked into her lavender eyes. "No, it was you who gave me what I needed. Your eyes gave me hope for a better way of living."

LouLou looked at him with worship in her eyes. He needed someone to talk to and laugh with. He was her task in life, especially as he gave her the one and only goal she ever had, mistress of a whorehouse.

"I'm going to make you famous as the owner of the best whorehouse in the world."

LouLou turned around and her svelte body gave another rip to the red dress she was wearing. She was tall for a girl, about 5 feet 7 inches tall. Her red gold hair shone in the light and her face was heart shaped and she had a pert little nose.

McGuire shook his head and stared down at Samantha who lay in his lap without moving. He came back to the present; he watched the trees get further apart. They were taking the easy way back to town. He had better give Ted a turn with holding Samantha. Ted was eyeing him with slit eyes now.

He stopped his horse and motioned to Ted to come over. He gently handed Samantha over to Ted. Ted held her close to his chest.

Why had he given Samantha to Ted? He was the one who would have her forever. She would say yes to his wanting her. She would always be his. He dreamed how it would be with her in his arms always.

*   *   *

Without Samantha in his arms his mind wandered back to the past and to Loulou. Why was he thinking only of his business and not the woman he loved? He was afraid to face the future. He was afraid that Samantha would not have him.

LouLou left town, in that same red dress. In fact, McGuire thought of her in that dress only and in nothing else. It was her trade mark to him. McGuire figured he would never hear from her again. He at least should try to find a cook for the Hotel. He would go to Tuscan to look for someone who could cook, more than a pot of coffee that was so strong it melted your teeth. People needed an escape from reality. Most of all, people need good food for fun and laughter.

He also needed a bar tender for the casino. After all, the drinks were the gravy on the meat that made the money for the casino. He found the whole idea crazy that he had to have a cook for the hotel to be a success. There was no one in the hotel at the moment. Why had his uncle settled here? It was a god forsaken place. No one with any sense would come here. He was the loser.

He gave up the idea of being a businessman,. His gambling casino was empty. He needed a bar tender and of course, people to play cards. He decided to ride to Tucson to gamble. At least he would keep his mind active. He doubted he had anything to bet. There was no way that people in Tucson would want to come to this town of his. They would not come even for a job. Heck, he needed a cook, a bar tender, and most important of all, he needed people who wanted to come to this empty place.

He rode Chip and his mind was a thousand miles away from what he was doing. He reviewed his old life and he didn't feel very proud of it. If he had done as his father had wanted, he would know business. He was a spoiled rotten son who loved the life of a wanderer.

He realized that before him lay a dead horse and a couple people. Odd to think of anyone sitting in the middle of no where with a dead horse and just sitting in the desert. He saw Oriental people. He wondered if he was going crazy?

He had many hallucinations in the past. Many of them to do with the old life had had let slip from his fingers. This was the craziest hallucination he ever had. He thought of his sister who loved the color white. She was wearing a white dress with little pink roses around the hem and waist.

He knew without speaking this was a mystery to be solved. Was his mind off on a tangent or were they real? He came to in a second and knew this was a true scene. He was not crazy. The people looked up at him on his horse. His eyes were playing tricks with him. A gambler, a true gambler never drank.

Why would people sit with a dead horse? Horses were meant to ride. No horse, no ride, no where to go! He stopped his horse Chip and slid off. He looked closely at the people sitting there. There was no doubt in his mind that he had gone over the bend in the road. He shook his head. He breathed deeply. They were still there with the dead horse.

He shook as he looked at them. Why would Orientals be here in no man's land? "You need help?" he asked. A dead horse, an oriental couple and the desert. The sand of the desert seemed to overwhelm the two people sitting there. Why sit in the desert with snakes and scorpions and who knew what?

Both the man and woman looked at him as if he came from outer space. They watched the way the sun sparkled on his golden hair as he pushed his hat back. The Oriental man rose from the sand. He pointed his finger at the horse. "Dead." He said.

McGuire laughed. His mirage talked. Maybe there was more to it than his going crazy.

"I sure can see that. Where you people going? I can help you get the where ever you want to go." McGuire thought. Maybe these were real people. He hated to see people lost in the desert without water or transportation.

McGuire looked at the couple and the dead horse. He was certain that they had stolen the horse. It was a poor choice of horse for the desert. It looked ready to die he was sure before they stole it, from the railroad, they were building to the West. The man worked for the railroad he could tell. He wore "tent" blue pants and a plaid, red. woolen shirt. It was a great idea to use tent material to make pants.

Why did They steal away at night? McGuire guessed it was slave labor that the railroad used every once in awhile. They grabbed every available man that they could find. He remembered seeing whips in the overseers hands. This man must have been so frightened. He was sure that the woman was his wife. He must have stolen away at night afraid for his life. He did not know that the horse he stole was on its last legs and about to die.

He looked at the woman. She was small, very small, and her face was the color of ivory. She wore a black dress that came down to her toes. It was a shapeless dress, but it covered her. She stood up for a moment and then sat down into a ball as if to hide from him.

The Oriental man pointed to himself. "I Kim. We cook. Find Work." Kim was thin as a weed, and his black eyes glowed as he talked. He was proud of the fact that he could speak this strange new language.

Shaking his head, McGuire watched the little lady curl up and stare straight ahead. "If you can cook, and I like it, you can come with me to the hotel. I have a hotel. Can you understand what I said. You cook."

The woman peeked at McGuire from her lowered lashes. She said something to her husband in Chinese. His gut feeling told him she was afraid that he would send them back to the railroad.

The Chinese man shook his head, said something in Chinese, then smiled. The woman smiled. "Woman say you angel. We cook. We make good meal."

McGuire laughed as he knew the woman did not call him an angel, maybe a devil.

"Cook" Expecting the couple to stand up and follow him, they started to gather some pieces of wood from the sand. They took out a pan, and brought out several items, meat, some sauce, eggs, garlic, and a long green looking weed. They started to stir the eggs and cook the meat over the fire on a splint they had made over the fire. They worked together, chopping and stirring. Finally, the woman took out a plate and put it all on the plate. She handed the plate to McGuire.

McGuire looked at the plate. He felt his stomach turn. Maybe it was poison? McGuire, figured he had nothing to lose by eating this food, he was broke and his brain was empty with ideas. He took the fork they offered and dug into the food. He was surprised at how good it all tasted. He ate every bit of meat and eggs and looked to see if there was more in the fire. He stared at them with his lake-blue eyes and blinked them several times to make sure he wasn't asleep.

"No question. You both are hired. Wait here. I'll get a buggy and take you back to my hotel in Cactus Gulch." Somehow he had to bury that horse, but all in good time.

He looked at the couple and could see they did not understand what he had said. He smiled his big smile and his white teeth flashed as the sun blazed in its setting ways. Somehow he had to make them understand he was going to get a buggy and take them back to his hotel. Finally, he handed them his silk white ruffled shirt. He waved at them and left in a hurry.

McGuire found his cook and waitress in a blink of an eye. McGuire wasn't far from Cactus Gulch and he only hoped they would wait. He jumped on his horse and made a dash back to town.

He fetched the buggy and the man and woman looked at him with his bare chest. They gave him back his shirt, and he put it on. The hotel was going to make it. He stopped in his tracks. The horse was no where to be seen. He looked at the desert sands and saw no marks of a burial. He wanted to ask the Oriental couple where the horse was, but he knew they would never answer him as they didn't understand. He shook his head again. No, they never ate the horse.

They got into the buggy. He knew his idea was working, they would be his new cooks. He delivered them to his hotel. He took them into the hotel kitchen. He watched them tremble with delight. They looked at the lovely kitchen and the dinning room. They smiled as if they were in heaven. He fired his old cook, who was ready to leave anyway, and toured the kitchen with them. They started to cook for the hotel, and before you could blink an eye, customers came from near and far. Their fame spread, that there was good food to eat. They cooked delightful food and people wanted something different. The word spread like wild fire as people wanted to celebrate with something special, and these cooks gave them something special.

If you liked Chinese food they specialized in this type of food. They made steaks and potatoes, chops and noodles a specialty. They made breakfast a feast, and tea time a treat. It was something the ladies adored. It was so wonderful to sit at the little tables and gossip and drink tea and eat little sandwiches. The little cakes were a miracle of delight. Ladies far and near made their way to this new experience. It made the hotel grow and as people spent the night at the hotel just so they could eat at the restaurant.

Lady Luck was smiling at McGuire and McGuire would never gamble away his luck. He knew he had found the treasure that people had long sought. His hotel was doing a land slide business, and he made the casino come alive with his gambling. He only wished he had a real bar tender to serve drinks so he could see about his business, Still, he knew his casino would never make a go of it until he found a bar tender. It was the life blood of the casino. He desperately needed someone to serve the drinks and watch the customers with an iron hand, a gun.

McGuire knew his whorehouse and his gambling casino were in big trouble. They loved the tea time. Fewer and fewer people came to gamble as there were not many men who came with their wives. His whorehouse was closed as there were no one to keep the men busy. The men would buy the whores drinks that they knew was just water It was the old game that men knew how to play.

McGuire was fortunate that he ate every meal in his restaurant. He felt His cooks made sure he was happy His hotel and restaurant were winners.

One cool day, as McGuire sat eating in the hotel, he noticed a tall, thin stranger there at one of the tables. The stranger sat with his back against the wall. McGuire watched him eat, and he knew he was either an outlaw or lawman. No one sat with their back to the wall except those who expected trouble.

The man had long fingers. His hair was brown and his eyes darted over the people in the restaurant McGuire took a breath, his eyes reminded him a LouLou. They were lavender. He remembered LouLou's eyes that looked like violets. She who said she would stay and left almost in a second flat. He had to watch out for lavender eyes. Why was he thinking of LouLou? He knew he would never see her again, and yet, she lingered in his mind like glue.

Why was this man in town? Thought McGuire. McGuire could stand it no longer. He shoved back from the table where he was eating, and left almost all his breakfast. He walked to where the man was sitting. He leaned over the table and looked at the man. The thin man easily reach for his guns.

. "Howdy, thought I would see how the food is? I'm the owner of this establishment, so I like to make sure the food is good."

The man put his hands back on the table. He put a bit of pancakes into his mouth. He smiled as he chewed his food. He then put his fork and knife down. His eyes searched McGuire for his intentions.

"Aren't you McGuire the gambler? I remember you. You use to live down south. You are a southern boy, who fought for the south. Heard your plantation is gone."

"That's me. I'm McGuire. And you are sir? Are you some northern bigot who wants to fight now?"

"Don't you remember me? I was the bar tender that stopped the Yank from shooting you in the back when you were challenging Buck Jones after the war."

"Did I ever thank you?"

"Sure did. You gave me a hundred dollars right there and then."

"Must have been richer than I am now."

"That's why the challenge if you remember. You said Buck Jones was cheating at cards. That's when he drew on you and man, I never saw a swifter draw then you did. One second and your guns were out their leather and the next second they were pointed at Buck. Your guns were pointing right at his heart.

I remember you said to him, "You were cheating. You want to make something of it? Leave now while I give you this chance."

The cheater at cards grabbed his hat and he gulped. He stared at you with wild hate, and backed right out the door. He was yellow. He then left the saloon, and I thought that was last we would see of him.

But he returned when you were playing at another table. You were winning. I remember that. That was when you turned your back to pick up your winnings. He came through the swinging doors. He never let the doors swing back, as he wanted silence. He stood there with his guns out, extended. His eyes were slits of hate. His shadow fell into the room. He was about to shoot you. I got hold of my shotgun. I raised it and I pulled the trigger of the shotgun right then and there. He fell back. And then he ran. Wherever he ran to I never looked. I just stared at you. I guess I didn't kill him, because he ran. But that was a slick trick to wait for you to win and turn your back.

You looked around as if this was normal. You smiled at me. It was a smile that could freeze you in winter. You took all the money you won and walked over to me. You put the money in front of me down at the bar. You waited till I put the shotgun down and back in its place below the bar. You put out your hand and pointed to the money.

"For you," you said in a calm voice.

I looked at the money on the bar. It was a hundred dollars. That hundred bucks you gave me was the money you won in the game. You gave it all to me."

"Hell, my life is worth a lot more to me, than that hundred. What are you doing in this town? Hardly any one comes here."

"Passing through. Someone said I could find LouLou here, but she's not here as far as I can see."

"Oh, she was here. Running from a man called Morales. I had to kill him. She's free to do what she wants to now. She left town about a few week ago."

"Too bad. Thought I could sort of find work. Seems I miss her every where I go. She's a hard one to keep track of."

"Your not another man after her like Morales was? Anyway, she's gone and I don't think she is coming back."

"Hardly, am a man like Morales. I'm her brother. Look at our eyes. They are the same. I am Alex Haxley. Not many people have lavender eyes."

"Gad, she sure has a following. Seems like everyone wants LouLou. You really looking for work? You want to work? I have work. You were a bartender. I do need a bartender."

"You mean you have a job for me?"

"You bet. But I can't tell you were LouLou is. She is free to do as she wants. I never make some one do something they don't want to do. She wanted to go and go she did."

"They call me Thin Alex. My name as I told you is Alex Haxley. You can call me Alex. I really need the job. I haven't been employed for a long time chasing after LouLou. She sure is a slippery cuss."

"Well, Alex, You just saved my life. I was looking for a bartender, and you showed up right on time. It's like some one is out there helping me." McGuire said as he put out his hand to shake Alex's hand.

"Now all I need is a Madam, and I have every thing I ever will need." smiled McGuire. "I'm not a business man at heart. This whole package was left to me by my uncle. But, he was my only relative, so he left it to me. He fought over a madam. He could not shot for his life, and yet, he challenged this bad guy to a duel. He was nuts."

"What happened?" asked Alex.

"Simple. He lost the deal, or better yet to say, he died. So they sent out a call looking for me. They found me in New Mexico. Anyway, it caught up to me and here I am. No knowledge of what I am doing."

"Hear tell your hotel is really rolling," smiled Alex.

"Lady Luck. For awhile I thought the whole thing was a bust. But lady luck came through for me. They can take hay and make it taste like steak. I found them in the desert. Yes, there they sat, with a dead horse and two tiny little people. Without hope. That was me, I could not believe my eyes, or should I say luck, when they cooked me a meal."

"Out on the desert, they cooked you a meal?" asked Alex.

"It was incredible. It was like a fantasy. They cooked out on the open range. No fancy tools or any thing. Just a fire and a fry pan. It was so, how can I put it? It was unbelievable."

Alex shook his head. He could not believe the luck that ran with McGuire. He was noted for his luck in cards.

"Why don't you sit down, and we can have a drink to our new working relations. I guess I have to give up on LouLou. She was always hard to keep track of."

McGuire sat down. His back was to the door. He did not bother to wonder about it, as Alex was on the alert. It must run in the family to come here and leave, never to settle down and stay.

"Here's to us," said McGuire. "I think this is a pleasure that is all mine. I am glad to see you again, and glad you remembered the time we met. Small world, to say the least."

Alex raised his hand and a waiter came over. He ordered a bottle of whiskey. Alex poured two glasses and handed one to McGuire. McGuire seldom drank whiskey, but this was a special occasion. LouLou's brother sparkled with her eyes of lavender.

"To life, love and liberty," said Alex in a low voice.

They raised their glasses to their lips and smiled. Then they drank the whiskey down. They banged their glasses on the table and sat back and relaxed.

*   *   *

Reviewing his life, while Samantha's life hung in a balance. He was ashamed of himself. He looked over to Ted who held her so closely to his chest. His eyes never left her face. Their horses seemed to travel without a sound. He turned inward to his thoughts. He remembered LouLou his mistress. Even as he stared at the white face of Samantha, he turned inward. He had to think of other things.

*   *   *

His mind turned back the clock. He thought he had lost the whore house, but that was Lady Luck. He remembered, it was several days later that he heard the racket of some kind of wagon being driven into town. He rose from his seat in the office and walked over to the door. He opened the door and he saw a wagon, loaded with women. Driving the wagon was a round black man, who waved and cheered on reaching the town. LouLou called out "I'm back. Back like I promised."

LouLou jumped out of the wagon and rushed over to McGuire. She threw her arms around his neck and kissed him right on the mouth. "Did you miss me? I missed you something awful"

"Missed you. Thought you would never come back," said McGuire as he pulled her closer to his chest. "You're dress is stunning. It's a royal purple to match your eyes. This fits you like a queen. I got a surprise for you. Your brother is here. He can hardly wait to see you. I told him you would never come back, but here you are. Truth, I thought I would never see you again."

"Alex, I can't believe my luck. My own little brother," cried LouLou as she hugged McGuire tighter. LouLou ran to the saloon. She ran through the swinging doors. She was inside the saloon and screamed, "Alex, are you really here?"

Alex came out from back of the bar. They hugged and kissed. They looked into each other's eyes. Their lavender eyes brightened with "I can't believe we are together again." Alex held her tightly in his arms. He smelled her perfume.

"I have to go now. I'll see you later Alex. I can't believe that we will be together again. It has been years since we were together. I thought we would never be parted. Then the war came, and I lost track of you. Now look at us. In the same town. Look, I have to go and set things straight for my girls and me. I got business to do with McGuire. I brought him ten lovely ladies. All first class!" smiled LouLou.

McGuire and LouLou got the ladies settled in. LouLou went into the office with McGuire. She snuggled up to him. "You look like a gambler. You got to change your looks. Long black coat, red boots, and holsters with silver guns, and those stripped pants, and ruffled shirt. McGuire, you own a hotel, a saloon and a whorehouse. You got to look like an owner."

"Can't see why I should change what I wear. I am a gambler. Just luck that my Uncle left all this to me. Luck, I found people who know how to run the business.

LouLou shook her head. She threw her arms around his neck. "I love you. Can't help that. You just have to bear with me. I have to take care of you. It is time for you to change, and you are going to change. Remember I'm boss here. My god, you are so beautiful. We are going to put you all in black from head to toe. I love you ."

His mouth opened, McGuire was going to say something, but LouLou shook her head. "We are going to the general store and get you black tight pants, so your great rear shows off, then black shirt and black Stetson hat. The boots and gun belt will have to be special made."

"I don't—"started McGuire.

LouLou took McGuire's face and kissed him. "I am yours. I love you. So let's go to bed. No, you don't have a choice. I decided you're my man from now on."

LouLou put her arms around his neck and kissed him with passion. She stood on tiptoe and pulled his shirt open. He seemed stunned, but then he started to unbutton her dress. The purple silk dress molded her figure and the large breasts she so proudly displayed. The purple silk slide off her shoulders and ruffled around her feet.

LouLou felt his firm chest and arms. She admired his broad shoulders, and McGuire was entranced with her breasts in her thin camisole. He pulled her tightly into his chest.

"My god, LouLou, I can't believe we are together. I want you something terrible." McGuire whispered as his hands moved over LouLou's body.

"Yes, I know. I need you. You're my knight in shining armor." Said LouLou as she hugged him to her breast.

She took his hand and brought him to her bedroom. The room wasn't fixed up the way she wanted it. but the bed was waiting. She pulled him over to the bed and smiled.

"I dreamed of this. Just you and I. Oh, it will be great. My love." cried

LouLou. She looked at the bed, and they tumbled into the soft down comforter.

They held each other tightly, and McGuire stopped and pulled his boots off. LouLou smiled like a cat and opened her eyes wide. Their faces touched and then their lips clung together feasting on each other.

McGuire just smiled and complied with LouLou's wishes. He could feel the soft skin on LouLou's back. He gently rubbed her back and his manhood became alive. He was as hard as a rock. He took her breasts into his mouth. He lapped their treasures. She trembled in his arms. Her lips kissed his breasts. The storm, raged in a whirl of lust as his breasts were kissed.

His arms tightened about her body. He used his hands to capture the soft folds of LouLou's body. His hands traveled down to her legs, and then up to the crease covered by soft hair. They kissed as if there was no ending of their love. Entering her warm body, it was an ecstasy that he hadn't felt in a long time.

"You are mine, always, mine," murmured McGuire.

"I want you forever. Oh, McGuire, you make me feel like a princess. You make me feel dreams can come true." whispered LouLou "I dreamed of our being one with you. McGuire you will never know what you have given to me. I love you forever."

They spent together as one, lovers, workers, and friends. She loved McGuire with all her strength and heart. Her lavender eyes were filled with so much love of McGuire that she never saw anyone else. He had given her the one thing she never had, -choice. She had her brother back with her again. She knew that she was lucky. She prayed that her luck would last forever.

Because of LouLou, McGuire became the man dressed in black, The Madam wore the styles from Paris with a flair. She was the dream that men dreamed of when they slept and when they were awake. She became known for the Parisians style, of bare half breast. Every man who saw her wanted to touch those magnificent breasts. She was McGuire's and untouchable to every one else.

McGuire refused to give up his silver guns. It was a matter of pride and loyalty that the guns remain as they were. They made it through the plantation days, the war, the gambler, and now the man who owned property. LouLou gave up on the guns, let him keep his silver guns. She made sure he got black boots and black holsters. He was a gambler and a killer. McGuire would always be the eagle waiting for his prey.

The year rolled by and everyone was happy. The hotel, casino and whorehouse were making tons of money. All the girls in the whorehouse were happy as they got a percentage of the trade, and LouLou had the only man she ever loved.

LouLou knew that McGuire and the school teacher had been close. She could tell that McGuire made the school teacher. Would he have to marry her because she was a virgin? She shook with fear. Was she always to be the one that fate kicked out?

Chapter XII

McGUIRE BEGAN TO THINK OF his mistress, LouLou as someone special. She was his best friend. He knew LouLou loved him. He also knew that LouLou would not stand in his way if he told her he loved Samantha. She made the whorehouse rich and of course, he became rich. She knew what to do to make things hum so it spread that the whore house was the best of the best. He knew LouLou would not be his mistress or friend, once he married someone else.

She looked great in red. LouLou knew that McGuire liked to think of her in red, being that was the first time he saw her. He liked to think of her as stuffed full of pillows. She had to laugh at how he looked at her red dress pulling at the seams and her so fat.

She was a beautiful woman and deserved better than being just a Madam. She insisted that was all she wanted out of life, and most important of all, being the love of McGuire's.

*   *   *

LouLou and her brother lived a happy life even though their parents were as poor as church mice. It was a hand to mouth existence but they managed to survive and have happy times. LouLou's given name was Louise and her brother's name was Alex. They were the lowly Haxley clan of hard workers who seemed to be out of luck all the time. He father would work where ever he could find a job. All of the money he made went for food.

Louise could not find a job as people thought she looked too fast for their beliefs. Louise at fourteen was five feet four inches tall. She had a striking red-gold hair that gently curled around her face. Louise had big breasts that stood at attention no matter how hard she tried to hide them. She use to tie old sheets to tie her breasts down so they would not be so obvious. Her waist was so tiny a man's hand could span it.

Her time was spent around garbage cans to find something to eat that someone threw away. She used arrows and sticks to round up the game.

The winter was terrible. The cold came into the small room that they rented through the cracks in the wall, the ceiling, and the door. There was a big bed and a small stove for heat, if they had money to buy coal.

Most of the time, the family was hungry. Hunger was a way of life until Father got a job and there was food for them to eat.

It worried Louis that the sniff sounded terrible to her, and they had no doctor to call. At first, her parents tried to hide their sickness One day they could not get out of bed. All four Huxley's would lie close to each other to stop the cold. The snow came down in large flakes and then it became a blizzard. The snow covered all the ground around where they lived. There was no food in the room they rented. Louise heard Alex's stomach growl. All they could do at the time was lie in the bed for warmth. It was useless, there was nothing they could do. First the mother died. The two children did know what to do. It wasn't very long by the clock, maybe an hour, the father succumbed to the flue.

Louise looked at Alex and they had no money to bury their parents. The cold bit into their bones. Their was no place to go. The hunger covered their lives. They had to better their lives some how. They understood they could not be together and make ends meet.

"We have to go our separate ways," said Louise in her torn overalls that Alex had worn. Her blouse was a gray mixture of old torn sheets put together.

"I can't leave you alone, Louise, What will you do? They will never hire you are a maid or laundress." cried Alex "They think you are too pretty. I can pick pockets.'

"Oh, and get caught. You know you are not good at that. We have to think about our parents. We have no money to bury them. We have to leave before someone finds they're dead."

"I have to do what I can, Alex." said Louise in a very adult voice. "The only job open for me is to be a whore."

"What? Lay on your back and become a whore?" cried Alex.

"Alex, if that is what it takes to eat, that is what I will do. It is you I am worried about." cried Louise. She hugged herself worrying about Alex.

"I'll go West." said Alex in a very small voice. "They have jobs there I know. I read about it in the papers people threw away. But Louise-

"We live in Chicago and there is nothing for us now. Our folks are dead, and we do have to eat and sleep. I think you should go where it is warm so at least you can live outside if you must." murmured Louise.

The snow lay heavily on the streets. Louise and Alex knew they had to leave fast and soon, so that their folks would be buried by the town, and not by them.

Louise watched as Alex shoved his hands into his torn pockets and then took them out. He hugged Louise.

"We'll find each other soon." said Alex as he headed out the door. Louise felt the tears fall from her eyes. She pushed back her red gold hair from her eyes. She never would see Alex again she thought.

"Alex, I love you. I always will. Take care of yourself and think of me," cried Louise.

"Louise, we will find each other again. I promise you. We will. I just know we will," said Alex in a very low voice.

Louise left the house in a rush. She wore a coat that was thrown away many years ago by someone as poor as she was, but it was all she had. She knew where the whorehouse that she wanted to go to was in Chicago. She tramped through the snow filling her worn shoes to the brim with ice. All the world looked so white and clean. Louise looked at the places she past and wondered why her world was so battered and without joy.

She found the mansion. The building was large brown stone with many windows for the light to shine in on the top floor. The bottom floor held one red door and no windows. It looked so strange as it stood alone on a meadow of snow with a tall gate around the entire structure. Louise knew she had no choice but this one. She was so hungry her stomach forgotten how to growl. She was so tired of wanting some place warm to sit in or sleep in.

She knocked on the door with the large brass knocker. A took a moment for the door to swing open. A lovely black lady answered the door. She was dressed all in black satin, with a tiny little white apron around her small waist.

"Yes?" said the lady in voice that sounded like silver bells.

"I need work," said Louise.

"Do you know what this house is?" asked the lady as she looked Louise over She could see the poor condition that Louise was in, as her clothing shouted she had no money.

"Yes, I do. Every one who lives in Chicago knows what this house is. It is the only job that I can take right now." answered Louise "I know I can do it. I am so hungry and tired of being cold."

"Maybe you should see the Madam," said the lady as she turned her back to show Louise the way. The maid's face held out a fraction of hope.

Louise followed the maid down a hall filled with pictures of naked women. They shone from the lights that lighted the hall. Louise was fascinated by the display of women. It was hard to tell what the real color of their hair was, as the pictures were all black and white. She tried to picture herself as one of the pictures, and here her imagination went dry.

The maid knocked on a very polished black door and she heard a gravely voice call out to enter.

The maid opened the door, "This child wants a job. She must be about 11 or 12 years old.".

"No, I am fourteen years old, and I am starving. I need heat and food. I know what I am doing." cried Louise. "please don't turn me away."

Louise looked into the room. She recognized it as Oriental furniture from pictures she had seen in the old papers that people threw away. She stared at the bed that was so big it could fit nine people in it.

Louise's eyes stared at the Madam. She was sitting on a stool of red velvet. She was a large woman. Her hair was black as coal. Her eyes were gray and flat. She wore a velvet dressing gown of gold. It hugged her big body like a wrapper on a Christmas tree. She leaned back on her stool of red and stared at Louise. She apprised the merchandize.

"So you know what this house does? Are you willing to lay on your back and enjoy it?" asked the Madam.

"Yes, whatever it takes to be warm and fed." said Louise in a soft voice.

"You are very beautiful you know," said the Madam. "Are you a virgin?"

"I am a virgin. Is that important?" asked Louise.

"Yes, but you are a child. I can not use you now. Come back a few years from now, like when you're sixteen." said the Madam as she picked up a silver hair brush and started to brush her hair. The Madam was losing her business; there was no sense taking on new people.

"I need work now. I am old enough. People will never know I'm not sixteen. Look, I can unbind my breasts. They are big. I need heat and food now. "cried Louise She pulled off her blouse of many colors and unbound her chest. Her breasts fell out of the binding and stood straight up.

The Madam looked at her naked breasts. She nodded her head. "You are a fine one. And a virgin." The Madam put down her brush and looked at Louise "I can give you food right now. I can give you heat for awhile. I can let you talk to the women who work here. If after all that, you truly want to work here, then we will talk. You should know, I am not making any money right now. I may be going bust at any moment."

Louise smiled her biggest smile to date. She was going to be warm and fed.

"Mary, take this girl to the kitchen and feed her. Let her talk to the girls to see if she really knows what she is getting into." said the Madam in a low voice.

Louise went into the kitchen with Mary. She smelled the fresh baked bread, and the butter that lay on the kitchen table. She pulled at the fresh baked bread that was on the table. Her hands broke the bread in two. She stuffed her mouth. It tasted so good to eat.

"Well, hello there," said a Southern voice. "I'm Kitty and who might you be?"

"I'm Louise Haxley. I want to work here. I have nothing to live for outside this house. My parents died and my brother went West or at least I hope so. I am all alone, no one to care if I live or die."

"What a stupid name you have. Is it real? Anyway, you should not talk with your mouth full." Kitty said as she sat down next to Louise.

Mary gave Louise a plate with meat, potatoes, and peas on it. She shoved it under Louise's nose. She took the food into her mouth and ignored Kitty.

Kitty watched her eat and then another woman came into the kitchen. Louise noticed that Kitty and the other woman wore dresses that was cut high against the busts, therefore advertising the fullness of each bust. The dress that Kitty wore was a Kelly green silk that spread out in fold of bold relief. The other woman smiled and ran her hands over her a yellow silk dress that floated as she walked. "I'm Darling." said the woman in the yellow dress, as she sat down opposite Louise.

What strange names you both have," said Louise. "I never heard any names like yours."

"No," said Kitty, "it is you that has a name that no one will remember. I never seen any one eat so fast as you."

"I am so hungry. I haven't eaten in days. I really don't care what I do, so long as I have warmth and food." Said Louise as she took another forkful of food into her mouth.

"You are a strange one," said Darling. "Let us find a name for you."

Kitty sucked her thumb. "How about Sweet stuff, or Lovely?"

'No," said Darling, "It should be something special. Something that one will remember. May be angel or rose red."

"Well the way she eats, she sure is a lou lou." said Kitty.

"That's it. It is perfect for her. Look at her breasts. She is a lou lou on that one." cried Kitty. "Her name is LouLou."

Just then the girls looked at the door. They were very quiet. They were looking at the Madam. She stood very still as she watched Louise stuff her mouth.

'Yes, I like LouLou for her name." said the Madam. "It fits her nicely. Well, have you decided to stay or go? It is up to you. I do not want you to cry to me later that you had no choice."

"I want to stay," said Louise. "Please let me. I have no place to go if you must know."

"You can stay, but your name is LouLou from now on. Forget that common name. We have to talk about your being a virgin. I get loads of money for a virgin. I can give you ten percent of it. By the way, these are the only girls I have right now. Most girls don't want to stay in a place that is dieing."

"More than ever. Can I have pretty dresses like them?"

"You'll have many pretty dresses. As much as you want. You are like a miracle for me. Men love virgins, but your hair, and your busts, they are the dreams of many men."

"If you stay, we will advertise the fact that you are a virgin. We will get bids for whoever will win you. Do you want to go without clothing? Better still, a see through night gown should be the ticket. Are you willing to do that?"

"If I get ten percent of the take, it will be more money than I ever had. I sure will do whatever you tell me to do." cried LouLou as she ran her hands over her mouth.

"Manners, manners," said the Madam very softly. "you must understand, manners are very important. Men adore women with manners."

"But I never had sex of any kind. How do I show manners?" asked LouLou.

"Ah, that is where it does not count. Men hope you don't know anything about sex. That is why they bid so high. If we get one hundred dollars for you,. Well, you get ten."

"Go for it. With ten dollars I can do almost anything." said LouLou in a low voice of marvel.

It got around there was a virgin, a very pretty virgin that was to be bid on the following week. Many old fat men came. The bids went on and on. The fat old men sat around in a circle of chairs. Their faces were filled with lust. The finale bid for LouLou was two hundred dollars.

She could not believe that men would pay so much for her. LouLou pranced around the room in her see through night gown. The men tried to touch her as she pranced by, but she was swift and gave none of the men time to feel her.

She went into the room set up for her and her bidder. The rest of the men had the two women. The two women were happy, they had business and that night, time and time again they had different men. No man had been around for a long time.

LouLou was a drawing card for the house. The Madam split the money she made with the three girls. Before long, many girls wanted into the mansion and the place became known as a special place for the lonely male. Now there were ten girls and every room was put to use. The Madam made sure that each girl was beautiful and thin.

The only thing that could not be mentioned, was the fact that LouLou kept growing. Finally by sixteen, she was five feet seven inches tall, and by many standards a real beauty. She loved her life and she was an asset to all the girls. They loved her like a sister they never had. She was a breath of Spring to everyone.

She lost her original name and became LouLou. She wore dresses of satin, silk, and velvet and she was so happy. The Madam and the girls were happy as they were making so much money they could not believe their luck. There was no way they would change their luck. They were not jealous of LouLou, in fact, they blessed her each and every day. It was because of LouLou that there was a load of business and good business. They were the toast of the town.

A month later that LouLou came to bless the whorehouse with her presence, that Morales came. He had come to kill a man he hated, and kill him he did. He went to the best whore house he heard about. He entered and he stood in the corner of the French Pallor,

The men wore tails as if they were going to a fancy dress ball. Many men and women sat on the coaches and chairs that were scattered around the room. The tables were polished so much that they gleamed. The glasses the drinks were served in were Waterford.

She wondered if her brother became a thief or a pick pocket tough, but then he didn't have the talent to take a man's goods. She prayed day to day that he was alive and well. She wanted so much to see him and hear what he was doing, but the West was big, and she was stuck smack in the middle of Chicago.

She was happy to be in one place and felt at home here. She had made friends with the other girls and their life was simple, sleep all morning, rise up at afternoon, and be ready for customers come the evening Sometimes, her mind would travel back in time and she would think of her first man. It was something she trained her mind not to think about. But she could not help recall her first man.

She though of her first experience of being a fallen woman. He just jumped on her and she shook. She was so afraid of making a mistake. The Madam of the house did not tell her what to expect. She left her in ignorance. Said she was too young to be a whore, and she certainly did not believe her she was a virgin. She would use LouLou, as LouLou wanted to be used.

"You are much too young to be in this business," shouted the Madam "But I need something to make this house more useful, instead of being dead. You realize that you are very pretty?"

"I swear it is true, I have no place to go. You are my only hope." cried LouLou "And I am a virgin, so I get ten percent of whatever I sell for the night. Don't you want to help me?"

"Well, we'll see. You know that almost all men that come here are fat and old. They are used up so to speak. And their wives are just like them. said the Madam as she picked a piece of bread from the table. "At least we still have something to eat."

LouLou remembered the night that she lost her virginity. The man was fat and old, but he was rich. He had to be rich to pay two hundred dollars for her. She wore a night gown that was see through, but silk and a shade that seemed to hum of sex, black. The room they went into was small, but the bed was big. It seemed to dominate the room. Fresh sheets made up the bed and it smelled like violets. She breathed a prayer that this was what she could do. It was all she could do.

The Madam watched as LouLou entered the room with the man at her heels. She watched as the man grabbed the small waist of LouLou. She waited to see if LouLou would scream and run away. She felt her heart hammer in her breast. Was this what she was meant to do?

LouLou looked at the bed and shuttered. Even though she said she knew what she was doing, she felt the knife in her heart. Would she survive? This was the only way she knew to make a living. She had to eat and so here she was. Slowly she turned to the man. She saw him smile at her. Her heart leaped in her breast. She smiled back and put her hand on his shoulder. He turned her face towards his. He pulled her closer and kissed her gently on her lips. She shivered as he pressed his lips harder on hers. LouLou was so nervous her body shook. He pulled her closer and took off the silk night gown. She stood before him naked.

He stared at her for a moment. Then he took her into his arms and started to kiss her breasts, her neck, her lips. She was unable to do anything as he held her tightly around her waist.

She felt his hot hands swiftly touch every part of her body. She looked at the candles that were around the room. They glowed in various colors to match any mood. She was lost unless she acted at once, she was glad the fat man held her closely. Gladly, she held her breath. She saw this as the price to pay for what she wanted.

She smiled at the fat man, and felt his teeth close over her breast. He was biting her. She wanted to scream, and then, almost immediately she put her arms around his neck. The vibration of his body shook as she leaned closer to him and kissed him on his mouth. He stared at her in amazement. He then took her body and held it closer to his.

"You are so very beautiful," he said in a harsh voice.

"I am yours," said LouLou as she looked into his dazed eyes.

"You are worth every penny I paid for you." he replied, "Will you be mine forever?" he said as he nuzzled her neck.

"For as long as you want me," said LouLou in a voice filled with desire.

"I want you now, are you ready?" asked the man.

"For you, forever," replied LouLou.

He turned and took off all his clothing. His boots gave him some trouble, but they came off as he tore at them.

He took her hands inside of his and pulled his penis up into her hidden sex. She felt a sharp pain, and then he stopped and looked at her.

"You're a virgin. They told the truth. How I wish I wasn't married to a nag, you would be mine forever," he whispered.

He pulled her close and tossed her body on the bed. They rolled around as his body stuck close to hers and his penis was inside of her body. The pain was gone. She felt a faint stirring of her body. He pounded and pounded on her body, and yet, she felt nothing amazing or abnormal.

She thought of the hot bread she would eat after this was over. The warmth enveloped her as she lay with his pounding of her body. She was some place else, a place of food and warmth and welcome. And then she thought of the money she would make doing this. Never had she any money. It was so wonderful to think of the money and what she would do with it. Money and freedom to do as she wished with the money.

"My wife is such a nag. You are wonderful. I want you again and again."

LouLou lay in the bed and looked up at him as she watched him gather his clothing. He looked so sad about leaving her. She was surprised that she could make a man like him feel any thing for her.

The old man pulled his pants back on and got off the bed. He huffed and puffed and started to walk out the door. He glanced at the white bed and the pillows that lay on the floor.

"I should stay here with you. I think I love you I am the first man to have you. Do you know what that means to someone like me? It is awe inspiring. I can not believe a girl like you could even consider a man like me. The money is nothing to me. I am rich. But you, you are beautiful, and could have anyone you want." The old man shook his head in wonder.

He did not look at her, and he did not even look at the room. He had done what he wanted and that was all that mattered. He knew he would never feel like he felt right this moment. He wanted to tell her goodbye, but that was too dramatic. He wanted to tell himself he would have her again. It was like a drug, he had to have her again. He was rich, but his wife was richer and smarter than he was. It was a miracle that he could bid on the lass. He had to remember what happened and how he felt.

Surprised, she looked at the red blood that stained around her bottom, and on the crumpled sheet. She got up and put her night gown back on. She wondered where the blood came from, but all she could feel was the need of a bath. The old man would be back she felt. Like a gypsy, she knew it would happen again. He had her in his blood.

As she finished putting her might gown on, the Madam walked into the room. She looked at LouLou. "You are made for this type of work,"the Madam said. "I never saw anyone take to it like you did. You are a natural."

LouLou looked at her. "So now what happens. I need a bath. Are all your customers old and filthy rich?

The Madam looked at the room. "I told you, I was going broke. We were lucky to get these men to bid on you. A virgin in a whore house. I think we will make it now. I think we can say we're on the roll. I have to get you clothing. I have to fix up the place so men will be happy to come here. I have to fix you up a great deal better than you look now. You're young and pretty. Men will want you even if you are not a virgin now. You are top drawer. You are a once in a life time deal. So let us get rolling. By the way, we want rich, fat old men."

"I'll have to find you clothing, give you a hair cut, fix it so it looks good, and not shabby. And teach you how to look at a man. Our clients are old, fat and rich. I guess you are hungry and need a bath. The reason you are bloody is because you were a virgin. You won't be bloody again, and I certainly won't let any man beat on you. You have to eat, but first, take a bath, I will give you a robe to wear, and then we will get you clothing."

It was introduction to the life LouLou chose. It was an easy life, if you forgot the men and lived to eat and drink.

"I can't believe I like this life. It is better than what I knew. I swear it is true," cried LouLou "And Madam, don't forget that I get ten percent of the take. The money was so easy to make."

"I am glad to you like it. It makes for a better relationship between us. I never push the girls to come here and do this. I once was a whore, but I moved up you see. I seem to be going broke. You might have changed my luck. They are used up so to speak."

Nothing wet her dreams, not the pounding of her body or the blood on the sheet and herself. She was some place else, a place of food and warmth and welcome. And then she thought of the money she would make doing this. Money and freedom to do as she wished with the money.

LouLou was a drawing card for the house. The Madam split the money she made with the three girls. Before long, girls came to the mansion and the place became known as a special place for the lonely male. Now there were ten girls and every room was put to use.

The only thing not mentioned, was LouLou kept growing. She stopped finally at sixteen' she was five feet seven and by many standards a real beauty. All the girls loved her like a sister they never had. LouLou was fun and even though she towered over most the men that came to the house, they waited in line for her and a chance to be with her. She was a breath of Spring to everyone.

On that night LouLou let her mind wander. She did not see Morales in the deep corner of the room She just let her mind stray for a second. She had money to spend which she never had before. She was rich.

She was wearing a silver silk dress with embroidery of silver threads. The dress emphasized her lavender eyes. She smiled as she looked around and found the place was crowded with men and women.

Morales looked at her as she entered the room. This was the lady of his desire. He could feel his erection come alive. His body shudder with desire. He stood in the corner of the room just looking at her. He looked at her red gold hair and he let out a silent sigh. Her breasts stood out ready for his hands. He strode over to her.

"I would like to have the pleasure of your company upstairs," he said.

LouLou looked at him. She had never seen him here before, plus, she was taken every night by her special customers. She did not take new people. She smiled, "Sorry, but I am taken for tonight."

"Break it," said the man. "I am Morales. The famous outlaw of the West."

"Famous or not, I am taken," said LouLou. "I am sorry, but there are other pretty girls here that may be free tonight."

"Maybe," shouted Morales, "I do not want other girls. I want you."

LouLou still tried to smile though she loathed this man she said, "I said, I am taken. And that my friend is that. In fact, I am taken for three months in advance."

"No," snarled Morales. "I always get what I want. I want you to be my woman. The heck with this place. Let's get out of here.

Morales grabbed LouLou's hand and pulled her body to his. He took one of his hand and cupped it around her breast. "I always get what I want. I want you and that my lovely woman, is that."

LouLou tried to pull away from him, but his grip on her hand was too strong. His face came down to her face and he kissed her hard and swift."

LouLou relaxed slightly and looked around for the bouncer they had gotten when they found that they were famous. He was standing by the door looking around. LouLou made a sign to him and he recognized her distress. He walked over.

"Think it is time you left," said the bouncer.

Morales let his grip on LouLou's hand relax. She pulled away and fled the room. Morales turned and before he knew it the bouncer was on top of him. Morales was a dirty fighter and he knew all the holds. The bouncer didn't stand a chance. Before he knew it, he was thrown across the room. They ducked and looked at Morales. Morales smiled and looked around for LouLou. She was gone.

He dashed up the stairs to the rooms above. He flung open the doors. He looked into the rooms, and the girls inside with their clients started to scream. He took out his guns and started to shot around the house. People ducked and hid from his rage.

LouLou had gotten her coat and money and left the house. She did not know where she was going, but she knew trouble when she saw it. The only thing she could think of was to head West and maybe find her brother.

LouLou traveled West. She had enough money to take her any where she wanted. She dressed differently but Morales seemed to find out where she was and were she was going. She could not shake the man. She wanted to go back to Chicago and the Mansion where she was so happy, but Morales was always in the way. She covered her hair; she put shoe polish on it; nothing helped. He seemed to find her no matter what. She did not know what she would do if he ever found her again. She heard the rumor of the silver eagle, and how he protected women. She also heard he was in dire straights and about to lose his whorehouse.

She wanted more than anything in the world to be his Madam. She wanted to rule the roost.

Her only hope was to get herself to Cactus Gulch and hope that the silver eagle, McGuire, was there and he would help her. He helped women in distress. She rushed to Cactus Gulch. She could not believe her luck that she made it all the way there. This time she was a fat lady. She knew it would never work, that Morales would find her again.

The encounter was not by chance, it was to LouLou the new meaning of her life. She did not realize that McGuire would be so handsome and strong. He was the most beautiful man she had ever seen.

Chapter XIII

THE SUN WAS PLAYING TAG with the clouds that gathered above the mountains. Samantha still lay still, like a broken doll without a heart. She was handed about several times between McGuire and Ted. Now, she rested in McGuire's arms. They had come out of the mountains, and in the desert, McGuire stopped and jumped off his horse, Chip, with Samantha in his arms, He handed her to Ted.

McGuire acknowledged that Ted would treat her like a queen. Ted was madly in love with Samantha. McGuire wondered if he would be good for her, or would he tire of her like he did of all his playthings? Was Ted the better man for Samantha. He pulled his hat over his eyes and rode his horse slowly trying to decide what he would or should do. Was he in love with Samantha, or was it just a dream?

McGuire tried to think of the future. Was he to be tied to a woman because he took her virginity? Was he like the tumble weed ready to blow away with the wind of time? He loved the feel of the breeze in his face. He was kin with the cards as they play.

He had taken Samantha's virginity and he would marry her without question. He was of the old school, and his parents would turn in their grave if they thought he took a lady's cherished possession and did not honor. She would expect him to marry her. He had no choice but to marry her. He really wanted her so badly he could taste it. He must love Samantha.

He just wasn't about to leave LouLou high and dry. Ted would never marry her if he knew that he, McGuire had taken her virginity. He would be too proud. Would he marry Ginger? Yes, no —, everyone thought Ted would marry Ginger.

McGuire thought about LouLou. Her soft lavender eyes that light with love every time she saw him. She gave herself to no one but McGuire. Even if she was a Madam, she was his responsibility. His to love and care about.

LouLou knew McGuire loved the feel of her velvet skin. He loved rubbing his hands down her back when she wore her formal dresses without a back for the working night. Sure, she knew he had other ladies on the side, but he always came back to her.

McGuire remembered so many nights with her. The nights following her return to the whorehouse. He didn't believe she would come back, but she came. He didn't know anything about running a whorehouse.

The first night with LouLou was magic. She had smiled up at him. She was wearing a purple dress that fit her body like a second skin. She wore her purple dress which flounced out at the bottom, but the top was just held in place by thin straps over her shoulders and down her bare back to her waist.

LouLou turned slightly and sat down on a sofa. She patted the sofa for him to sit.

McGuire looked down at her. He could tell she was trying to make him feel at ease. No one ever tried that. This was a new experience for him.

"Oh, McGuire," laughed LouLou. "I want you. Can't you see that? I want you as my man. You have to see that I'm ready for you any time you want. I know you had me already, but, I want only you."

McGuire sat down next to her. He took her hand. He looked into her lavender eyes. "I'm a rolling stone, LouLou. I don't stay long in any place. I may leave any time. You just can't trust me."

"If it makes you feel better, I will never hold you captive. Just like you gave me a choice, I'll let you go when the time comes. But right now, let's enjoy being together. I can tell you like me. I make you laugh. You like that?" LouLou said as she put her hands on McGuire's face.

LouLou pushed away from McGuire and stood up. She walked over to the dresser and got two glasses down. She brought up a bottle of whiskey. She poured whiskey into each of the glasses. She glided back to the sofa and handed him a glass. She sat down next to him and they clinked glasses and drank.

LouLou took her glass and threw it into the fireplace. It shattered in a million pieces. McGuire laughed and threw his glass into the fireplace. "You do make me laugh and feel like I'm free like a bird." McGuire said.

"You are a bird; you are an eagle?" LouLou put her two hands onto McGuire's face and kissed him long and deep.

McGuire pulled her body close to his and rubbed his hands over her back. His right hand held her breast and his left hand went lower down to her rear. He kissed her tenderly at first and then his kisses heated up. His tongue darted in and out of her mouth. She shuttered with his touch.

She pulled down her straps of her dress, and the dress fell to the floor. She was left with a thin bit of material at her bodice, and nothing else.

McGuire slowly pushed the material off her body. He held her breasts with his two hands. He pushed away from her. McGuire pulled off his boots, his shirt and trousers. He was naked.

They lay on the floor and his hands dwelt in her nest of hair by her legs. She breathed a deep word of prayer and then she was all over McGuire as she gently stroked his long shaft. Her body rubbed and swelled with his attention.

They shattered as he entered her. She cooed and he opened his eyes wider as he looked at her. "You are so beautiful. I have never seen anyone like you before."

"Oh, McGuire, I'm yours, always You want me. You want a woman who is willing to give up her soul. I give you my soul forever."

McGuire tugged at her breasts and feasted on them again. He felt content for the first time in years.

"I love you." whispered LouLou. "You don't have to love me back. Even if I know it is only a small part of you that cares for me, I still am very happy."

"LouLou-"started McGuire.

"Please, don't say anything. Don't spoil it. I know you. You are a free soul. Let me have you every once in awhile while I can. You can go any time you feel you must, but McGuire-"

"Don't say anything LouLou," said McGuire. "Let us just take what we can at this moment of time. I do not think I am capable of love. You are brave, and funny, and lovable."

LouLou took his face into her hands and kissed him. She kissed him with passion and with love. It was a big night for the two of them. They never got to sleep. They started to make love again and again. This time slowly and with a great deal of feeling but not thinking of the future.

Chapter XIV

McGUIRE SMILED AND HIS BIG white teeth sparkled in the sunlight. He was happy. He believed that he had found what he was always looking for-a woman to keep him happy and in line. Children would come soon enough and he would have a family again. Of course, he never was proper and right even when he lived and worked on the plantation. He had no choice now, he had taken Samantha's virginity. For once in his life, he would do what was right, and damn the consequences.

The posse jogged along at a slow rate, because of Samantha. It felt good that he and Ted had saved Samantha, and the bad guys were dead, Black-Hawk and Coyote. Most of the town had been afraid of Black-Hawk and kept out of his way, but kidnapping a schoolteacher put things in another light. The posse dispersed once they came into town. Ted carried Samantha into Kate's house.

"Oh, you poor girl. Here, put her into my bed. No! No! She can not go upstairs with the children. Why, she is burning up. We have to call the doctor. Does her Pa know that she is sick? Look at her face! It is black and blue." Kate said as she rushed into her room and pulled down the blanket.

Ted lay her on the bed. "Guess you'll have to undress her. I'll go for the doctor. Forget her Pa. He knows she is sick. I think he is sicker than she is."

Kate paid no attention to anything Ted said. She was so flustered seeing Samantha looking like she was dead. She looked at Ted. "First get me a towel that is wet. I'll wash her face. It might bring down the fever some, but you must go for the doctor."

Ted went into the kitchen and pumped some water onto a towel. He stared at the towel. He knew that McGuire had taken Samantha's virginity, but it didn't matter. He loved her with all his heart.

Ted brought Kate the wet towel and left. Kate looked around the room and saw only the bed and two shelves where she kept her clothing. She wondered why Samantha's Pa just stayed away from her. Kate finished undressing Samantha, and then put her into her own nightgown. Kate slowly washed her face, and then moved down into her breasts by opening the top buttons of the nightgown.

"Why would Black-Hawk kidnap you?" asked Kate. Why does her Pas hate her?

"Nothing I can do until the doctor comes, except cool her down some with the cool water." Kate said as she went into the kitchen. She looked out the window and saw the doctor and Samantha's Pa coming up the path. Ted was running to catch up to them. Ted looked worried.

They all barged through the door and into the house. Kate showed the doctor where Samantha lay on the bed. "Ted," said the doctor, "you go on out now. I'll let you know what's what, when I know it."

Ted shook his head. "I'm staying no matter what. Especially if her Pa stays." Ted's heart lurched in his body. He wanted to knew that Samantha was his, and his alone. He wanted to marry her, and love her, and have children with her. He worried that she might bet pregnant with McGuire's child. She would marry McGuire and Ted knew he could not allow it to happen.

The doctor was a small, round man, with a big beard and a baldheaded. He took out of his bag his stereoscope and listened to Samantha's heart. He felt her face, and he whistled. "Hot! I think she just needs some rest"

The doctor rubbed his hands together and thought. Finally he said, "I think if you have one of your girls wash her down, her fever will finally go away. She sure is bruised up. Did she get those bruises when they brought her back from where they found her, or did those outlaws mark her up like this?"

"It was the outlaws that bruised her like that. They are dead, thank God. I don't know what I would do to them now looking at the state Samantha is in.," Ted said.

"My," said Doctor Weed. He certainly wanted to hear more to tell it to the boys at the bar. "What happened?"

Kate didn't trust doctors, but she did not know what do with Samantha. She felt a chill as she thought of Black-Hawk beating Samantha in the face. She looked at Clarence. "What do you think, Clarence, shall we just let her rest awhile and have one of my girls sort of wash her down? There's nothing we can do for the bruises as far as I know. Tell me doctor, is there any thing we can do to take the swelling down?"

Clarence shrugged. Kate put her hands on her hips and glared. She turned to the doctor and said. "Yes, we'll do like you say. But you will come back here again, I hope."

Doctor Weed smiled and his beard stretched out. "Sure, I will," I'll be back in a few hours. Now just wash her all over in cool water. I think I should hear more of the story to see if I need to do anything else."

Ted shook his head. "Not now Doctor. When you come back we'll be glad to fill you in/ Just know Black Hawk beat the lady."

"Maybe I'll leave some medicine to take the hurt away. Do think she'll need some of this medicine to take the pain away?"

Doctor Weed put his bag together and turned around the small house. He hated it was a small house, which meant he would not get a big payment for his services. The whole town was watching him and what he would do. Maybe he just will forget his payment. The whole town would remember that the doctor helped the schoolteacher.

Doctor Weed left the house. He only became a doctor when people started asking him questions. As a dentist, he just sort of told them some old fashioned remedies his Ma he told him. But the remedies worked and everyone decided he was a doctor. More money in being a doctor. He decided maybe he was a doctor. Thus a doctor was born.

Kate turned to Clarence. "I have taken all I am going to take from you. Now you tell me why you hate Samantha?"

Ted said nothing, but took a seat opposite from Clarence. McGuire came banging into the house. He took a seat next to Ted. Ted and McGuire glared at Clarence daring him to tell some tall story.

Clarence squirmed in his seat. He pulled at his braces. He coughed. He dusted his pants. He looked out the one window in the kitchen.

He stood up, but Ted pushed him down. "I want an answer now, and no more this game you are playing. The whole town knows you hate the girl.

Why did you put her in an orphanage with the nuns? In fact, tell us why you wanted her dead. Believe it or not, that is the prize question."

Ted and McGuire looked like the devils from hell. Clarence turned white and his face squashed like mashed potatoes. McGuire jumped up and walked around the table. He pulled Clarence from the chair and punched him in the face.

"I am tired of you avoiding all questions. I am tired of you trying to kill Samantha. Why did you want Samantha dead?"

Ted rushed around the table as Clarence was still standing and Ted punched him in the stomach. "I don't understand what you want out of life. We are waiting for you to tell us."

Kate screamed. "What are you both doing? You get no where trying to beat him. He is like a frightened stalk of a man."

"He paid Black-Hawk $1,000 to kill Samantha But Black-Hawk liked the way Samantha looked and he was going to take her to Mexico. He would have made a slave out of her." said Ted as he sat down again on the chair.

Clarence covered his face with his large hands, and seemed to whither right in front of them. He held his stomach and then his face where he was hit. His eyes started to tear, and he rubbed his hands over his eyes. His round nose tweaked like a mouse.

"Speak up, Clarence. I want to hear it all," yelled Ted then bunched his fingers into a fist and pounded the table.

"It isn't a pretty story. I can never forgive or forget I. It eats me," Clarence said. "I hate Samantha, do you hear me."

Clarence's large hands clenched into fists. His thin mouth thinned in his hate. His eyes were filled with an unholy light.

"I don't know where to begin, except at the beginning. Elizabeth was the prettiest girl in Philadelphia. Our fathers both worked in the factory making chairs. She must have been all of sixteen when I fell madly in love with her. She had so many men who wanted her and I had nothing to offer her. I remember her in her dark black skirt and a brown sweater. Her family like mine was poor. She hated dark colors but loved light happy colors. Most of the clothing the family had came from the nuns. They got most of the clothing from the rich people's servants.

Elizabeth had the joy of life in her face. She liked to laugh and have a great time. The men in her life were poor but they wanted to possess Elizabeth.

They spent what money they had on Elizabeth to take her dancing or buy her candy. Elizabeth wanted to be rich more than candy, she wanted bright colors, beautiful clothing, admiration, and love.

Elizabeth was lovely. Her long black hair fell around her hips, a velvet curtain that closed her off from real people. She reminded me of Spring time and flowers. She was the loveliest flower that grew in a garden. I wanted the flower.

She had a straight small nose and her eyes were bright as stars. Everyone knew she would never marry any poor slob. She was destined for greatness. A husband with money was what she desired. As much as I hated the thought, I knew she would achieve her wish.

Elizabeth hardly looked at me. I was ugly as sin and still am. But I loved Elizabeth with a love that was all consuming. She had a million suitors to pick from but they were poor. Why would she look at a skinny man? She wanted to live royally. She wanted a man that was not only rich, but good looking. She wanted to live among the stars.

I had no way to court her properly. You know candy and flowers. That sort of thing. I needed money. I saved a little money I made by selling newspapers. I started to bring her candy. She took the candy and ate it right in front of me, but still refused to go out with me. She laughed at me as she ate the candy.

"Why would I even think of going out with you. You are so small and skinny like a stick." she laughed. "Only a demented person would go with you."

I brought her some flowers. I stole the flowers from a yard next to where I saw them growing in a rich man's house. I was afraid one of the other suitors would steal her away from me. I got up the nerve and asked her if she would marry me. She said a loud no.

You wonder why I hate Samantha, because Samantha looks exactly like Elizabeth God, there wasn't anything I won't do for Elizabeth. She was sweet to everyone but me. She only laughed at me, and said I was a joke, a clown, a nobody.

I finally found a good paying job in an ice factory. Not much, but enough to feel rich in this poverty-stricken area. I asked Elizabeth if she would marry me again. She kind of thought about it for a moment, then looked at me with those big hazel eyes of hers.

"Clarence, are you always going to deliver ice, or are you going to make something of yourself?" she asked.

I didn't know how to answer her. I could see she was not thrilled about marrying a gawky kid weighing only 128 pounds. "What do you want me to do?" I asked.

"I need a new life. I want pretty things. I don't want to be stuck here for all time." she said. "I want to be rich."

I looked at her and nodded. What else could I do? I didn't know of any way out of this poverty.

"Go to school and become something. Use that time, instead of wasting your time coming to my house. There are so many men in my life, but none of them want to do anything about their future." Elizabeth answered "Maybe, just maybe I would be interested in you. That is, if I could have the things in life I want."

"What kind of school? I would have to use my money for school. Don't get mad, Elizabeth, I'll do anything you want me to do if you will marry me. Just say what it is you want me to do."

Elizabeth swirled around the room and then sat down. The dark skirt she wore rose above her knees and my heart froze in delight. She sat on a torn loveseat. "I am so tired of living in this place. You would make a good telegraph operator. There are so many openings out west, I read it in a newspaper. I'm not sure I want to go with you, yet any thing to get out of this place. Maybe I'll even marry you. God, that is a fate worse than death."

"Gee," I said, "I'm not so bad. Really. I would do anything for you. You want the West and will marry me, I'll go to the ends of the world for you. I never thought of leaving here because the folks, both yours and mine, are here. But listen Elizabeth, I would do anything you want."

"I am just tired of being in this slum. Telegraph operators are needed in the West. I want air I can breathe, and a place that will be mine. I do not want an ugly apartment like our folks have with hand me down old furniture. I want fine dresses, and pretty coats. I am pretty and deserve it."

"If you want me to go to school, I'll go. If you want to go West than we will go. Elizabeth, you have to promise to wait for me to graduate school, so I know you're mine. You want pretty dresses, I'll see that you get them. Will you marry me?"

Elizabeth shrugged her slender shoulders. "Of course I will marry you, if you graduate from school and get a job out West, with a decent salary. I can marry some good looking guy if nothing else will do. You are the ugliest man I know."

So many men wanted Elizabeth but none wanted to go west with the Indians and poisonous snakes. That was why she was willing to marry me, if we go West. Some thing in my brain said it is too good to be true or last.

Elizabeth's long black hair shone like obsidian as she dug it into my heart. Her skin parchment white is forever part of me. I will love her until I die. Her large hazel eyes sparkled like the sun. I stared into her eyes and knew I was in heaven.

Her mouth was like wine ready to drink and be licked. I wanted to kiss her so badly, but she never allowed me near her. I wondered when we married would she still keep me away from her person? I worried and worshiped her at the same moment in time. The earthly pleasures she presented to my mind were filled with lust for her body.

I looked at her and would commit murder, if that would get her to marry me. It was a matter of pride I be first in the class and get the job she wanted. Being first in class was not hard. Not many men wanted to be a telegraph operator. In spite of it, I had to be first to get the best job, and have Elizabeth marry me.

The ring I gave to her was a bronze little thing. It had no stones, but Elizabeth wore it while I was with her, which was seldom. I knew she took it off when I wasn't around.

I graduated school, first in my class. Elizabeth kept her word. The job I was offered, and the salary were the selling points for Elizabeth. The salary was more than the money that her father and my father made together.

We were married by a priest. Only the family came. Our families brought food, and the church was decorated with golden ribbons. Elizabeth wore a soft pink dress. The dress hugged her small waist, and then it billowed out in acres of material. I have to admit I paid for the dress. I wanted her so much and she wanted the dress more than she wanted me. The dress cost almost all my savings, but it was worth it.

She wore a crown of daisies and carried a bouquet of daisies which we got next door to us. The rich had gardens and flowers and grass. We were lucky to have food on the table.

I got a job in El Paso. The salary was very good to what we made at home and Elizabeth was pleased. For the first time in our lives, we felt rich and free of the slum that we had lived in. We arrived in El Paso where we not only had a job, but also a place we could live in. We got a little house near the telegraph office. It had two bedrooms, a kitchen, and a pallor. Not only did we have the house, but we were lucky, the house was furnished. There were even curtains on the windows Eastern people feared Indians and snakes and such. It might seem strange, but we never did see any Indians or snakes. It was a dream come true for Elizabeth but mainly for me. I had the woman I worshiped.

With our first salary, Elizabeth bought new clothing; dresses, shoes and a coat. She went wild about the clothing. I was so happy to have her; I just never said a word. I never seen Elizabeth laugh and smile so much. Her eyes lightened up and her body sang with her love of new things to wear. She even let me kiss and hold her close. All this time we had a sterile relationship. I knew if I waited, Elizabeth would let me love her. She spent all my salary on clothing, but so what? I had the woman I loved.

Elizabeth dressed in new, beautiful clothing. She was taken into by the town's elite group. Her eyes sparkled and she was so fetching in her bright colored clothing. There wasn't a man that did not notice her. I was a little jealous of the men looking at her, but she loved it and let me make love to her all the time. There was no way she would be unfaithful to me. I knew she had pride.

She danced with the rich people and seemed to be having the time of her life. The men in town seemed to take to her like a fish to water. The men were rich and very good looking. She laughed and flirted and was happy. It was what she wanted. Most of the time I got time off from work, and she just wasn't there. I had to make my own lunch or dinner. I knew I was no prince, so I let it all happen and that is where I made my mistake.

I finally got fed up with the whole thing. It was time to have a family and settle down. She had her fling. Now it was time for us. I caught Elizabeth's wrist while we were in bed.

"We should settle down now and have a family. I let you play and have fun, but Elizabeth, fun is over for now." I shouted. "It's time to stop all this dancing and worrying about your hair and clothing. Now it is time you did what I want."

"What do you expect, me to just stop and be a home body? I came out here to live," shouted Elizabeth. "I told you before, I want to dance and have pretty things."

"No, I want you home with me. I don't want you flinging yourself to all these people in town." I cried. "Elizabeth, it is time for us now."

She fumed and left my bed. "You just can sleep by yourself Clarence, until you see things my way. I am not some ordinary woman. I am very beautiful and the people in town appreciate my beauty. I don't know why I stay with you You are ugly and pitiful."

"No, Please don't leave me. I love you with all my heart. Forgive me. Stay here. I won't say another word. I want you here with me." I cried. She huffed and puffed and would not listen to my cries of woe. Her heart was hardened against me.

It was about eight months, Elizabeth would not come into my bed. I was so afraid she would go back to Philadelphia that I didn't complain. She would not go back, but she might leave me. Elizabeth grew more beautiful as the days went by. I noticed that she wore loose clothing. I wondered about that, as I knew she liked to flaunt her figure.

One night, Elizabeth came over to our bed. "Clarence," she said, "maybe we should not be apart. I'm sorry I left our bed."

My eyes devoured her, there seemed to be something different about her. She came into my bed and stayed there until she informed me she was pregnant.

I was over whelmed with joy. We were going to have our first child, and she had come back to our bed.

She really had come back to my bed. Elizabeth made love with me. I could not believe she loved me so much, but I was so happy. One day, she told me she was eight months pregnant.

"You're eight and a half months pregnant, but how can that be?" I asked,

The tears fell from her large hazel eyes. "Oh, Clarence, I was raped. I need you. I love you. You do not want me to die?" Her hazel eyes stared into mine.

"Raped? Who did this to you?" I screamed.

"I do not know. I had too much wine to drink. Please forgive me. We will love the child, it is mine, and if you love me, you will love the child also."

Lord help me, I loved her so much I forgave her and promised to love the child. The child was born, and she looked just like Elizabeth. I was happy she looked like my love. Elizabeth made my lunch and dinners. She made special breakfasts for me. She was wild in bed. The child, Samantha, had so many beautiful clothes. I asked Elizabeth about it, she smiled and said I made a wonderful salary. I believed anything she told me. I will never love anyone like I loved her, with all my heart and soul.

I noticed Elizabeth wearing clothing I knew I could never afford to give her, but she was so loving, especially in bed. Her clothes varied from floating chiffon to velvet. She laughed and smiled and joked around the house.

I was afraid to break this warm loving spell she gave to me. Elizabeth was home when I was at home and she dotted on the child. I knew the child was not mine, but I didn't care. As long as Elizabeth let me near her, that was all that mattered in my life.

It was a thin Elizabeth that floated and danced about the house. I never saw any one that happy. I felt that it was because we had settled down. I did not think of the clothing of hers or Samantha.

One day, along came this trader. The man was fat and had a bald head. His nose was wide and big. His clothing were rich velvet and black leather. He had a big smile, pasted on his face. He had horses, and gold. I came home, and saw Elizabeth packing her clothes.

I watched as she folded and packed her dresses. "Where are you going?" She smiled and she licked her lovely pink lips. "I'm leaving."

I rushed over to her. "Please, no! I'll do anything you want, but don't go. I love you Elizabeth." I grabbed her arm and her dresses fell from her hand.

Her eyes narrowed. Her lips became a sneer. "Let go of me now."

I dropped her arm. I was so scared of her leaving that I started to shake. I picked up the dresses from the floor and laid them on the bed. "What about the baby and what about me? We are married."

"I am leaving you. What have you to give me. A telegraph salary, that hardly covers my wants. What about baby? She's not my responsibility now. I want fun, fine things, dancing and champagne. You take Samantha. I'm going to have clothing and diamonds and a house to be proud of. I put up with you all I can and that's that. Henry wants me to go with him and marry him. I am beautiful and smart."

I can't forget her picking up her bags and her red satin dress swishing ready to go out the door. I looked at her and the dress that hugged her body like a second skin. The skirt was a thin chiffon and really did float in the air. I could not live a life without her, she was my reason for living.

"What about Samantha?" I cried. She did not answer. She turned her back on me.

I certainly wasn't going to keep that brat. She didn't want it so why would I want a bastard? So that was how I sent her to the nuns and changed the town I worked in."

Kate looked at Clarence and tears streamed down her eyes. "I am so sorry for you. Why didn't you tell Samantha you weren't her Pa?"

"I always wondered who her Pa really was and I know it wasn't me."

Kate got out of her chair and went to the stove. She got a pot filled with coffee and brought it to the table.

"So she'll leave me in peace. I don't want her to remind me of Elizabeth. I loved Elizabeth with all my heart. I would take her back even now but the girl; I hate her with all my being. Who gave her the pretty clothing that she wore?"

"You wanted her away from you. Is that why you paid Black-Hawk to kill her?" Ted asked.

Clarence turned red, and then white. He stared at the wall blankly. They sat and watched him keeping their tempers on hold. Ted and McGuire wanted to kill Clarence right that moment.

With pleading eyes, Clarence asked, "How did you find out about all this? How did you find out that Black Hawk had kidnapped Samantha? I knew she would be my down fall."

Kate rubbed her hands together. "To kidnap a woman who was going to be a teacher in this town, is not done. The Town went wild. We needed a teacher like we need air."

"Mike saw it happen," McGuire said in a strained voice. "Black-Hawk knows to stay away from my woman. You paid him to kill this woman. You assured him, that I would not trail him for days. They both were killed, so you believed that no one would know what you had done."

"How did you find out I paid them?" asked Clarence.

"We heard them talk at the window," replied Ted "They were telling how stupid you were to think they would kill Samantha. They wanted her like a lion loves her cubs."

Clarence said "We can leave the whole thing drop. I won't try to kill her again."

"Of course we are going to tell everyone what an inhuman being you are," Kate said as she smiled with her teeth."

"Look, if you keep this quiet, I'll marry you, Kate. You have five kids that need stuff. I will give you my salary from the telegraph office. And-"

"Stop right there, You are such a liar." Kate, said as she got up and leaned over the table so she could be close to Clearance's face. "I won't marry you if you had a million dollars and you looked like- McGuire."

"You'll never get away with it," shouted Ted and McGuire at the same time. They jumped at Clarence opening the door. Clarence fell face down on the floor.

Clarence turned. His face was blotched from the fall to the floor and his hate of everyone in the room. "You both think you're so smart. I was going to give you, McGuire a telegram saying that there was a batch of new whores for you to pick up. Think you would please LouLou with that new batch of women. And you Ted were suppose to be on a cattle drive. Who expected you to return to town? Everyone knows you love your cows. You were the last person I expected to see in town."

Clarence got up from the floor and turned to Kate. He balled his hands into fists. "She never left me. Do you think I would let her leave me? I killed her. Do you hear? When she told me she was leaving and packing her things, I stabbed her with a kitchen knife. I was going to kill that little goodie Samantha, but I heard someone at the door."

Clarence put his hands to his face. The tears leaked from his eyes. "Then later that night, I carried her to the desert and buried her. I hated her so much for making me lose control and killing her. I wanted the coyotes to eat her, by not burying her. I buried her deep in the desert sands. The sand was hard but I shoveled it deep so she would not be found. She never left, but everyone thought she had. I fooled them all. I got rid of that kid, Samantha. I knew she would be my downfall. When I saw her, I knew that everything would come out about Elizabeth being killed by me. Some day she would remember, and tell everyone what I had done."

He knew he was lost. There was nothing left for him. Ted and McGuire had heard enough about all the things Clarence had done. It was time to take the man to the sheriff and let them hang him. Elizabeth only used him as a way to the West, out of her poverty.

"You dirty rat, you sold Samantha to Black-Hawk. How could you do that to anyone?" McGuire said as his mouth became a straight line and his long fingers cradled his guns in their holsters.

Clarence was scared. He started to hyperventilate. "I hate her. Who her father is no longer matters I went to school like she wanted me to do. I went west like she wanted me to do. I bought her whatever I could afford. She was shocked when she discovered she was pregnant. That is why she stayed with me. I was her cover story. I had no life after Elizabeth was dead."

"Come on, I heard enough. I'm taking you to the sheriff. He can do whatever he wants with you." Ted said as he grabbed hold of Clarence.

Clarence shrunk like a bent twig. "No one was going to have Elizabeth if I couldn't have her."

McGuire on one side and Ted on the other side pulled Clarence from the house. He could have sent the child back to her grand parents. Clarence had a twisted mind, and that was what Elizabeth must have found out after she married him. Who was to tell Samantha this?

Chapter XV

Kate watched as Samantha twisted and turned in the bed. Kate put her hand to her forehead and Samantha was burning bright fire. Kate called to Mary. "Bring me a wet dishcloth. Fill the bathtub with cold water. She is burning up and maybe the cold water will help her."

Mary came into the bedroom and she handed her Ma a dishcloth that was wet. "Will she live?" Mary let her silver eyes shed a single tear.

Mary finished filling the cast iron tub. Kate undressed Samantha and then carried her to the tub. She gently put her into the water. "Oh, Mary, I just don't know what to do or where to turn. Must I tell Samantha about her father? I mean that he is not her father. How will she take it to find out that she is well—illegitimate? That Clarence tried to kill her just as he killed her mother."

Mary put her arms around her mother. She leaned her head on her shoulder. Mary cast a worried look at her mother. She rubbed her face into Kate's shoulder. Mary turned her face to Kate's. "Mom, you never said what happened to Pa. Did he just run away? Did he hate being responsible because of us kids? You have to tell us some day; I have waited so long for you to tell me."

"You have a right to know about your Pa. I loved him so much and he loved me. His name of course was Mike."

Mary shuttered. This was the break she had waited all these years. She wanted and needed to know about her Pa. Kate sat very still and looked into the silver eyes of Mary.

Kate took a deep gulp. "He just loved to sit and watch the sun set. It was one thing he loved, besides you kids. It was what made him leave."

"We came here just a stop in the road. He went on for the land rush, and he came home in a coffin. So we stayed here."

"I will miss you so much," cried Kate. "I do not want to raise the children alone. I want you. Do you understand. Nothing is worth while if you are not here."

She thought of Big Mike walking over to her and kissing her hair. He wanted to hold her, but he knew she would not let him near her now. She was angry and nothing would suit her about him leaving her alone with the children. Her pregnancy reminded her that soon there would be another child. A child that Big Mike would love and lavish with all his heart.

He left that afternoon on the old horse. He saddled the sway back horse and still he looked towards the door where Kate stood.

"You're Pa was off to homestead. He was going to get us all a big acre of land. He'd been there before he married me. He use to trap with the Indians in his young days. He traveled a great deal over the West. He knew that land. He had seen the place he wanted to settle. It was perfect as far as he was concerned. It had black soil and the lake for water and beauty. You know how much water is worth out here. It is more precious than gold. But your Pa always looked at the beauty of the land, the sun and the moon. He was a romantic. He loved life, his children and me.

He went into the homestead rush with thousands of others. He was going to build us a mansion. I was to wait here in Cactus Gulch till he came back. He would tame the new land, but never this land we live on. That's like holding a tiger by the tail. This is desert land and so it shall always be."

Mary took Kate's hand. "He left us here, is that why we still live here? Is hc coming back? Is he building us a mansion?"

Kate put her hand around Mary. She stared at her child. She shook her head slowly. "Oh, NO. He did come back. He came back in a casket. He did find land out there that he wanted. A man followed him. He knew that your Pa knew where he was going. He knew that would be the best land to own. He wanted the same land Big Mike wanted, and the stranger killed your Pa. They caught the man and found him guilty. They hung that man who killed your Pa, as an example to others. Naturally the land went to someone else. All was lost for us.

Some people were good and thought of me. They sent Big Mike back here. All of him back. Back to his wife and now five children.

Kate let go of Mary and turned to the window in the kitchen. She looked at the table and the stove. She stared at the way her life was now. She cried, "Oh, why didn't I at least kiss him goodbye or wave my hand?"

Kate turned around Mary and gripped her stomach and started to cry, softly so as not to have anyone hear her. Mary pulled Kate close to her body. She kissed her mother.

"Mom, it's O.K. We're all here together and we love you. I would have wanted to know more about my Pa, but he was a good. Mom, you have to tell the rest of us about Pa."

"He loved his children so much. He wanted you all to have the best. Mike was seven, you were six, John was five, Sally was three, and little Kate to be born. Kate never saw her Pa."

Kate knew her love of Big Mike would last forever. It was something that rounded out her heart and head. She could still hear his voice if she listened really close. His arms would wrap around her body as she stood very still and waited for the special moment of time She would met him again when the time for her to leave this earth came.

Kate sat down on her rocking chair. She let the tears flow down her face. It was a release she did not know she needed. It was time to talk about Big Mike. It was time to make her peace with what she had done before he left them all.

"Big Mike liked sugar. Even though it was expensive it was one of his few weaknesses. He was a hard working man. Always working first for his family and then for something better for all of us."

"It was strange how we met. Big Mike was going to the hardware store, well, it really was the general store, and we both entered the door at the same time. We squashed together in the doorway. He looked down at me and smiled. I noticed his eyes then. Never had seen silver eyes before. He pulled me through the door. He took off his cowboy had at just stared at me.

"You're the prettiest lady I ever did lay my eyes on," Big Mike said. "I have seen so many women in my life, but only you are the one and only one that I want to keep forever."

I sort of hid my face. It was burning up by turning red. I blushed so easy in those days.

"I was going through here but I think I'll stop, that is, if you're not married or engaged or something." Big Mike said.

I looked up to his face. "No, I'm not married or engaged. I just turned sixteen, so give me a chance."

He laughed and laughed. "You are now. You're engaged to me. I love you little lady, whatever your name is. I want to marry you and take you away to some place out West."

I shook my head. I could not believe what this cowboy was talking about. But I very slowly said. "My name is Kate."

"Kate. What a beautiful name. We will name our children Kate the first and second and third."

"You are fooling now," I said.

"No Kate, I do love you and want to marry you. I guess I better talk to your parents. You live around here?"

Needless to say, that is how it started. At first my folks did not like him. He seemed to tumble around the place. But then he set his mind to making them like him and he worked and worked like a dog. My that man could work when he set his mind to it.

I lived up north near Chicago. The earth was black and good. Even a stick in the ground would grow. I was a farm girl from way back. You see it was nothing new to me to farm.

It happened when he took me into his arms and kissed me. My whole being wanted to blend into his body. He touched my hair in a special way he had and he smiled down at me. I thought I would die of happiness when he touched me. I never told my folks about his kissing me or touching me. It was a private time in my life. I loved him so very much. Sometimes in passing, he would grab my hand and kiss it like it was the most precious thing in the world. Shivers would run up and down my spine.

My folks were not use to seeing a cowboy and working. But we finally married and he took me away from the land I knew. It was a bad experience for me, but I loved Big Mike. I really loved that man. Sometimes, I can not believe that he is gone. Why ever did I let him go without us? Her mind turned to the time of the first night they were married.

He came into the room at the hotel they were staying at. He looked at her with those silver eyes and smiled. He crossed the room and held her hands, and then he pulled her close to his body. She could feel the wonder of his love.

She put her hands around his neck and he smiled with the dimples showing around his cheeks.

"Better undress and get ready for bed. Because I sure am ready. Kate, know I love you so much. I'll go down and come up in about twenty minutes. Is that alright with you?"

I held my breathing. I nodded my head. I knew I was entering territory I never had been at. I felt cold and hot.

Kate stood up from her rocking chair. She gave Mary a real big hug. "Bet you will soon be leaving the nest. I saw the way you and Barry looked at you while you were dancing. He came by the other day and asked if he could court you. I told him it was up to you. Do you like Barry? Are you going to let him court you? What do you want Mary? It is up to you to make the choice."

Mary laughed and her young slim body did a dance around the room. "Mom, I have to marry soon or become an old maid. And yes, I do more than like Barry. I love him."

Kate shook her head. "I'm not surprised. The way you two acted, I'm surprised you are still here with me."

"Barry said he loves me. I believe him. He wants to go to Denver to live and I sure would like to leave this place. There is nothing here, Ma, just sand and more sand. The mountains never even come close to call it home."

"I expect I will leave here also. I am tired of this place. I just am too lazy to move. I still think I'm just waiting. I am waiting for your Pa to walk through that door and love me once again. Mary, it is time we all left this place. It is a no where place."

"Ma, I think we all should just move out and start over. It is so blank out here. Nothing to do, and no where to go"said Mary. "I guess if you are a gambling man, or some one who likes the ladies, if you call them that-? Maybe eat in that fancy hotel. It's not for us."

"We better bath Samantha while she is in the tub. Maybe that will wake her up." Kate said as she walked over to the tub. They bathed Samantha with a very soft cloth. Very carefully they lifted Samantha from the tub and carried her back to the bed. They dried her. They dressed her into the nightgown that was Kate's. Samantha quivered and opened her eyes. Her eyes were not in focus and she shook and trembled.

Kate massaged her shoulders and then her back. "What happened? Where am I?" asked Samantha. Her black hair swirled around her face, wild and unkempt.

"Are you all right? Can you hear me? Should I give you some medicine to take the pain away? You are here at Kate's house." said Mary.

Samantha started to struggle. Then she stopped and looked around. "Where is my Pa? Did he come? Why am I back with you Kate?"

"All in good time," Kate answered. "Let's get you under the covers. Did you know Mary is sweet on Barry?" Kate picked up the blankets and pulled them over Samantha. "Can you imagine Mary is afraid of being an old maid? She has a great many more years for that to happen. I saw all the boys waiting for Mary to just look at them. I doubt she will ever be an old maid with them silver eyes. Mary, you have your pick of any man you want right now."

Mary felt her face turn red. "I'll tell you. Samantha, one rancher drove 30 miles just to dance with her. Mary doesn't know how pretty she is. Woman are scarce out here, and a pretty girl is worth more than gold." Kate said.

Samantha moved her head back and forth. She looked at Mary and could see how beautiful she was. "Is it true Mary? 30 miles?"

Mary Laughed. "I'll bring you some water to drink."

When Mary left the bedroom, Samantha turned to Kate. "Please, tell me what has happened? How did I come here? The last I remember is Black-Hawk slapping my face."

"In a little while. Let's just get Mary sort of calmed down. She thinks she will be an old maid. When she comes back with the water, I want you to take this medicine the doctor left for you. It will take away some of the pain that you have."

"No, it is more than that Kate, what is it?" Samantha asked "My mind is in such a whirl. I do not know up from down. I wish to know."

Mary came back into the bedroom and handed Samantha a glass of water. Kate took a teaspoon and poured the medicine into it. She then held it out for Samantha to take. Samantha took the medicine and then the water.

"That rancher that traveled 30 miles is an old man. He must be all of 30."

"You will have men courting you from here to Fresco." Kate hugged Mary. "Tell me Mary, why is Mike so up tight lately?"

Turning her back from Samantha, Mary whispered into Kate's ear. "Don't you now, he's in love with Samantha. But he'll get over it. She's going to marry McGuire I bet."

Kate patted Samantha's arm. Kate leaned over Samantha and watched her close her eyes. She started to doze off. The medicine was powerful. "Poor thing! I hate to think of her marrying McGuire. He will break her heart. He also will break LouLou's heart. What a mess the whole thing is."

Ted came back into the house as Samantha dozed in the bed. He took her slim hand into his large one and stared down at it. His heart raced as he looked at her hand. He turned to Kate.

"Whose going to tell Samantha that McGuire has a mistress? Are you going to tell her about LouLou?"

Kate looked at Ted. "I don't think so. I just don't have the heart. I hear tell he took her. He plans to marry her I also hear"

"Her marry that two timer. She better not. I love her. I want her as my wife. I don't care what happened before we marry, I only know I love her."

"McGuire is sure she will marry him. I was told he was going to tell LouLou about her. They will marry. He is an old fashioned plantation man and he will do what is right." said Kate.

Ted stood up. "I better leave. I can't see Samantha marrying that gambler. I aim to stop it from happening."

Samantha jerked awake and started to sit up, "I'm not marrying McGuire. He has a mistress. Why would he marry me? I need some one to love me, for myself only."

"Why not? He helps you, and he would do any thing you ask. Plus he looks at you like you're his already." said Mary as she pushed Samantha down into the bed and recovered her. She wondered why everyone was so concerned with Samantha.

Kate came into the room and looked at Samantha. She looked so lost and pale. Kate opened her mouth and then closed it. Some one had to protect this poor child.

"I don't trust McGuire. He's too good looking and he's too smooth for my taste. I hope you marry a man like Ted. He's hard working and he's steady. Not a flash like lightning." Kate said. "Now you sleep for a while, and then I'll answer all you questions."

"You promise," said Samantha as her eyes closed by themselves. Her mind whirled away into the land of dreams. Ted watched her. He sat down and cradled her head in his arms and kissed her slowly. Only a dream! She fell asleep with the knowledge that she belonged here. The medicine was strong, but she had dreams, good and bad but her head whirled about as she thought of Ted and how kind he was to her She wanted more out of life, a love that was forever. McGuire could never give her the lasting feeling she wanted and needed .

Kate and Mary left the room; Mary spoke softly to Kate. "Come on Ma, why Ted? He's always working, and lives way out of town and I thought he was going to marry Ginger. You know Ginger has her heart set on him."

Kate turned to look out the window and shrugged. What ever will be will be, thought Kate. There were worse problems ahead to be solved manly what Samantha was going to think about all that happened, especially about her Pa. Kate was busy in the kitchen making breakfast when she heard a sharp sound. "Where am I? What happened?"

Mary rushed into the bedroom and gave Samantha a big smile. "Thank the Lord you are up and awake. Your eyes are normal. You have been out of it for two days. Fever, cold, whatever. We called the doctor; not that he did anything. But look at you. You are up and I bet you are hungry."

Kate rushed in and hugged Samantha. She kissed her black hair. She held her tight. Samantha felt the beat of her heart at the same time as Kate's heart. She was alive and ready for action. She was ready to find out what happened to her.

Samantha closed her eyes, and then opened them. "Black-Hawk and Jose, they had me in a cabin. He, he slapped me so hard I don't remember any thing. I think I passed out. Besides he hit my rear so hard my body felt like an earthquake had just passed by. Did they, did they, well you know. Did they rape me?"

Mary was surprised that Samantha asked the last questions, but then, she just woke up and didn't know what had happened. Mary patted Samantha's arm. "No, nothing like that happened. McGuire and Ted made sure of that. In fact, it was both of them that saved you. You have nothing to worry about from Black Hawk or Coyote anymore, because McGuire and Ted shot them dead. \They will never bother you again/"

Samantha closed her hazel eyes. Her face was colorless. "Does my Pa know what has happened? Did my Pa come to see me?"

Mary glanced at Samantha and then at her Ma. It was Ma to tell her what had transgressed. "Ma tell her what happened. She has a right to know."

Kate coughed and smiled at Samantha. "Welcome back to the living. I wasn't the only one worried about you."

"My Pa?'"

Kate sat down on the corner of her bed. "Samantha, I'm not one to beat around the hay stack. I don't think your Pa and you are exactly like being the best of friends ever. I have to tell you things you won't like or believe. It was your Pa that paid Black-Hawk to kill you, not to kidnap you. It was Black-Hawks idea to keep you and take you to Mexico."

"No, no. It can't be right," screamed Samantha.

Kate pulled Samantha to her breasts. "Oh, my dear. There is so much more I must tell you and none of it is very nice."

Samantha pulled away from Kate. Her hazel eyes filled with tears. "I have no one. No one to love me."

Kate shook her head. "You have us. You have Ted and McGuire. You have all the students you are going to teach. You have the whole town in love with you. What do you mean you have no one to love you?"

Samantha looked at Kate. "Tell me what happened? Tell me what is going on right now. I have a right to know."

Kate wrung her hands together. "Do you want to know every thing or should I just forget it all?"

Without a sound, Samantha's hazel eyes met Kate's black eyes. "I must know it all. What happened. Tell me what happened."

Looking out the window, Kate hesitated. "Clarence was not your Pa. One of the reasons he hates you. He is not related to you in any way. Your Ma had an affair with some one in El Paso. Your Ma was very pretty and could get away with any thing she wanted. And she wanted money and power. Pretty clothing. Love!"

Samantha wrung her hands. She looked at Kate with a bewildered stare. Clarence hated her? He was not her Pa? What had the world come to? Who was she really? Samantha brightened up. She smiled. Her eyes gleamed.

"Maybe I can find my mother She was beautiful. How wonderful. She wanted out of her poor state. No wonder she wanted money and power. It was her right to have. She should never have married my 'Pa' No wonder Pa hated me. I wasn't his. No wonder I was left with the nuns and Pa didn't have to pay. I wasn't his kid. I was a bastard. No one knows who my father was, or is?"

Samantha swung her head and stared at the white sheets on the bed. Kate continued. "You look like your mother, according to Clarence."

"Mother, she might like me some," whispered Samantha." Maybe I'll find out who my real Pa is. It would be wonderful to belong to someone."

"No, dear child," answered Kate. "Clarence killed your mother when she was going to leave him. He could not take the fact that she did not love him and would leave him. He would never let anyone have her if he could not have her. He said he buried her some where outside of El Paso. I doubt that he buried her. Probably just threw her body into the desert, hoping the wild animals would finish off any evidence that he killed her. It was a long time ago. The wolves or the coyotes probably ate her bones by now."

Tears slid down Samantha's cheeks. They left a trail down her face, but she did not bother to wipe them away. She put her hand into her mouth and wailed. "I have no one. I belong to no one. The nuns knew what I was, even if he did not tell them. The Nuns always know. That is why they told me where to find Clarence. They always said retribution is the Lords. I am a bastard child. I am the sin the Bible talks about. Even though my Ma wanted out of poverty, why did she have me? Why not get rid of me? Why did she give me to Clarence?"

Kate smoothed the blanket over Samantha. She gently pushed Samantha down into the bed's pillow. "Sleep, you need to get better. Remember school will be starting in a week and the children need you. You are wanted right here. We love you."

Pulling the blanket over her head, Samantha wanted to hide in the dark from the world. Some how she was the walking dead. Deep in her heart she knew that she belonged to no one and no where in this world. She was never to know happiness.

It only took another day and a half and Samantha was out of bed and dressed in her black skirt and white blouse that looked like it had a battle with the dirt and lost. Samantha smiled and felt like she was reborn. It was good to be whole and well. Perhaps she had no one, but the students needed her. Most important of all, she was alive.

She was ready to go back to the schoolhouse to live. She wished for the first day of school and all her new students. She kissed Kate's cheek and all the rest of the family as they lined up to see her leave. She felt brave that she was going back to the school house. She knew she had to face the world as it floated by in the air.

"Kate you're right. I am lucky to have my teaching to keep me busy. Mike thanks for saving my life. If it weren't for you, Black-Hawk would have had his way with me. It was you who brought McGuire to the trail to save me. I can never thank you enough. But most of all, thanks for making me part of your family. You, Mike, are a hero."

Looking at Samantha with worship, Mike's face blotched as he watched Samantha search him with her eyes as if he was the most wonderful hero in the world.

"I'm glad if I helped you. I am glad I was there when all this happened. I, Oh, Samantha, I don't want anything bad to happen to you ever."

Kate spoke up in her gruff voice, "You don't have to leave. You can stay a few more days. You are part of this family you know, now and forever."

The five children shouted, "You are part of our family, now and forever."

With shinning eyes, Samantha laughed. "I have to get lesson plans going and I know this is not a bright idea, but I have to think about what happened to me all alone."

Mike spoke up shyly, "Is there something I can do to help you?"

"Thanks, Mike, but all my things are at the school already. But if you want to walk with me, I sure could welcome the company."

Mike and Samantha looked at each other. She smiled at him.

Mike became all puffed up. Walk with Samantha was his dream come true. To have her all to himself was like heaven. But, before he could answer, McGuire came riding up in a buggy.

"I'm here to take you to school. Thought you would be ready by now. I think we have to talk. It is important. You knew that I had to talk to you, didn't you?" McGuire said as he jumped down from the buggy to swung Samantha up into the seat.

Her mouth opened. Samantha had not thought that McGuire would know she was going back to the school. She did not want to be alone with him again. Her skin jumped into a hundred little bumps. Her lungs filled without air. She could not speak or think.

"Mike is going to walk me to school," she said.

"Mike knows you're not strong enough to walk. Don't you Mike?" asked McGuire.

Mike glared at McGuire. His idea of being alone with Samantha was smashed. Mike said, "Maybe I should go with you and help you put up the bulletin boards and such."

"No need to Mike," said McGuire as he turned around to Samantha. "I'll see she has whatever she needs. The buggy only holds two people with comfort. You don't want Samantha to be crowed? I want to talk to Samantha privately if you must know. In fact, I waited too long for this talk."

Quickly, she looked into his lake-blue eyes. "Don't say any thing you might regret. I want to be by myself if you don't mind. I don't want to talk to anyone now."

McGuire put his large hands around Samantha's waist. She could feel his warmth. He pulled her closer to him in the seat of the buggy. He laughed as he looked at her face. "We belong together you know." smiled McGuire.

Cold wind swept through the veins of Samantha. Would she be able to stop his loving her body? She was powerless when it came to some one loving her.

McGuire and Samantha rode in silence to the school. They did not make any contact with each other. She moved as far away from him as possible in the two seated buggy. How did she end up with him again? At the school, McGuire took hold of Samantha, and swung her out of the buggy. He looked at her as he held her in his hands. "Samantha, there is so much I want to say to you." He could feel her nearness and the heat from her body penetrated into his body. His eyes smoldered.

"Please, McGuire," Samantha said as she pulled away from him. "I am not ready to talk right now. Do you mind?"

McGuire leaned over and kissed her hair. Her black hair glistened in the sun and sparkled like diamonds framing her face. He wanted to pull his fingers through her hair. He wanted her so much. He knew his heart was doing double time. He put his finger under her chin and raised her head. She closed her eyes. He watched as the tears streamed down her face.'

"Don't cry sweet heart. I do love you. I really do. Later," McGuire said and jumped into the buggy and drove away. Samantha opened the school door and went in. Slowly she climbed the steps to her bedroom. She looked around the bedroom and saw the bed was still all messed up from when McGuire and she had made love She had made love to McGuire or had it been McGuire made love to her. She was beaten and kidnapped, and almost killed. She had passed out and could not remember anything that happened except her body was like some one had beaten it with a large rock.

She threw herself on the unmade bed and cried, more tears. She lie still as the day became night. Her mind whirled and whirled. She did not try to stop it. She let it take her were ever it wanted to go.

Her mother was killed by the man she though was her Pa. She was kidnapped and beaten because the man she thought was her Pa hated the sight of her. The reason he hated her was that she looked like her Ma. Should she go to El Paso to find her real Pa? Whom did she love if anyone? Ted or McGuire?

She touched her face as she felt the tears falling down again. She was so mixed up. Suddenly, she knew in her heart of hearts, that she did not love McGuire. In fact, she knew he stood for the old life of the plantation. He did what was required of him. He was an example of the old South. He had taken her virginity She had helped him to her body, she wanted love. He had a mistress. A beautiful mistress that loved him! He looked perfect, so tall and handsome. He was a gambler, a man who loved to roam with no ties binding him. She pictured his broad shoulders and his bright blue eyes. He was so handsome and so prone to think of the qualities he was brought up and believe. He was not what she wanted in life. She wanted children, a home, a white picket fence, and a husband who loved only her.

He would feel trapped in time. Maybe they would be happy a year, or more, but finally, he would want to roam. He was not made for marriage. He did not know it. He was the wind, the tide, the hurricane. He had helped her no end, and he felt an obligation to help her more. She had to let him be free and not worry about her.

Chapter XVI

McGUIRE FELT SO GOOD. THE day reflected his feelings, so bright and sunny. He knew finally, in his heart of hearts, that he truly loved Samantha. She was the best thing that ever happened to him. He had mistress, LouLou, who was loads of fun. He knew he owed her the success of the whorehouse, but that was business. The way he felt right now was bliss, happiness, and expectations. He was going to make it right that he took Samantha's virginity. He was going to marry her. He could hardly wait to tell her his plans for the future.

He could see how happy she would be when he told her he was going to marry her. Her smile would be like a million wild flowers blooming at once. He just knew that she was waiting for him to ask her to marry him after what he did to her. He had to be absolutely sure that he wanted to marry, and he was sure he wanted to marry Samantha.

His horse Chip danced over the ground and McGuire had a big smile on his face. He wondered if he should pick some flowers along the way, but saw there were none in bloom. He would tell her he was willing, no wanting, to marry her. He could just see her eyes turn green with happiness. Lucky girl! Lucky him!

On the side of the road, he saw yellow flowers pecking out from the rocks. He stopped his horse and jumped off. He pulled his knife from his boot and started to cut the few flowers just blooming. This will show her that he thinks of her all the time. Women loved flowers. He got up on his horse again and started to sing.

The old schoolhouse was right in front of him. He tied his horse to the hitching post and ran into the schoolhouse. He caught his breath as he watched Samantha putting little slates at each desk. She was so petite and slim. Her black hair was in a tight bun at the back of her head. She wore the same black skirt that he had paid Kate to make for her, and the white blouse from her trunk.

He could picture her with her hair falling around her face and cascading down her back, as she lay naked in bed upstairs. He felt his shaft growing bigger. He would give her the flowers, and they would go upstairs again. She would be so happy they would be married. He could hardly wait to feel her skin again. Her skin was like velvet, so soft and smooth.

"Samantha," whispered McGuire'

Samantha jumped and turned around. She saw McGuire at the door of the schoolhouse. His golden hair gleamed as he stood with his hat in his hands. She noticed the golden flowers he held in his hands. He stretched his hands out and walked over to where she stood.

McGuire handed her the flowers. "This is for you. You are so beautiful, more beautiful than any flower that grows."

He placed the flowers into her hands. He opened his arms for her to step into. She stood very still. She looked down at the flowers and looked up at McGuire with a question in her eyes.

"Samantha, we need to do some serious talking," McGuire said as he reached out and put his hands on her shoulders. Samantha flinched back a step. Her hands let the flowers fall to the floor. She shrugged her shoulders in order to make his hands fall from her. McGuire put his hands down to his sides.

"Look, I know I should have talked to you before this, but-"McGuire said as he reached for again.

Samantha put her hands up before her face. She backed to the blackboard at the front of the room.

McGuire stepped forward and stood before her. His lake-blue eyes held a question. "Aren't you going to talk to me? Honestly, you'll like what I have to say to you. In fact, I should have said this to you the day we- well – you know, when we went upstairs and-"

"McGuire, I don't want to hear any thing you have to say. If you think you can come here and we would go upstairs again, just because you gave me some puny flowers, you are mistaken."

"No, No. You have it all wrong. I wanted to say we would marry. That is the only reason I came over today. So you would know my intentions are pure."

"You'll marry me?" laughed Samantha. "Without asking what I want and if I want to marry you? Who do you think you are? Someone so great that it is an honor to be asked by you to marry?"

He walked over to her and brought his body next to hers. "I didn't mean it that way," McGuire said as he kissed her hair, her nose, and then lightly her mouth. "I meant, I know it is my duty to marry you after taking your virginity and all. I know you expect me to marry you. You trembled so on our day of love making. I thought of you constantly. I love you."

"Your duty? Yes, I trembled. I have never had such a guilt feeling in my life. I think I will never have that feeling again. The day of our love making? I wanted you as much as you wanted me."

"I promise you, you will feel and tremble again, but from love. I love you Samantha. It wasn't guilt that made you tremble; it was love. It was excitement. We were meant for each other right from the very beginning of your arrival here. That was why I saved you from the mud. We can marry as soon as the preacher comes to town. Will that please you?"

Samantha walked to her desk and sat down. Samantha played with the papers on her desk. She looked up into the eyes of McGuire. McGuire came over to her chair by the desk. He wanted to run his hands through her hair. Take it down. He wanted to take the pins that held it so securely in place. He smiled at her big and bold. He felt his heart stop at the thought she might not marry him.

"I do not plan to marry you, ever. I do not love you. You are the brother I never had. Do you understand, I do not love you, and will never, marry you. You took what was mine to give, but I gave it willingly to you because I owed you my life. I will always owe you."

He stepped back from the desk. He put his hand on his heart. He could not believe that she did not want to marry him. Something was so terribly wrong here. "Wait, now that you thought about it, you see we have to marry. Don't you think it would work out? I mean I made you undesirable for any man who desires a virgin."

"I know McGuire. But no thank you, I do not want to marry you. I shall become an old maid. Don't you understand, I love you like a brother?"

"What do you mean by "no thank you"" McGuire screamed. He pulled her out of the chair she was sitting in, and put her into his arms and kissed her long and hard. He could feel her shutter the way he was holding her. His hands pulled her shirt and the buttons flew in all directions. He put his hand into her blouse. He rubbed her breasts. "You must marry me. I am the man for you. I love you. I never loved anyone before."

He gently kissed Samantha's lips. He looked deep into her eyes. "Say the word and we can marry as soon as the preacher comes to town. Samantha there is no one I love as much as you. I know you heard about LouLou. But she is a friend. I mean, well, OK she is my past. I promise you I shall never be with her again. LouLou understands this. She even said when I fall in love, she would give me up to the woman I loved."

"Brad, it is not LouLou that concerns me. It is the fact I do not love you. I like you as a friend, brother. You have helped me more than anyone I know. I am grateful for all you have done for me. Believe me, I know how much you have done. You even saved my life. If I had a brother, I would want him to be you."

"Brother? Samantha I love you with all my heart. Did you consider the fact that we made love and you might be pregnant? If the child is born, I want to be its father. I want it so much. It is time for me to have a home, children and the woman I love."

"Pregnant?" she said, and tears came into her eyes. "I could never leave a child to have the horrid life I had. Yes, Brad, I would marry you than. But you must know I love another. I do not think he knows it, but as I am without the means to prove my love and innocence, he will never know I love him."

Samantha walked to the door of the schoolhouse and looked at the sun shinning so brightly. "Never would I have a child suffer as I did. Never would I take away its father." Samantha stared at McGuire. "I may not love you, Brad, but if I am pregnant I will make you a wife to be proud of. I promise you that. If I am not pregnant, than I shall expect you to forget me—"

Samantha walked back to him. He put his hands around her waist and she struggled away, as her blouse ripped. She gazed away from his face that bore the failure he felt. She would do anything to keep him happy, but she knew she did not love him, but she loved Ted.

"I do love you and want children with you. I want to settle down and be a family man. I want to build a house for us anywhere you want."

McGuire stood in stony silence. He felt defeated. He knew in his heart that she was in love with Ted. He did not want a woman who was in love with Ted. He knew now she would marry him if she was with child. But did he want her like that. Yes, he wanted her. He wanted to have a family. He loved her. He never realized how much until now.

McGuire pulled her to his chest. He kissed her lightly on her lips. He felt the hunger fill his soul. Somehow or other, he knew that she would never marry him. She was not pregnant. No, he wasn't that lucky. "I'll not bother you again unless you call and tell me we are going to have a child. I know you love another, and it is Ted. Ted is lucky."

"No, I shall never tell Ted I love him. It would not be fair. I am not a brave woman, nor foolish to think he would not know I am not a virgin. If it so happens I am – well as you say, oh, Brad. I am so mixed up. I do not know what I am doing."

McGuire knew he had lost. He knew she wasn't pregnant, and he knew he was left to linger without his love. Strange, he did not know how much he loved her until it was too late.

McGuire walked out the door and then slipped the reigns from the hitching post. He jumped on his horse Chip and rode slowly away from the school. Somehow or other, he seemed to never have any lucky, except in cards. He was sure LouLou knew that he was in love with Samantha.

Chapter XVII

McGuire wasn't surprised to see LouLou at the door of the whorehouse. She was wearing red. His favorite color on her. She smiled at McGuire as he slid off his horse. "Fine day," she called

McGuire looked at her and shook his head. "I asked Samantha to marry me. She refused, but she said she would if she is pregnant. I really love her, LouLou. I don't know what I shall do. I didn't know I loved her so much. Seems I was too concerned with myself then with her. I think I'm just a bastard. Never thinking about other people and all that stuff."

LouLou stepped over to him and took his hand. "Come inside and tell me all about it. I want you to be happy. If marrying Samantha is what you want, I will never stand in your way. But McGuire, if she won't have you, you still have me."

"Oh, LouLou," cried McGuire as tears formed in his eyes. LouLou pressed his head on her breast. He would never realize that she, LouLou, loved him so much she would give her life for him. "It will be all right. You'll see. I'm sure she will change her mind. Who could resist you? She's just playing hard to get. Serves you right after taking her-"

"She loves Ted." McGuire said in a whisper.

LouLou ran her hand down his back. She patted him as if he was a baby. She hoped that this was not the end of her and McGuire no matter what happened. She was dry-eyed as she smoothed McGuire. McGuire was her one and only true love. She hoped that Samantha and Ted would be happy, and she would be left with her true love, Brad McGuire.

"Ted won't have her if she's not a virgin. She will never tell him she loves him so she'll come back to you. He's too straight laced to have her no matter how he feels. Wait, I'm sure she'll come around and love you if you just wait." LouLou crossed her fingers in her back and hoped that Samantha and Ted were in for the long haul. She did not want to lose McGuire. She hoped Ted and Samantha married.

*   *   *

Samantha watched the month go by slowly. She was so afraid of what would happen. Her classes started. She was proud of her classes. The class ranged in age from six years old to nineteen years old, and all of them could not read. It was her duty and her love of teaching that made her sure to win. She walked around in a daze, hoping she was not bound to McGuire in any way.

She knew the reason they could not read was because the teachers always married and left the classroom. She was determined no matter what happened to her, she would teach these kids to read. Hopefully she would not have to marry McGuire, and Ted, well Ted would never know she loved him.

At night, Samantha walked back and forth in the schoolroom. She wanted a child, but she wanted the child to be Ted's. Still, there was nothing for her to do but wait. She clutched her aching head and wanted to cry, but what was the use? She loved Ted because he was honest, brave, hard working, and not a wanderer like McGuire. McGuire would always wander. It was in his blood. As much as she liked him, she could see he would never be still. She knew she owed McGuire her life and her love, but she did believe he could sit still? She had lost too much in the last few days. Her Pa, her Ma, her life, her love.

Near the end of the month, Samantha could not get out of bed. She felt so terribly ill. It was good that it was Saturday, and there would be no class to worry about. She got up to get a glass of water, and then she noticed her bed. It was bloody. She had her period. She was not pregnant. She did not have to marry McGuire. She would be an old maid schoolteacher.

She could not contain her happiness. She threw herself into making new lesson plans. She sang and she danced at night by herself. She understood she had to tell McGuire that he did not have to marry her. She would send him a note, no; it would be better if she told him herself. He had done so much to help her.

She sent McGuire a note to see her. She did not want him to think she was with child, so she wrote in the note briefly, she was just herself with no other one to worry about.

McGuire came and she told him she was sorry, but she was not marrying anyone and she was not with child. McGuire nodded his head. He pulled her close, and kissed her nose. "I knew I never would be lucky and have you. I wish you all the happiness that is in this world."

Samantha laughed. She kissed his cheek. "You will always be my friend."

"Yes, I know, but it is not enough for me." said McGuire. "I want all of you." He shrugged and walked to the door. "I do love you Samantha, no matter what you believe."

McGuire left, and Samantha hugged herself. At school, she played games with the students. She was a new person, without any responsibilities.

Winter came with it cold and snow and wind. The air frosted the small schoolhouse. Samantha awoke and knew she had to bring in wood for the class today. She felt chilled as she felt the warmth of her bed. She dressed quickly and ran down the steps.

She put the kettle on the stove to boil. it was very low on wood. She hated the thought of going out in the cold. She threw the knitted shawl that Kate had made for her and opened the door. The wind howled and the snow hit her face. It was good that the woodpile was near the door. The sun rose in the horizon and the snow glittered blinding Samantha as she reached for the wood. Her hand was ready to grab a piece of wood when she heard the rattle. She stood perfectly still. Her heart beat into her brain. She was so afraid of snakes. She closed her eyes, and knew the snake was ready to strike. It was winter, and snakes were suppose to hibernate during this time. Still, here was a snake.

In the terror of the moment, Samantha did not hear the sound of hoofs coming closer. She only heard the beat of her heart. Ted rode up and anyone could see Samantha was in trouble. At a glance he saw the rattlesnake. He slide his gun from his holster and in one quick move, he shot the snake in its head.

Samantha heard the shot, and opened her eyes. She saw the bloody stump of the snake still wreathing in the wood. She stepped back and started to crumble from fright. Ted jumped off his horse and caught her in his large hands.

Ted held her tenderly in his hands. He drew her closer to his body. He wished so hard that she would be his. He was afraid McGuire was the one she wanted and loved He told him all about how Samantha loved him when they hunted the kidnappers.

"Samantha, don't be afraid. The snake is dead," said Ted as he nestled her body close to his.

Samantha turned in his arms and looked into his black eyes. She felt so safe just seeing his eyes and feeling his hands around her waist. She smiled up at Ted.

"Ted," she said. "Oh, Ted." The tears filled her eyes and she seemed to blank out the world. She could feel the tears falling down her face. She knew that Ted knew McGuire had made love to her. She knew she was damaged and her reputation hung in threads if McGuire told what he did to her to everyone.

Ted could not love her after what she had done with McGuire. She knew she was alone in the world and no one would ever love her. Her Pa wasn't her Pa, and McGuire had taken her one gift that she could give her husband. She was ruined. She felt the large hands of Ted smooth her back. Then he pulled her closer to his body. She was in a half daze, and let him feel her body tremble. Her eyes fluttered close. It was time that would never happen again, she thought as she lay at in peace in Ted's arms.

"Thank you, Ted. You saved my live. You are always there when I need you. I can't thank you enough. You saved me from the kidnappers, and now a rattlesnake."

Ted steadied her on her feet. Ted kicked the ground with his boots. He looked at the top of Samantha's head. "When are you and McGuire going to marry?"

Stepping back from Ted, she shook her head. "I'm not going to marry McGuire ever. No, not ever. I do not love him, and- he did ask me, but I told him I do not love him and would not marry him. He is like a brother to me. He has helped me so many times. It is hard to believe how much he has helped."

Ted was stunned. Samantha brushed her skirt from the snow and walked into the schoolroom. She turned her face away from his face. She finally said, "Come in out of the snow. I didn't think I would ever see you again."

Ted came into the schoolhouse and carried some wood that he put into the wood box. He closed the door. He came over to where Samantha stood. He looked into her eyes. His body felt the weight of years leave him and free his soul.

She brightly said, "Would you like some tea? I was making some for myself before the wood pile incident." Her heart beat furiously waiting for his answer. She hid her face from his as she did not want him to see the love that gleamed in her eyes.

Ted's face beamed. He smiled. His heart was singing with joy. He had a chance with Samantha. He would not blow it this time. "Love some tea, or anything you have to offer. Samantha, are you going to stay and teach school here? I was hoping you would stay. I-well-I"

Ted sat down in the teacher's chair. Samantha brought over the tea in cups. She pulled a student's desk and chair over to her desk and sat down. Her hands shook so badly, she almost spilled her tea.

Heavy silence filled the room. Samantha squirmed in her seat. Both of them did not know how to start this conversation. Samantha knew she had made the tea all wrong. The water wasn't boiling and she added the tea to the cold water. She felt like a fool. "Don't drink the tea. It is not ready yet."

Ted bent his head and picked up his teacup. "The weather is cold now."

"Yes, it is snowing." She said.

Ted nodded his head. He twisted his hands together as he watched Samantha. His mouth became a stern line. He picked up his cup and put it down. He watched the tea floating in the cold water. "Are you wondering why I came?"

Samantha nodded her head. She felt too sad to talk. She knew he came to tell her goodbye. How she loved the way he carried himself. She loved the way he stuttered when he stumbled to say whatever he came to say. She could help him out, but she was too shy to say anything.

Ted stood up from the desk. He walked over to Samantha and lifted her from her chair. Her cup fell on the floor shattering it in a million pieces. "I could not stay away from you. I love you. It's simple as that. I want to you have my children, and to live in my house. I am a ghost without you. I want you to marry me."

Her hazel eyes were filled with tears. He bent his head and he kissed her hard. Then his kisses softened and he kissed her as one possessed. She answered his kisses with a passion she did not know she possessed.

Ted's hands gently rubbed her back. He pulled her closer. She closed her eyes as she felt his need of her on her belly. She wanted him like one wanted life. She knew she would go to bed with him no matter what happened. He raised his face from her lips. He gently smoothed her hair. "I love you Samantha."

"Oh, Ted. I can never marry any one. I am not a virgin. I am a fallen woman." Samantha pulled away from Ted and leaned on the wall. Her face was covered with tears as she looked at him. She would never lie to him. She wanted him, but knew she could never have him.

"Samantha, I know about McGuire. He told me how he had you, and how he was willing to marry you because of your lost innocence"

"He, he told you? Oh, God, did he tell everyone?' cried Samantha as she turned away from the wall and went to the door and pulled it open. She was about to step out into the snow when Ted pulled her back into the room.

"Samantha, I don't care what happened with you and McGuire. It was something that happened because he helped you and you were so alone. I understand. It will never bother me. I swear. I love you so. I don't know what I will do if you do not love me and marry me."

Ted held her hands in his large hands. He held her hands tightly and then he pulled her to him. He smelled her sweet smell of her hair. His heart soared in his chest. His hands fell to her breasts and he cupped them. She gasped as she felt his hands kneading her breasts. His tongue slid into her mouth and she followed suit with her tongue. She knew she would never marry Ted, she was not good enough, but she would have one day with him. One glorious day to remember the rest of her life. She would give him her body and her soul.

Stars filled her eyes. Her mouth moved up to his mouth. His hands opened her blouse and he dipped one hand into her blouse to feel her naked breasts. His kisses so gentle at first became hungrier and hungrier. His large hand pulled at her nipple and then he slowly took off her blouse. He threw it on the floor with her chemise. She stood near him without any clothing to grace her top. She did not hide her bareness but proudly pushed out her chest. She stood still as he looked at her.

"Oh, God," cried Ted. "You are more beautiful then I ever dreamed, and I have dreamed of you so often. My life is in your hands. I want you, I must have you. I want to marry you. Please say yes. Stop this torture of my heart."

He bent his head and sucked her breast. He pulled her to him as his hands moved down her skirt. He opened the back of the skirt and it fell to the floor. Her petticoat fell to the floor and she was left with her bloomers. His hands untied her bloomers and they too fell to the floor. She stood before him as a goddess without any clothes on except her little boots.

Ted looked at her with all the love he had ever dreamed about. She was exactly what he dreamed about all his life. He stopped touching her and stepped back. His eyes devoured her like a hungry wolf. He felt his manhood jut out against his trousers. He knew that his love was his to take and keep.

Samantha looked at him and she felt cheap. He didn't want her. She had let him do as he wished and now he was sorry. She had wanted this day, and even that was denied her. She gasped as she turned her head so he would not see the tears in her eyes.

"I want you so very much, I would like to take you upstairs and make you mine. But Samantha, I can wait till we marry. I will not cheapen our love. I love you so much. I want you to want me and love me. Can you love me? I do not want you to marry me because you are pregnant. I want you to marry me because you love me. And me alone. I want you so very much."

She felt his eyes on her. She could see he loved her. She could see he wanted her by the bulge in his pants. She was surprised that he would wait until they married. She was over whelmed that he wanted to marry her. She wanted to have Ted's children. She wanted a real home. Samantha moved over to him. She put her arms around his waist. She stood on tiptoe and raised her face to his. She kissed him slowly and with all the raging passion she could feel.

"I love you, Ted. I love you so very much. I was willing to have one day with you to last me forever. I would give you my body and my soul now. Even if we never marry. I love you so much. I am not pregnant."

She put her hands around his head and then ran her hands down his back. She wanted to feel this was real and not a dream. Her pout turned into a wide smile. Her eyes sparkled with fire. She stepped back and looked Ted full in the face. Then she stepped closed to Ted and she snuggled into his arms.

"Ted, do you mean it? Do you really love me? Can you truly forget about McGuire and me? I would marry you if you-"

"With all my heart and soul I love you. You are my lady fair. As far as you and McGuire are concerned, I told you it was something that could not be avoided. You trusted him. I want you to feel love. You are a goddess so beautiful and proud. Put your clothing back on and let's tell the world you are mine. I can't believe that your Pa never loved you and wanted you dead. Oh, Samantha, I wish your Ma was here to let her see you now. I am so happy."

"I can't believe my wishes are coming true. I love you so. Yes, I will marry you." They both kissed and blended as one.

She put her clothing back on and knew that she had found the love that she had looked for all her life. It seemed to wrap around her body as she looked at Ted. She could feel his desire across the space between them. She knew the for the first time, that she was safe and would be always be loved.

Epilogue

The sun was shinning brightly. The church as packed with everyone in the neighborhood from miles around. Even the cacti seemed to bloom with orange flowers for the occasion. They were big flowers that welcomed Spring. Men and women came in their best clothing. This was a happy occasion. It was because everything came in three. And threes were suppositious to all present.

It was hard to believe that today there were three weddings held at the same time. Three weddings to be given to love when Priest James came to town. All three brides wore the same style wedding dress made by Kate. It had kept Kate busy for hours. But she would not deny the dresses she was asked to make to any one of the brides.

The dresses were made with white cotton eyelet and covered with lace at the sleeves, hem and waist. All the dresses had three petticoats made with white cotton and they had lace at their hems. All dresses flowed out in yards of material, but the waist of each dress was tight to show off their small waists. The girls were all slim and beautiful.

Everyone came to town bringing food and drinks. There was music and dancing and so many hardy congratulations. Samantha smiled up at Ted as they recited their marriage vows. Ginger looked at Jim who adored her with all his being. Mary married Barry. and would move away to Denver. They were all in blissful contentment as they looked at their flowers in their hands. They were old fashioned and threw their flowers to the waiting people. The flowers came from Denver and they were roses; white for Samantha, Red for

Ginger, and pink for Mary. The future was bright for all the young ladies, but brightest for Samantha. It was the first time in her life that everything she wished for came true.

McGuire was the only one who did not attend the wedding. It was he who rescued Samantha from the mud, who gave her clothing, and who cleaned her schoolhouse. He had rescued her from the kidnappers. He that would love her with all his heart, and she did not love him. He wished her the best, because he did love her. It was time for him to leave town, as he could not stand to see her married to Ted.

The hardest thing he did was talk to LouLou. He looked into her eyes, and he read her love of him there. He liked her a good deal, but the truth of the matter was, he did not love her. He loved Samantha, and she did not love him as he wanted. He could not stay and so he spoke to LouLou. "I am giving you this whorehouse for keeps. I'm leaving town for good."

"Brad McGuire, I love you. Don't leave me. I don't want no whorehouse without you. Let me go with you. I don't care where we go, just let me go with you."

"No, LouLou. I like you a great deal. You deserve this whorehouse. I wish I could give you more. I don't love you enough to stay. I'm a gambler and so I have to go. I hope you find yourself another man to love."

LouLou turned to the window of the sitting room. "I'm happy the way it is. If I can't have you, I don't want anyone else. I know you don't believe it. But that is the way of life. If I can't have you, I want nothing. The business will be my life. Thanks McGuire, you gave me my life. Let me let you go free, as you want. I shall always think of you with love. If you ever decide to come back to me, I will be waiting." He gave her the deed to the whorehouse and she held it next to her heart. "This is my new love."

McGuire looked at LouLou and knew she meant to live as a hermit. He wanted her to have a life, but he was not one to give it to her. It was the least he could do was give her what she had dreamed she wanted. The whorehouse and to be a Madam!

LouLou's brother Alex was given the deed to the saloon. Alex could not believe that McGuire was going away. He wanted to go with him. Alex longed for the life of a rambler. He wanted to be free, and here he was given the saloon. It was something he could not pass up. It was a way of life he had always dreamed that he would have. His own saloon.

To his cooks he smiled and told them the best he could that he was leaving. He gave Kim the deed to the hotel. Kim knew he was an angel sent by Buddha to live their lives with joy. Kim was not surprised at the gift, he knew in his heart that this was bound to happen. It was written in the stars.

Sadly, Brad McGuire looked at the town he was leaving. It held the memory of his love of Samantha, but some how, he knew it he was not destined to remain in his town. He had places to go and things to do.

McGuire with his packed bags jumped on his big black horse, Chip. He looked once again at the town he was leaving and one that he would never come back to. He galloped away towards the East. A gambling man should head right to New Orleans If one was to gamble, there was no place on earth like New Orleans.

But then again, things did not go as McGuire expected. There's always a joker in the deck. That's what happened after he got to New Orleans and surprise, his sister, Helen, was on the way, but that's another story in the life and times of McGuire.